"What I find strange, Miss Riley, is that you were able to keep your mouth closed for more than a minute."

"I don't think it necessary to be so negative. You don't need to address me as miss. You may use my Christian name. Mr. Cruz?"

"Gracie, I've been traveling all day. You're a nice girl, but I'm tired. I don't want to talk."

"Oh." Gracie swallowed. "My apologies." A nice girl indeed.

She was more than a girl—she was a woman. A capable, independent woman who didn't need to rely on her parents or some unwanted fiancé for survival. And she'd prove it. She would find Striker and write an amazing article so the *Women's Liberator* would hire her as an investigative reporter. Then she'd tell Striker what she thought of him.

A man should know when a woman fell madly in love with him.

JESSICA NELSON

In keeping with her romantic inclinations, Jessica Nelson married two days after she graduated high school. She believes romance happens every day and thinks the greatest, most intense romance comes from a God who woos people to himself with passionate tenderness. When Jessica is not chasing her three beautiful, wild little boys around the living room, she can be found staring into space as she plots her next story. Or she might be daydreaming about a raspberry mocha from Starbucks. Or thinking about what kind of chocolate she should have for dinner that night. She could be thinking of any number of things, really. One thing is for certain, she is blessed with a wonderful family and a lovely life.

Love on the Range

JESSICA NELSON

Love Inspired

LOVE INSPIRED BOOKS

Recycling programs
for this product may
not exist in your area.

ISBN-13: 978-0-373-82914-9

LOVE ON THE RANGE

www.LoveInspiredBooks.com

Printed in U.S.A.

And ye shall seek me, and find me,
when ye shall search for me with all your heart.
—*Jeremiah* 29:13

Many thanks to my awesome family and friends, who have supported and encouraged me from the moment they found out I wanted to write books for a living.

I am in deep gratitude to those who have helped refined my writing skills while encouraging me to keep growing. These wonderful ladies have read my awkward sentences, plot holes and mean characters yet still managed to make me feel like my stories were important. Huge thanks to my Friday Crit Group: Linda Glaz, Camille Eide, Emily Hendrickson, Cheryl Linn Martin and Karla Akins. You girls rock!

Love to Anita Howard, my POM, a fabulous author who has read everything I ever wrote and still says I'm a good writer.

Big thanks to my blogger pals Eileen Watson and Terri Tiffany. Their advice for this story was invaluable to me.

To my agent, Les Stobbe, who is knowledgeable, supportive and always available to answer my many questions.

I'd like to give a heartfelt thank you to my editor, Emily Rodmell, for liking my manuscript enough to make me a published author!

The biggest thanks to Jesus, who put this love of writing in my heart. He's Awesome!

Chapter One

Harney County, Oregon, 1918

Obsession was the way in which madness lay.

Despite that annoying truth, Gracelyn Riley couldn't stop scanning the train platform for Special Agent Striker as she disembarked. People bustled everywhere, stirring up dust. Nearby, a mother held her toddler close while passengers crowded around her. Boards groaned and voices rose as people scattered, looking for their luggage and rides.

The whistle shrieked a warning to those lagging on the platform. The train had stopped briefly at this desolate Oregon county station before continuing on to California.

Gracie had hesitated traveling to this vast and untamed land until she'd learned Special Agent Striker lived here. He was the only reason she could endure going to a place as dreary as this. Though her parents considered traveling alone unsafe, even in these modern days, the threat of influenza loomed larger than their worries and prompted them to send their only daughter west. Had the fear of grippe not been so severe, her parents would surely still have her strapped to their sides.

Once she'd learned Striker made his home here, her

plans changed. She'd finagled the promise of a coveted position as a staff writer with the *Woman's Liberator* if she could procure an interview with the elusive agent. Sweet independence was within her grasp.

Unfortunately, she didn't see among the passengers anyone who looked dangerous enough to be the mysterious Striker.

She stood on the platform until the crowds thinned and the train rolled away on a cloud of steam. Squinting, she turned a slow circle. Though several wagons parked nearby, they all looked full and their drivers busy.

Where was her ride?

Gathering her things, she walked to a bench situated outside the station door and sat. Her trunks remained inside. No doubt when the driver arrived, he'd go in and retrieve them. In the distance, mountains jutted into a never ending sky. Sparse landscape surrounded her.

She shuddered and pulled *Jane Eyre* from her Dotty bag.

A shadow fell over her.

"Ma'am, is this seat open?"

She looked up. The man beside her waited for an answer. With the setting sun behind him, the broad brim of his cowboy hat shadowed his face and hid all but his straight nose and strong chin.

"Yes, it is." The bench at the other end of the platform held a family whose kids shrieked and laughed. Smiling, she moved to the side for the stranger. She remembered seeing him on the train, a lone figure in a back seat. Aloof and unapproachable.

Some exotic, spicy scent filled the air as he sat, and she slid him a look. He was rather handsome, though not in the way she was used to. This man wouldn't fit in at a fancy Boston dinner party. His broad shoulders and tanned skin spoke of a ruggedness to which she was quite unaccustomed. These attributes intrigued her.

What did he do for a living? For the first time since embarking on this wretched trip, her fingers itched to jot down observations on the small pad of paper she always kept nearby.

The stranger must have felt her scrutiny because he took his hat off, placed it in his lap and eyed her in return.

A jagged scar traveled from above his right brow, down his cheekbone to the hairline near his ear. Striker was also rumored to be scarred, though she'd not heard of where in particular. No doubt Striker bore many evidences of his heroic feats. Her gaze traced the puckered skin on the stranger's face. Perhaps she should've felt embarrassed to have been caught staring. But after the emotional upheaval of being forced to leave home and left to flounder alone on a loud, smelly train, the tiny flicker of interest flaring within caught her by surprise and loosened her tongue.

"How do you do, sir?" She held out her hand in the way she'd lately observed others from the barren West do.

He didn't shake her hand. Instead, one thick black brow rose.

Gracie struggled to keep the polite smile on her face as she withdrew her unshaken hand. Shame flooded through her. So much for skirting her gentle upbringing. She fiddled with the folds of her dress suit.

The stranger's gaze was dark, his eyes shards of obsidian. His strong jaw emphasized narrow cheekbones while that wicked-looking scar slashed angrily across his features. Not a face as perfect as Hugh's or Father's, but overall, quite an interesting study. He stared at her in such an odd way, cold and intent. Her throat clenched.

Say something. Anything.

"This grippe outbreak is horrible, isn't it? My parents

are sending me to stay with an uncle until the influenza clears up," she blurted.

His scar crinkled with his forehead but he still said nothing.

"I don't mind the trip, though," she continued, "because I've heard Special Agent Striker has been spotted in Burns several times."

"You heard wrong."

He had a wonderful voice. Deep and masculine. Warmth spread across Gracie's face. "I'm quite sure I have not heard wrong, sir. My sources are reliable. I assume you're familiar with Striker and his many feats?"

The man's mouth compressed into a thin line. "Do you usually hold conversations with strange men? Don't have much common sense, do you?"

"Sir, I'll remind you that *you* sat beside me. I have plenty of common sense, thank you very much." Her shoulders stiffened. "And I do have protection."

"Who?" The stranger made a pretense of looking around, then he pinned her with a dark look.

"God protects me."

"God." The stranger's eyes glinted. "If someone snatched you right now, no one could stop him."

Interesting words. Gracie peered more closely at him, determined to find out more. "If you're referring to Mendez, the notorious kidnapper of women, I must inform you Striker will finish him for good. He's from the West," she added.

"Mendez?"

"No, Striker. He enforces the Mann Act of 1910 by chasing down kidnappers and criminals who perform evil deeds." Also known as the White Slave Traffic Act, it had been established to keep women from being transported across state lines for immoral purposes. "My uncle's home is near Burns, a town Striker is rumored to frequently visit. I'm hoping for an exclusive interview designed to prove his honor." And to jump-start her career.

"Honor?" The man beside her snorted. "From what I hear, the man's a skilled assassin."

"Rumors." Her lips clamped tight.

His fingers steepled. "You haven't heard of the Council Bluff skirmish?"

The fiasco had made only a few papers back East. Government officials didn't want the public to hear how the innocent died during a routine raid of an outlaw's hideout.

"Striker did what was necessary. He would never kill in cold blood."

The stranger's mouth twisted. "But, they say, that is exactly what he did."

"There's an explanation." Gracie clutched at the pocket in her skirt where she'd placed her news articles. "I intend to prove it."

She forced herself to relax and took a deep breath. A subject change was in order because she did not intend to argue with a stranger. Not about her beloved Striker. "Where are you heading, sir?"

He studied her, and she thought he might continue in the controversial vein, but he didn't. "I've been out of town on business, but I'm heading back to Burns. The name's Trevor Cruz."

"I'm Gracelyn Riley, of the Boston Rileys who came over years and years ago." She paused for breath before continuing. "That is quite the scar you have. Do you mind telling me what happened?"

When his eyes slit into narrow cracks, a sense of foreboding crawled down Gracie's spine. Perhaps it was a painful story and her question intruded on his grief. Mother's voice echoed in her mind: *Always asking questions. Try to pretend to be a lady for once.*

Mr. Cruz's expression cleared. "Got it when I was twelve, cutting some barbed wire for a fence. I sliced it wrong and the wire snapped up and got me right there." His finger rubbed the scar lightly. "Guess I was lucky not to lose my eye." He shrugged. "Never met a lady interested in my scar."

"Perhaps because it makes you look dangerous. In a good way," she added, not wanting to further offend him.

Her gaze lit upon his scar again and she frowned. "It's such an evil-looking scar that I rather thought something horrendous must have happened for you to get it. Something besides being cut with barbed wire."

"I'm sorry my scar is not more exciting for you, Miss Riley…Gracelyn."

Had she spoken aloud? A horrible heat rushed through her body.

"That's okay," she stuttered, unable to meet what would surely be a disapproving gaze. If only her uncle would arrive. She searched her surroundings. The family was leaving and the approaching dusk whittled their shapes into shadows as they climbed aboard a wagon.

Two tethered horses waited at the edge of the platform. Their harnesses tinkled every few minutes with their movements and the sound reminded her of music. She turned to Mr. Cruz, hoping to distract him from her rudeness.

"Do you enjoy the music of Joe Oliver, from New Orleans? My father says he wouldn't be surprised if Mr. Oliver becomes known as the king of jazz, he's that good. Jazz is lovely, much better than classical, don't you agree?"

"I prefer the outdoors, ma'am."

"You do not enjoy music, Mr. Cruz?"

"Not jazz or classical. I like natural sounds."

"Oh, yes, nature's music. Do you mind explaining?" Might as well enjoy the conversation because there was no escaping the scourge of her thoughtless tongue.

Mr. Cruz's eyes bored into Gracie. Her chest constricted. This man affected her in quite a strange manner.

"I'm not articulate. You'd have to hear it to understand." His lips curved into a wry smile. "You're young."

"I am only twenty, it's true." She held his gaze. "But perhaps I understand your meaning."

Mr. Cruz's eyebrow rose. Did his raised brow mean he invited more conversation?

"I'm well acquainted with the sounds of nature. Before dawn I like to walk down to the ports. The fog is often thick and when I first reach the docks all I hear is the water pushing and lapping against the wooden posts. Then, slowly, the world awakes. Seagulls call to each other, high, piercing shrieks." Feeling faintly encouraged by the steady attention he gave her, she continued. "The sounds of fishermen drawing up nets and shouting orders drift to me. And the sun slices through the fog like a blade through fine silk. On those mornings, I am certain God is much more than the boring entity talked about in stuffy, silent churches. I am certain He's beautiful, and that He sings through his creation. Is this like the music you mean?"

He jammed his hat back on his head. "I was referring to nature, not God. Do your parents know you go out in the mornings like that?"

Bristling, she lifted her chin. "Mr. Cruz, must you keep talking as if I'm a child? Does it really matter what they know about? The point is, God made nature and we see His glory through it. If you enjoy the sounds of nature, you're really just enjoying an aspect of the character of God."

That annoying black brow of his arched again. Then

he leaned back and tipped his hat over his face, as though dismissing her.

"Miss Riley," he drawled. "I don't believe in God."

A shocked gasp escaped Miss Riley's lips and for a moment Trevor thought he might be given the gift of silence. No such luck.

"Oh, Mr. Cruz!" From beneath the rim of his hat he saw Miss Riley's thick-fringed eyes widen. "How lonely you must be."

Trevor's jaw clenched. Time to stop being drawn in by her big brown eyes. He stood up, shoulders stiff.

"I think I'll get a paper. Pleasant meeting you, Miss Riley." He walked to the station's entry, turning back only once to see her staring after him, sympathy twisting her soft features.

Was he going to have to put up with her for months on end? He couldn't believe his senior partner, Lou Riley, had agreed to let his niece stay with them. And then he'd sent Trevor to check her out and make sure she wasn't followed back to the ranch.

Trevor bought a paper in the station and then returned outside. Miss Riley bent over a book and didn't appear to notice his exit. Quickly he turned on his heel and claimed the bench newly vacated at the other end of the depot. He cast Miss Riley another glance once at a safe distance.

A mass of flowing, dark hair covered her profile as she read. He groaned, wishing Lou had sent him on business anywhere else but here.

Truth was, he'd rather run the risk of contracting influenza than have to deal with some shallow socialite spouting nonsense about her nonexistent God. And there was her interest in Striker...

He settled back and opened the paper. It was unfortunate this Miss Riley knew so much about Striker's whereabouts. Maybe something had been leaked to the papers. He thumbed through but found nothing except a small paragraph focusing on Mendez's latest foiled kidnapping attempt.

His mouth quirked.

Mendez didn't have the success rate he used to. The knowledge almost made him happy. Almost, but not quite, because on the train a grizzled man had caught Trevor's attention. Though the man pretended to look out a window, Trevor had felt his perusal.

The watcher had looked familiar, the stink of an outlaw settling about his person.

Trevor rubbed his chin. The man had gotten off at an earlier stop, but that didn't keep his suspicions from being raised.

A clatter diverted his thoughts as a well-used wagon rolled up to the platform. Finally. He grabbed his traveling bag and sauntered over.

"'Bout time, old man."

"Stock got out." James, Lou's cowhand, among other things, grunted and took the satchel from Trevor. He nodded toward the station. "That the girl?"

"Yep."

They turned to look at Lou's niece. She must've seen James's arrival because she hesitantly picked her way toward them. Probably reluctant to believe she'd be riding in a wagon, if he had to venture a guess.

"While she's getting settled I'll grab some water for the horses," Trevor told James.

By the time he lugged two pails over, Miss Riley was nowhere to be seen. He plopped the water in front of the team and squared his gaze on James. "Where'd she go?"

"Said she's got luggage."

Trevor glanced toward the station. Sure enough, she

stumbled off the platform toting the biggest piece of luggage he'd ever seen.

Women.

Biting back annoyance, Trevor walked over to her. Apparently she thought pulling the trunk might work better than lifting it.

"Why don't you let me handle this?" he said to the back of her head.

The trunk thudded to the ground. Miss Riley fell with it, sprawling in an unladylike heap. Faster than he could draw his Colt revolver, she bounded to her feet and frantically began brushing at her clothes.

"Mr. Cruz...?"

"We have the same destination. Allow me to help you." He gestured to the trunk.

She stepped aside. "Thank you."

They walked to the wagon, and he stowed her trunk in the back. He offered her his hand. She took it.

The warmth of her hand was discomfiting. With his help, she climbed easily into the back of the wagon where a blanket lay bundled near the bags, waiting for her.

She smiled down at him, her lips a soft curve in the deepening night, and for a fraction of a second he found himself tempted to smile back.

He released her hand, gave a curt nod and headed to his side of the wagon. Night had arrived and stars filled Oregon's sky, lighting the vast openness surrounding them. He emptied the buckets and stuck them in the wagon next to Miss Riley, then hopped up to the front.

James snapped the reins. "It's not proper-like for a lady to be traveling at night with two men. Best get moving before someone sees and starts yapping their mouths." He spit a stream of tobacco juice toward the ground.

They set out, Miss Riley quiet and still behind him.

Was she thinking about Striker? Making plans to find him for that outlandish interview?

Trevor's jaw clenched. As long as things remained in his control, Striker would never be found.

Chapter Two

Oregon might not be so awful. As the wagon lurched forward, the deep sea of stars speckling the night sky filled Gracie with awe.

Gracie grabbed a thick blanket and draped it over her shoulders, making sure it bunched behind her back to protect her from the rickety wagon sides. This was the oldest Studebaker she'd ever seen.

Mr. Riley and James sat at the front in silence. For a while the only sound was the occasional snort of a horse, the clop of their hooves and James spitting.

As James drove, Gracie wondered about Uncle Lou. She hoped he was interesting. She and her best friend Connie had discussed all the qualities he might have—humor, irony, mischievousness. Gracie liked to think of him as a funny old man, a little on the heavy side with tufts of hair sprouting from unlikely places. But he couldn't be too old as he was her father's little brother and Father was only forty.

Mother didn't like Uncle Lou, and Father had nothing good to say about him. In fact, now that she thought about it, the reasons for their dislike had never been made clear. She had only heard Uncle Lou was unfitting, a rascal and irresponsible. He must be poor, also. Why else would he pick her up in some outdated wagon when he could send a motor vehicle?

His quirks, however, might very well work in her favor when she unveiled her plan to him.

After five minutes of interminable boredom, she decided to initiate a conversation. "Mr. Cruz, it is coincidental we're heading the same way. Don't you find it strange?"

"What I find strange, Miss Riley, is that you were able to keep your mouth closed for more than a minute."

An odd gargled sound came from James's direction, and Gracie frowned into the darkness.

"I don't think it necessary to be so obtuse. Besides, you don't need to address me as 'Miss.' You may use my Christian name. People call me Gracie." She took a breath. "Do you live near Uncle Lou?"

More noises came from James and his shoulders began shaking uncontrollably. The sound of his hoarse wheezing filled the night air.

Alarm spiked through her, tingling to her fingertips. Was James suffering heart palpitations? She leaped to her feet, despite the bouncing floor, and grabbed the reins from his slack hands. The horses tensed and, sensing a strange driver, began to gallop. A miraculously recovered James jerked the reins from her hands.

"What're you doing, woman? Are you mad?" His angry voice snapped at her.

Ears burning, she pulled the blanket over herself and huddled on the floor of the wagon. James hadn't been having a heart attack, only a laughing fit. At her expense. What a rude man. And Mr. Cruz let her stand there and make a fool of herself.

Men from the West had bad manners.

Gracie shifted. Just because no one had taught these two

how to act in front of a lady didn't mean she would forsake her polite upbringing.

The temptation to pout passed. A few moments later she felt brave enough to pop her head out from beneath the heavy blanket. "My apologies, James, for stealing your reins. As I was asking earlier, are you my uncle's neighbor, Mr. Cruz?"

"I manage things for him. My own home is half a mile from the main house."

"You said nothing of your relationship at the station." Silence greeted her comment. Frowning, she studied Mr. Cruz's profile. He evidently didn't wish to speak of his personal life.

Well, people were entitled to their secrets. She'd have to take care not to pry. Ignoring the curiosity that made her tongue itch, she forced a jovial tone. "My parents have called Uncle Lou a rascal."

"Oh, he had his day, missy. He had his day," James put in.

"I'm surprised he hasn't provided a female escort. I feel perfectly safe with you but if this happened in Boston, my reputation would suffer."

"This from the morning wanderer."

"I didn't say my reputation was perfect, Mr. Cruz." Gracie smiled at the thought. Her torch-carrying for Striker had set tongues wagging. Her former beau Hugh disapproved immensely.

"Some say Striker lives out West, despite what you told me, Mr. Cruz. Others hypothesize the villain Mendez roams the Western deserts, too." She gazed up at the star-studded sky. "Do you suppose I might meet Striker while I'm here?"

"Doubt it," James said.

Gracie set her chin. Perseverance would be the key. So would the coordinates Connie planned to send.

"You'll like your uncle, Gracelyn. He doesn't follow all the rules of society but he's a good man." Mr. Cruz turned and looked down at her, his profile outlined by moonlight.

Heart thumping a strange, uneven rhythm, she met his shadowed gaze. For a moment their connection held before he broke it by facing forward. A relief. She could breathe again. He incited such oddness in her.

Thank goodness she'd ended her relationship with Hugh. She'd had none of this attraction for him. In truth, their relationship was based on nothing more than the mutual machinations of their parents. They'd hardly courted before she spotted a betrothal announcement in the local newspaper. Aghast, she'd confronted her parents but they'd waved away her protests in favor of their own agenda.

Just thinking about how Hugh and her parents tried to swindle her into an engagement heated her blood. William and Edith Riley thought Hugh the perfect social match for their sole child, and Hugh's parents were probably eager for all the money they imagined would come into the family.

Gracie sighed. She hadn't benefitted by having an on-paper fiancé. Not even a real kiss. He pecked her cheek once before she'd seen the announcement. A most boring experience. She wanted a kiss like Connie had experienced. Connie said kissing was terribly exciting, but risky, and Gracie should wait until she was married to try it out.

But she didn't want to wait. She wanted to grab life by the steering wheel and drive until she ran out of road. Connie was most likely right, however.

Gracie also wanted to please God. Pleasing Him was of the utmost importance.

"Are you still alive down there?"

"Yes, James. But just barely with all this bouncing around."

"You almost made five minutes again."

"The fact that I did not is your fault, you know," she teased. "I'd really like to hear more about Uncle Lou."

"Look, missy, ya gotta meet him to know him." James cackled. "His stories rival a good Tom Swift tale."

"How intriguing." She smiled. "I enjoy Twain myself. He's swell."

"Silly women," James muttered.

She waited for Mr. Cruz to speak, curious. But he didn't say a word. "Mr. Cruz?"

"Gracie, I've been traveling all day. You're a nice girl, but I'm tired and I don't feel like talking."

"Oh." She swallowed. "My apologies." She arranged the blanket to make a pillow out of it and laid her head down. A nice girl indeed.

She was more than a girl—she was a woman. A capable, independent woman who didn't need to rely on her parents or some unwanted fiancé for survival. And she'd prove it. Her fingers found the hidden pocket in her skirt and she squeezed, relief coursing through her when she heard the rustle of papers. She would find Striker and write an amazing article so the *Woman's Liberator* would hire her as an investigative reporter. Then she'd tell Striker what she thought of him.

A man should know when a woman fell madly in love with him.

Gracie coughed. A cloud of tobacco-stained breath wrenched her from sleep, had her rubbing her eyes. She pulled herself to a sitting position and sneezed.

"We're here, missy," James said, straightening away

from her. The wagon bounced as he jumped out and rounded to its side.

She rose, letting him help her from the wagon to the ground. Both Mr. Cruz and James had picked her up easily. Perhaps she wasn't as heavy as she felt.

"What you got in that get-up, missy? Felt like I was unloading a sack of potatoes." James guffawed.

Gracie shot him a glare and snatched her Dotty bag from his grubby fingers. She glanced around. Mr. Cruz was nowhere to be seen. It was rather rude to not help with the trunk. Then again, he did load it.

Annoyance passing, she looked around with interest. Her breath caught in her throat.

Flat land stretched before her, frosted beneath the lunar glow. Dotting the landscape were trees surrounded by a sea of flowing grasses and scrubs made turquoise by the moon. Long-fingered shadows reached toward rugged mountains on the horizon. A soft breeze fluttered through her hair.

This place felt different than Boston, more arid and vast, yet the pressure in her chest mimicked what she experienced on mornings she dared venture to the harbor. She was overcome with a desire to raise her hands to the heavens and laugh.

"You gonna stand there all night, missy? Bed's a-calling."

Gracie turned and followed James to the house, noting with a quiet thrill of relief that it appeared large and modern. She'd been secretly afraid her uncle lived in a shack with an outhouse. She didn't know if they had outhouses in Oregon, but the West was a more primitive place than Boston. One could never know about these things.

A chill rushed through her and she shivered. "Is it usually this cold in September?"

"We're heading into winter soon, maybe an early one."

Although shorter than she, James walked faster, even holding her heavy trunk, and she hurried to catch up to him.

"It's so dark already. Where's Mr. Cruz?"

"Trev gets up early so he's gone to bed down for the night. Lou's waiting for you. You both talk more than a roomful of women. You'll get on real well."

"This is a beautiful home." Gracie stopped to gaze at the splendid pillars that flanked each end of the porch. "You must see all kinds of animals. Do you have bears here?"

When James snorted loudly, Gracie tamped down her frustration. What a grumpy man.

They climbed the porch stairs, their steps a hollow clumping on the wood. The door looked to be made of heavy oak, with a diamond-shaped glass placed in the middle. Just like home. A sharp, unexpected pain of homesickness squeezed Gracie's chest. Drawing a deep breath, she squared her shoulders. She had a plan, and focusing on that was her best course of action.

She turned to James. "Does Uncle Lou own a telephone?"

James grunted and pulled the door open.

"I really need to reach Connie," she continued, hoping his grunt was not a negative. She absolutely had to obtain those coordinates.

As they moved into the house, warmth embraced Gracie. James turned on the lights. When her eyes adjusted, she saw a young man standing at the end of the hallway, shaggy blond hair framing a handsome face and eyes like sapphires. He strode toward her, and Gracie realized he was not as young as he appeared from afar. Lines wrinkled around his eyes as his mouth curved into a mischievous smile. A light spray of scars pebbled one cheek, though she might not have noticed if she hadn't been studying him so hard. He was the spitting image of Father, minus the gray hairs and stately air.

"Uncle Lou?"

"You look just like Edith." He strode forward on long legs, though he stood only an inch or so taller than she, and grasped both her hands. "How was the trip? Not too boring, I hope. And the wagon?"

"Just fine." She smiled at him. "No one ever told me I look like my mother. Do you really think so?" It was a compliment indeed to resemble a woman as attractive as Edith.

"I thought you were her at first." He shot her a wide grin, exposing straight white teeth. "Let's go into the sitting room." He motioned to a door on her left. James, grumbling about being chauffeur, escaped through a door at the far end of the hall.

Gracie followed her uncle into the sitting room and settled on a couch. She glanced around. Comfort was the first impression she felt, followed by loneliness. The room looked barren of personal mementos. Curiosity stirred.

"I apologize for the wagon ride," Uncle Lou said, after a striking Indian woman brought a tray of refreshments. "James refuses to drive my car."

Gracie reached for a cookie off the platter. "Quite all right. I'm here now."

"It's a shame about this influenza going around. But don't worry, my dear girl. You'll be safe here." The crackling flames from the fireplace highlighted an impish twinkle in his eyes. "Now let me tell you of my travels…."

They spent the rest of the evening together, eating as they talked. It didn't take long for her to realize how alike they were. He talked quite a bit for a man, and she learned he'd owned his ranch for ten years and never intended to live back east again.

Uncle Lou delighted her. She could not fathom why Mother and Father disapproved of him. He regaled her with remarkably funny jokes and adventurous tales. Despite their camaraderie, she held back on unveiling her plans for finding Striker. When the hour grew late, he promised to continue his stories tomorrow and showed her to her room.

Weary, Gracie readied for bed. She grabbed the papers from the inner pocket of her soiled suit and set them on the bed. She washed from a small basin on the dresser, and then donned her undergarments. They were silk and, after the grueling day, their smooth coolness was a luxury that made her sigh. After recording the details of her day onto her notepad, she slid into the welcome comfort of bed. She slipped the articles mentioning Striker beneath her pillow.

Connie thought she was crazy, but Gracie couldn't help but be intrigued by the elusive government agent. Rumors said he was an older man, and without conscience, but Connie's cousin reported otherwise. According to her, Striker had rescued her from a band of uncouth men who'd snatched her from her very own backyard in California.

Gracie needed to secure an interview with him if she was ever going to break free from her parents and live her own life.

Snuggling against her pillow, she breathed deeply and prayed for success.

Chapter Three

Trevor sat his mount high above Lou's ranch and inhaled the crisp morning air. Below him Lou's housekeeper, Mary, hung laundry. Gracie probably still slept, tuckered out by her long trip. He studied Mary. Was she happy here, in constant hiding?

She seemed content in her role, happy to clean and have a quiet life.

Not like Gracie. He remembered his impressions of her on the train, long before she'd officially met him at the station. Trouble, he'd thought.

Like Council Bluff.

Because the screams from that fiasco still rang in his ears, he focused on Lou's niece.

So far, Gracie had proven curious but easy. He had to just keep her from going into Burns and stirring up interest in Striker.

He scanned the horizon. Mendez and his men were holed up somewhere in these mountains, searching for Mary, waiting for a chance to snatch the prey that had escaped Mendez so many years ago.

Trevor would make sure the only chance they got was to meet an unofficial noose.

That was Striker's job, after all. He chased down criminals that the higher-ups didn't have the time or knowledge to find, apprehending them and bringing them in. As the investigator beneath Lou, Trevor both reported to him and received cases from him. Lou was a senior investigator who'd been with the bureau since its formation beneath Chief Examiner Finch.

Bringing in Mendez was Trevor's longest-running case but he'd determined to do it this year. Based on what he'd seen on the train, Mendez was getting loony. In the last year, Mendez had ramped up his efforts to find Striker. Sending henchmen to scour the countryside for Mary, wanting to use her to find the man who'd rescued her and foiled his kidnapping.

Mary had been Mendez's first victim. A spontaneous deal that started an illegal thousand-dollar enterprise the government was still working to shut down. Quietly, of course.

But Trevor wanted to be done with all that.

The land called to him. It was time to settle down, own a ranch. No woman deserved the baggage he carried, though. Could he be content on his own? He'd been alone too many years to count. Maybe since he'd been a boy, even. His parents hadn't offered any kind of protection or companionship, had never given him a reason to want a relationship with anyone, but the urge for a family niggled at him.

He pushed the feeling to the side. With a past like his, he didn't deserve a wife. His mouth relaxed as he watched Mary go into the house. A short career, one he excelled at but didn't love, would end with this assignment, even if the guilt didn't.

And he'd get the one thing he longed for more than a home.

No more blood on his hands.

* * *

Gracie awoke to warm light streaming through large, arched windows into a spacious bedroom. She stretched her arms above her head, yawned and absorbed her new surroundings with all the famed curiosity of a cat.

Simplicity made the small room lovely. A bright, multicolored rug covered the honey-hued oak floor. A gilt mirror hung over a large wooden dresser in front of the bed. The bed had four large posts and the ivory quilt that draped it was warm and soft.

She swung her legs out of the bed and then began tidying up. Her jewels went into a far corner of the closet, shadowed by angles. They'd come in handy should she need to travel across the country in pursuit of Striker. Better yet, if she procured an interview and the *Woman's Liberator* sent her on assignment, she'd be financially sound. She'd brought only some of her valuables; a few for sentiment, a few for wear and a few for hocking, should the need arise.

After they were stowed safely away, she unpacked her clothes into the heavy dresser, and then set about trying to make the bed, a chore usually taken care of by maids at home. *But this is a new place,* she reminded herself. Her fingers tucked the sheets beneath the mattress. There were still wrinkles in the middle of the bed.

She tugged on the sheet.

More wrinkles.

In the end, she contented herself with straightening the covers across the mattress as best she could. She'd just dressed in an olive-green blouse and matching skirt when a knock sounded.

"Coming." She pulled the door open.

The Indian servant she'd seen last night stood in the hallway, holding a pile of linens. "May I come in?"

Gracie nodded and the woman glided into the room,

more graceful than a monarch butterfly. Dozens of questions sprang to Gracie's mind but she bit her lip and waited for the servant to speak first.

"I'm Mary, the housekeeper." She rolled the *R* in her name, her sentence ending with a charming lilt. Dark brown eyes rested on Gracie. "I've brought you some clean linens, and breakfast is waiting downstairs. I hope you like omelets. Lou didn't tell me anything about you so I just mixed up something quick."

"Omelets sound wonderful. You have a darling accent."

Mary stepped forward, holding up the pile of linens. "Where would you like these?"

"Wherever you wish. Don't let me get in the way. Are you Indian? You sound Irish. You dress just like me." Gracie frowned down at her own subdued clothing. "But you're much more beautiful. How many languages do you speak?"

Mary looked a bit taken aback, her mouth rounding into a soft O. Gracie flushed and bit hard on her lip to hold in any more nosy questions.

"Three languages," Mary finally said, regaining her soft smile. "I'm Paiute and Irish. Do you want help unpacking?" She walked to the dresser and started straightening Gracie's clothes. "I hope you brought some wool underclothes. It gets cold here. Biting cold."

Gracie's stomach rumbled loudly in the quiet room and she grimaced. Mother often found her appetite a source of embarrassment. "I apologize. Perhaps you can tell I need my food."

"Nonsense," Mary said briskly, as if she saw Gracie's discomfort and sought to comfort her. "I'm hungry, too. Follow me."

They walked to the dining room on the first floor and sat at an exquisite mahogany table loaded with dishes.

"I thought you made only eggs," Gracie said.

"Oh, that's the main meal. Lou, Trevor and James eat quite a bit. I've got to make plenty of biscuits and pancakes to go with the omelets."

While Gracie admired Mary's glossy black hair and exotic eyes, the men shuffled in and sat. Her impressions last night had been accurate. James looked just as grizzled as ever, offsetting Uncle Lou's handsome features and Mr. Cruz's dark ones. She wished belatedly that she'd taken more care with her appearance. She felt large and frumpy, especially sitting near the luminous Mary.

The men grumbled their greetings. Mary rose and bustled around the table, filling cups with coffee and orange juice. Gracie wanted to help, but had no idea how. She had never served anything more than tea. She also didn't want Mr. Cruz's attention on her. In the light of day he looked more appealing than ever, and the last thing she wanted was for him to notice her plain attire.

The men began devouring forkfuls of food, and Gracie stared in horrified amazement. All thoughts of remaining inconspicuous deserted her.

"Is anyone going to pray?"

Quiet descended. Forks stopped in midair and four pairs of eyes turned her way. Uncle Lou spoke first.

"We don't put much stock in prayer here, Gracie. You're welcome to, of course, silently. Morning, by the way. Like your dress." He resumed eating, and so did the others, while Gracie sat paralyzed with shock. She wanted to mind her own business, she really did, and her polite upbringing struggled valiantly for several seconds before it surrendered to her emotions.

"Are you jesting, Uncle Lou?" she asked carefully.

"He's not jesting, missy. Life is harsh. If'n there's a God, He's a cruel one and not who we'd like to follow."

Gracie didn't know whether to weep with pity or laugh outright at James's response. She stared down at her plate, silently entreating God to give her some words, some hope for these people. She looked up at last only to find everyone eating and conversing, all thoughts of God shoved to the back of their minds.

"Tell me about your business, Uncle Lou," she said when she had regained her composure. For the rest of breakfast they monopolized the conversation with talk of business, politics and the suffrage movement. Uncle Lou, it turned out, was in favor of women getting the vote. "1912," he said, pride swelling his voice. "We gave women that right years ago."

"Gracie here's a fan of jazz." Trevor pointed his fork at her. She flushed. He'd remembered.

"Really?" Uncle Lou winked at her. "I like Jelly Roll Morton myself."

The heat in her face hiked up a notch. "I've heard his morals are questionable."

James busted out laughing. A smile played over Uncle Lou's face. Gracie's brows drew together, and when she glanced at Mary she noticed the other woman's cheeks had turned scarlet.

Gracie saw Trevor studying her, a half grin catching the corners of his mouth. She caught her lip between her teeth. He found immorality amusing but seemed angered by her belief in God.

Maybe his perspective might change as they traveled the countryside searching for Striker.

Gracie almost went stir-crazy.

Four days passed before Mary agreed to take her around the ranch. She'd managed to steal a few moments each day exploring, but had spent the bulk of her time helping Mary with chores. And slipping in a few questions about Striker. Mary didn't say much about him, though, and Uncle Lou proved exceptionally closemouthed.

After hanging laundry on the fourth day, Gracie borrowed one of Mary's leather coats and soon they were strolling across the flat land, watching the mountains roll in the distance.

"What is that one?" Gracie pointed to a shrub near her feet.

"Bud sagebrush. It's common around these parts. There's some red top grass and winterfat over here." Mary gestured to her right. The wind caught strands of hair and blew them across her high cheekbones. "Paiute use winterfat sometimes to treat fevers. The sheep eat it, too."

Gracie studied the hoary white plants. By itself the plant looked ugly and bare. But where winterfat grew in bunches, the plant took on the appearance of a silver bouquet. The whole of Harney County took her breath away and she hadn't even explored the mountains yet. It was unfortunate this land was so far removed from civilization.

They ambled along, Gracie listening closely as Mary pointed out various species of plants and gave little tidbits of information about the area. Then Mary stopped abruptly, her gaze resting on a peak in the distance.

Gracie squinted in that direction but saw nothing out of the ordinary.

"I just remembered ironing I need to do." Something like regret flashed across Mary's face.

"Oh, how disappointing," Gracie said. The brisk breeze caressed her face, carrying new and exciting scents. "Do you have to go?"

"I'm sorry."

She didn't want to offer but forced herself to anyway. "Can I help, then?"

Mary grimaced. "No. You've almost been insane trying to get outside. Enjoy your walk. You've done more than necessary." She hesitated. "Be careful. If you see anyone, come straight to the house."

"Wait! Do you suppose we'll be going into Burns anytime soon?"

"If you're really looking for Striker, you won't find him there." Mary turned and picked her way to the house.

"But I need a telephone." Gracie frowned as Mary retreated without an answer. If she knew Striker's whereabouts, and understood why Gracie asked questions, then why had she been so evasive?

As soon as Mary became a dot on the bumpy horizon, Gracie's gaze circled back to her surroundings. Steens Mountain rose in the distance, its snowy tips glowing in the crisp air. Mary had told her the mountains were really a single fault block, rising almost ten thousand feet in places.

Good details to get down. She pulled out her map, guessed her coordinates and refolded the map. She drew out her notepad and jotted the numbers, adding a description of the terrain. Could there be caves and hidden dwelling places in these rocks?

The back of her neck prickled. Criminals of the vilest natures could find refuge here. Would Striker? It explained the sightings in Burns and other Oregon towns.

Striker wouldn't hide with criminals, though.

She slipped the pad of paper and folded map into her coat pocket and began to walk, stripping off the coat and tying it around her waist. In Boston she was often stuck indoors sewing, knitting, learning how to run a large household and how to balance the books. With the war going on she'd been inside much of the time, doing good deeds that left her with sore fingers and crooked stitches. Despite her longing to serve her country, there seemed to be no place where she fit.

She had wanted to join the military but her parents expressly forbid it.

Gracie had considered becoming a wartime operator but her French made people cringe.

The sight of blood caused her to faint, which ruled out nursing. Thus the uneventful good deeds such as sewing came into play.

Thankfully, there were rumors the Great War would soon end. She hoped they were true for the soldiers' sakes as well as her own.

The sound of hooves broke her thoughts, scattering them as surely as the approaching horse shook dust from the horizon. A horseman pounded toward her, gaining ground by the second. The rider's form sharpened into a broad-shouldered man.

Chapter Four

Heart slamming against her sternum, Gracie backed up, then realized the futility of such an endeavor. Her imagination set sail as the rider's shape morphed into a more recognizable figure. One who wore Trevor's conspicuous hat.

Relief rushed through her so fast her knees trembled. Trevor often came to meals but she had not been alone with him since their conversation at the train depot. She fumbled with her skirt, the memory of feeling dowdy the first morning here flustering her into a nervous state. She took a deep breath.

That was ridiculous. Gracelyn Riley did *not* get nervous. Especially over a man.

She straightened her shoulders, willing some starch into her backbone as the horse thundered up to her. The beast stopped mere inches from her nose. Swallowing a squeal, she stepped back.

"Hello, Trevor. What are you doing out here?" She looked up at him, shading her eyes from the morning sun.

"That would be my question for you." His deep voice carried a sterner note than usual.

"Is there a problem with me walking in the grass?"

"Let's just say you know nothing about the Oregon

desert. Anything could happen to you out here, and you wouldn't know how to deal with it."

The rich scent of horse and leather floated to her. The sun warmed her cheeks and his hat cast a shadow over his face. No doubt he wore that stubborn look he'd sported on the bench.

A hot flush of anger zipped through her. Finally out from beneath her parents' confining rules, no man was going to tell her what to do. Her shoulders stiffened. "Your presumptions about me are astounding. Move your horse so I may continue on my way."

Trevor's stallion shuffled in front of her, heavy hooves pounding the dirt. He looked ready to break into a gallop. He snuffled, a loud, wet and hungry sound. She eyed the large teeth warily as the horse chomped at the bit.

Perhaps a more mannerly approach would work best. "Please move your horse."

"Why don't I give you a ride back?"

"No, thank you. I am enjoying myself, and you seem…" She didn't want to finish. Offending him was not in her best interests.

"Seem what?" he asked, scar quirking upward with that annoying eyebrow of his.

She backed up another step. "Uh, like you'd rather ride than walk." She banished the word *irascible* to the back of her mind.

"I like walking."

He slid off the saddle. They walked together, the horse trailing them. Gracie wanted to talk to relieve the silence, but her mind had become curiously blank. No need to talk his ear off as she'd done at the depot.

Trevor shortened his stride to match hers. For a time the horse's plodding footsteps and the whispers of the grass in the breeze were the only sounds to keep them company.

He finally broke the silence. "What do you think of the ranch?"

"I find it charming. Have you lived here long?"

"Lou and I go way back. I knew him when he bought the place and I came to work for him shortly thereafter."

"Do you enjoy it?" Gracie glanced at him, admiring the determination that marked his face. "The work, I mean? I've always thought business, besides mathematics, would be dreary."

"I like order, structure. The thrill of competition and hunting out the perfect stock."

She laughed. "You don't seem adventurous, but I suppose you are, in a different sort of way." A sigh escaped. "It is unfortunate that adventure is difficult to come by out here. A desert has little in the way of exciting activities. I fear I'll be dreadfully bored until spring."

Trevor snorted.

She ignored the derisive sound. "Do you plan to own your own ranch someday? Being someone else's right-hand man is not the same as being in charge."

"Someday I'll buy a ranch."

"You'd do well with it, I'm sure."

A flicker of emotion crossed his face. "Thanks. How's everything going for you at the house?"

"Lovely. Uncle Lou is a real sport. It's wonderful how he financially supports the suffrage movement. Women deserve the right to participate in the choosing of our elected state representatives. Don't you agree?"

"Change subjects quick, don't you?"

She grimaced. "I apologize."

Something like a smile snagged the corners of his lips.

"Women are citizens, just like any man," he finally said after an interminably long silence.

An enlightened cowboy. For a moment, Gracie didn't

know what to say. Dragging in a deep breath, she looked over at him. "A man's treatment of a woman's basic rights says much of his character."

Her toe caught against a rock and before she knew what was happening, she landed on her elbow. She winced at the sting and moved to stand.

Rattling filled the air. She stiffened, confused. Within seconds she saw the snake poised in front of her. For a second it seemed as though her heart stopped beating.

Then Trevor was beside her, raising his arm. He moved so fast she didn't understand what he did until the rattling stopped and the only sound was gunfire echoing across the uneven landscape.

Breath shallow, Gracie stood carefully. "Thank you." She clasped her hands tight but their shaking wouldn't stop.

He holstered the gun, expression unreadable. "You okay?" His fingers reached toward her, then withdrew. By unspoken assent, they began to walk again, skirting around the area where the mangled carcass of a rattler must surely rest.

She wouldn't know as she kept her gaze averted. "I see what you mean about dangers." Good. Her voice sounded normal.

"Actually, most rattlers are curling up in crevices by now. That was strange." He glanced at her.

Still shaky, she attempted to give him a smile and for her trouble, stumbled over a shrub again. She instinctively grabbed Trevor's arm for support. A bright spot of red on her sleeve snagged her attention.

Blood.

The ground shifted below her. Trevor's muscles flexed beneath her fingers as her knees lost their strength. He hauled her up and his fingers dug into her shoulders.

"What's the matter with you?" His eyes, so very dark in the morning light, searched hers.

"My pardon. The sight of blood—" she gulped "—makes me faint."

Trevor released her and ran his hand across his chin. "You're saying you can't handle blood?"

Gracie knew her face must be crimson. She looked away. It was a most embarrassing disorder. "Again, my apologies." She searched for a new topic and blurted out the first thought that came to her. "Your arms feel as though they're hewn from rock."

"I have reasons to stay strong." He smirked. It transformed his face from rugged granite to soft strength.

Her heart fell faster than she could catch it.

She cleared her throat. "I suppose ranching does require strength." She had to be mindful of her goal to find Striker for an exclusive interview. She should pick Trevor's brain. Anything to calm her racing pulse. "Some say Striker frequents this area."

"On to another subject now, huh?"

"Well?" They picked their way across the ground, Gracie careful to keep a respectable distance from her attractive companion.

"Who says these things?"

"The papers, people who've claimed to see him."

He quirked a brow. "That so?"

"I have reason to believe he lives close by." She studied him for a moment. "You don't know the man, do you?" He kept walking and she shrugged. "Of course not. You do exude a dangerous edge but I don't think you have the wild spirit to hobnob with government agents. Don't get me wrong," she added when he shot her a disgruntled look. "I'm sure you could handle any situation, but it's obvious you're a bit on the stodgy side. Besides, Striker is rumored to be an older man."

Trevor stopped and she almost stumbled into him. He planted his hands low on his hips, looked up at the sky and groaned. His hat hung down his back. "I'm stodgy? Miss Explorer can't find adventure in a wilderness."

"Well, Mr. Cruz. I certainly did not mean it as an insult."

"I know what you meant, Miss Riley."

"Oh, look, we're almost to the house." Gracie pointed out the obvious and quickened her pace.

"Slow down, woman. Just meant you got a little bit of snobbishness about you."

Snobbishness, indeed. She twisted around and eyed him. "That may be. At the moment, I do not care to debate it."

"Ya got your skirts all twisted in a knot, don't you, Gracie? Bet your mama wrinkles her face that way when she gets her dander up."

Gracie didn't remark on his outrageous words, or his sarcastic, exaggerated accent. She had one question, then she'd head up the porch steps and escape the rude man. "Do you always carry a weapon?"

"Yes."

"Is there a reason?"

"Seems obvious enough to me. This is dangerous territory, home to more than one kind of snake." His eyes turned serious. "Don't go wandering by yourself, Gracie."

"If you are referring to Mendez, Striker will take care of him. In the meantime, I'll speak with Uncle Lou about looking around." She used a polite but distant voice to cover her annoyance. "Thank you for walking me back."

They parted, but once Gracie was in the warm house she rushed to the front window of the study and watched Trevor leave.

* * *

Later that day, Gracie visited Uncle Lou in his office. He had a smooth voice and smelled of sandalwood. He gave her an earful of stories about his life and local gossip but he didn't mention Striker. As he spoke, Gracie pondered the rift between him and her parents. He seemed charming, successful, everything her parents admired. But even with all his blessings he despised the mention of God. That made her curious, too. She didn't ask him about it because she didn't want to be pushy.

She exercised restraint once in a while.

Eventually Uncle Lou had to leave, but not before giving her permission to use his stationery and pens. On his way out, he flicked an envelope her way, and she squealed when she recognized Connie's tight handwriting on the front. She'd force herself to write a quick note home first, then read Connie's letter.

If only she had a telephone, but she'd been told this area of Harney County was too distant for telephone wires. Somehow she'd get to Burns. Even if she had to walk. The coordinates she'd been given were only a guess. Connie was supposed to verify them and send more—perhaps in this letter…

Gracie finished writing home, making sure to inform her parents once again that she wouldn't be marrying Hugh.

She left the envelopes on Uncle Lou's desk, and then went into the hallway. A scarred oak bench sat against the wall. She sank down on its padded floral seat and ripped the letter open. Connie's dark, bold letters jumped out. Gracie smiled and read with haste.

Dearest Gracie,
It is incredibly boring here without you. Elizabeth

and Laura do not have your sense of adventure. I am writing this the day after you have left. You see, I am already resorting to letter writing to keep myself from yawning.

My dearest friend, please come home soon. I am staying indoors for the most part, as rumors of the influenza are increasing. I have heard that Anne Holbrook has it. Pray for her.

I am planning a huge party for my twenty-fifth birthday. You'll be back by spring, no doubt.

I should have come with you to Oregon. I suppose you are having grand adventures while I am trapped in the rigid society of the Bostonians.

Not so rigid anymore, perhaps. I have bought another set of trousers. I love them, Gracie. I am convinced they are here to stay.

I love you, dearest friend. Have a wonderful experience, and I shall see you soon.

Love Always,

Connie

P.S. It is rumored Striker has gone west. Oregon or California. The ladies are all atwitter about your idea for an article. It is high time you were paid for your writing. Cousin Jane couldn't find the coordinates she promised you. She fears they've been lost for good. Beware Mendez. Sources claim he's been seen in Oregon for what could only be nefarious purposes.

Gracie lowered the letter. No coordinates? Nothing?

Footsteps sounded in the next room. Tall and lean, Trevor strode into the hall, glowering. "Is Lou in?"

"He left to go somewhere with James about an hour ago." She stood, the letter still clutched in her grasp, and forced a smile even though her insides had sunk to her feet.

Trevor glanced at her hands. "A letter already?"

"Oh, yes, from my dearest friend, Connie. She sent it the day after I left. I suppose it came rather fast."

"How are things back home?" He'd stopped in the middle of the hall. His hands pushed through his hair in an agitated motion—eyes distant.

"She says rumors of influenza are increasing and one of our acquaintances has caught it. Other than that, she is wondering if I have had any adventures. She longs to meet Striker, as do I." Disheartened and a bit wary of Trevor's mood, she rambled on. "Unfortunately, adventures in the desert are unlikely. Do you ever wish to live in the city? Somewhere exciting?"

Trevor's eyes snapped into focus. She wished she'd bothered to straighten herself after lunch. She squared her shoulders.

"The country is just as exciting," he said flatly.

"Perhaps I need to explore a bit more." At least in Burns, where someone *must* know something of Striker. "It is dreadfully boring here, is it not, Mr. Cruz?"

Trevor frowned. She thought it boring? For a moment Gracie sounded just like Eunice and Julia. The comparison to the women he despised made his chest clench up. The fact he'd begun to like Gracie only made things worse.

He stepped forward until he towered over her. She was tall for a woman, with curves that couldn't be hidden beneath the popular dresses, but there was something about her large doe eyes and thick brown curls that caught him unaware.

Then there was the contrast between her tendency to chatter and her ability to hold an intelligent conversation on a number of topics. At least what he'd observed during meals. He'd considered her a decent woman. Sure, he'd only known her a bit but he usually counted himself a good judge of character.

And Lou liked her.

But, barring Mary, she sounded as superficial as all the other women he'd known.

He stepped forward and Gracie backed up against the wall, rosy lips parting in surprise. He wanted to intimidate her. Unfortunately, she didn't look cowed, just flustered.

"Do you usually become angry when people do not care for your desert, Mr. Cruz?"

"It's not your opinion that bothers me but the shallowness inherent in your tone."

"Me, shallow?" She visibly blanched, and then recovered by lifting her chin. "I apologize for my attitude. I hadn't meant to offend you. It's only that I've important things to do and instead I am stuck in a desert when I need to find Str—people, lots of people, and I cannot do that here."

Gut tight, Trevor stepped away from Gracie. He'd heard her slip of the tongue. Considering the intelligence he'd received today, things were going from bad to worse. And now he had to deal with this…socialite. His teeth ground together. He had the sneaking suspicion she thought Oregon was home to old-time sheriffs riding down outlaws.

But beneath anger lurked interest and with effort he reined it in. She was his boss's niece. Disregarding everything else going on in his life, that was reason enough to back away.

"Too bad you're *stuck* here," he said disdainfully, then spun to leave.

"Wait," she called after him. "Aren't you going to tell me why you're so angry?"

Trevor turned and crossed his arms.

"Connie tells me I'm a good listener. She shares all her

little dramas with me." She caught her lip between her teeth. "It's true. Connie has tons of men trouble." Nodding, she tapped her chin with her forefinger. "Most people grow defensive because they've been hurt in some manner. What was I saying that irritated you? That the desert is dreadfully boring? Or was it something else entirely...?" She stopped chattering when he advanced swiftly.

A ferocious need clamored through his chest, locked his jaw.

"Are you angry again? I was just trying to help," she stuttered, backing up a few steps.

"Gracelyn, I would suggest you go to your room and start a quilt before I do something...unseemly."

"I assure you, Mr. Cruz, unseemly doesn't faze me. And my sewing skills are atrocious, anyhow." She stood rooted to her spot.

Frowning, he crossed his arms. If he suggested she don a pair of trousers and run into the mountains, she probably would, just for the fun of it.

She made a little squeak when he moved closer. Looking flushed and sounding breathless, she said, "You're an intriguing man. Why aren't you married yet?"

The hurt that lassoed through him was unexpected. He felt his features freeze into something tight and painful. "You just can't help being nosy, can you?"

Then he strode down the hall and slammed out the front door into the brisk October breeze.

Chapter Five

Trevor mounted Butch in one smooth move. He nudged the stallion into a hard gallop and set out for his house. He wanted to rid himself of the tension in his shoulders. Confusion didn't sit well on him. It was an emotion he likened to weakness.

Once at the house he let Butch graze while he grabbed his garden gloves and headed out back to yank persistent weeds from the hard soil.

The garden was his refuge. He could think there, process things. He knelt, his scuffed Levi's kissing the dark dirt with familiar ease. He began to pull out the unwanted elements of this private world, the earth cool against his fingers. The act of working in the soil relaxed him, making him long for the simplicity that had escaped him for too many years.

He thought of the letter he'd picked up this morning. Life just kept getting more complicated.

Gracelyn Riley. What was wrong with her? What was wrong with him? One moment she acted little more than a schoolgirl, brimming with innocent optimism and naivety. The next, her soulful eyes seemed to see straight to his core. For her to ask about marriage…somehow she'd looked right into him and known he was lacking.

If she really possessed the ability to look into a soul, his would surely horrify her.

He sat back and surveyed his small patch of privacy. Not much grew now, not with autumn's crisp breath cooling the land. Some broccoli, winter squash. The few weeds he'd pulled lay scattered beside him. The rest of the plants sprouted in straight rows across the garden, lined up in pristine order. The way he liked them.

He scowled. It'd be nice if the rest of his life would follow suit. A little less than a week of knowing Gracelyn Riley and it felt as if a tornado had come barreling through his tidy little world, destroying all sense of order and moving everything out of place.

The woman went outside at night, a dangerous habit he planned to report to Lou. Burned the clothes she ironed. Dropped dishes and couldn't make edible biscuits. Mary oughta convince Gracie to go muck out the stables. Anything to keep the socialite away from the food and clothes.

"Trevor?"

He leaped up, fingers brushing his holster.

"Mary told me where to find you." Gracie stood at the edge of his garden, hair askew, eyes wide. Her gaze darted around his sanctuary and for a moment he saw it through her eyes. The neat little garden, the rocking chair on the back porch and an endless view of sagebrush land ending in dark mountains situated against bright cobalt sky.

He crossed his arms. "Mary knows better than to send people here. What do you want?"

"Uh, yes." Her fingers twisted in her skirts and a wary look crossed her face. "I know I'm nosy, have been told it a thousand times or more, but I didn't mean to cause you pain."

"I'm fine." Trevor pulled his hands down his face, throat suddenly drier than the dirt at his feet. He gestured her toward his house. "I need some water."

They walked in and he filled two cups before handing one to Gracie. She took it, a slight smile on her face. "You have a beautiful home."

Trevor grunted and drank from his cup, the cool slide of water relieving his thirst.

Gracie set the glass on the kitchen counter. "Your house inspires good feelings. Are you the one who decorated?" She ran her fingers across the countertop. "Teak, right? So classy, elegant." Her tone became serious. "I spoke without thinking. I've never tried to hurt or offend anyone purposefully with my words. Nevertheless, there is no excuse for my blabbering. Will you forgive me?"

Trevor leaned against the counter and shoved his hands in the pockets of his blue jeans. "It's been a hard day. Broken fences and loose cattle put me in a bad mood." And a letter that put everything dear to him in danger. "You've got nothing to be concerned about."

Gracie chewed on her lip again, obviously not believing his paltry excuse. "Thank you for the water," she said. "I'll see you at dinner."

"We call it supper here." He shifted his hip against the counter.

Gracie blinked.

Trevor saw her silent scrutiny and had to brace himself. It had been a long time since he'd felt an attraction for a woman. Gracie pulled at his emotions, though, and he stamped the knowledge down with force. There were a lot of reasons not to care for her. He counted them in his head.

One, she was the boss's niece.

Two, she was young, probably inexperienced. Though looks could be deceiving.

Three, a hypocrite. He couldn't forget the trace of snobbery in her voice when she'd been lecturing him about the benefits of the city.

Four, he'd known the girl a short time. Yep, plenty of reasons.

Her pale hand rested on his kitchen counter and he resisted the urge to touch her skin, to see if it felt as smooth and warm as it looked.

"I need to get back. Thank you for the water," she repeated. Her gaze slipped away, scanning his counter and stopping on a letter he'd meant to burn. It lay propped against where the counter met the wall, the handwriting legible from where he stood.

"I'll let you out," he said quickly.

Gracie looked up, and he could tell she'd seen too much. She didn't ask questions like he'd expected but rather waggled her fingers at him and stepped out the door. A blast of cold slammed the door shut behind her.

Trevor watched her from the window in his living room, a lone figure huddled against a harsh wind. The sky was streaked orange by the setting sun. He should take her back in his Ford. It would be the kind thing to do. He reluctantly grabbed his hat and yelled out the front door. "Gracie, let me give you a ride. Wait up!"

She turned, the wind lashing her skirts against her legs. He led her to the back of his house where he kept his truck. She wore a small smile as she got in. The engine coughed to life, and they drove over the rough terrain, bouncing in awkward silence. He trained his gaze forward.

Gracie cleared her throat. "I didn't notice the lack of a road when I walked over."

"No need for one." Trevor concentrated on avoiding

shrubs. It helped him ignore her perfume, some flowery scent that made him think of spring.

"Thank you for driving me back. The weather turned colder than I expected."

"Winter's coming," he said, voice terse.

"I've always loved winter, how it shows God's goodness, His faithfulness." She smiled, her eyes glowing in the sunset like a newly oiled rifle stock. He loved his rifle. "I can feel how close He is and how small I am in the desolation of winter."

He looked ahead, jaw tight. "What I sense is the harshness of this place."

"But the plants grow. He provides sun and rain, and despite the harshness, there's life. He is good." The unbridled optimism of youth rang in her voice.

"Time will temper that outlook."

Gracie studied Trevor's sharp, lined profile, wondering how to respond.

His face reflected him in many ways. Strong, stern. Weary of soul, as if the winter of life had deadened within him all ability to grow. The hope was that good seeds still lay in the frozen soil of his heart, waiting for spring.

Back in the kitchen, before seeing that intriguing letter on his counter, she'd observed how Trevor filled out his earth-stained Levi's with muscular strength, and how his plaid shirt stretched tight against his broad shoulders. She was unaccustomed to noticing men in such a physical way, but at that moment she'd had trouble removing her gaze.

What would have happened if she'd leaned forward and kissed him?

The thought brought a stinging blush to her cheeks. She wasn't so bold. A woman simply didn't kiss just anyone, especially a man known for such a small time. Most important of all, it was Striker who she longed to forge a relationship with, not some taciturn cowboy.

The truck jolted over an uneven piece of land, bringing her attention back to Trevor's profile. "Why don't you believe in God?"

He shot her a glare. "I don't believe in a God who lets people live in a world like this."

She rolled her eyes. "I'm not even going to ask what's wrong with it because I'm sure you'll have a whole list of doldrums to recite. Nevertheless, you should consider the good things."

"It's not that easy, Gracelyn. You can't just simplify pain and suffering."

"I'm not. I am not trying to, at least." She cocked her head. "You have a good life, Trevor, in a place you love. And yet you're bitter?" She was fishing, she knew, but it was in her nature to probe. He awakened something within, and she found herself longing to discover more of him.

Trevor parked his truck next to Uncle Lou's wagon, then turned to Gracie, eyes blazing. Her curiosity withered beneath his hard gaze.

"'God is so good,'" he mocked. "What do you, socialite of Boston, know about pain? I could tell you stories that would shock you. You're lighthearted and completely unaware of the suffering around you. We don't believe in God around here for good reasons." Trevor struck the wheel with the palm of his hand. The sound ricocheted in the truck like a gunshot. "What do you know about a drunken father who beats his kid unconscious every night for smiling the wrong way, mothers who prostitute themselves and then spend the money on whiskey and opiates. Do you know why Mary doesn't go to church? They won't let her in because she's part Paiute. That's some God you serve."

Gracie pressed herself back against the passenger door, a faint tremor working through her stomach. No wonder Trevor hardly smiled. He was obviously a man tormented.

She frowned. She didn't like his implication that she was a shallow child incapable of empathy, ignorant of evil. She was torn between defensive anger and deep sorrow.

As he glared at her, the scar on his brow stark white against his skin, perception filled her. She straightened from the door and leaned toward him.

"You do believe in God," she said slowly. "You just hate Him."

A shocked expression crossed his grim features, then a look of dawning knowledge.

There was silence as he looked away from her. "You're right," he said, voice low.

Gracie wanted to say more, but he looked so defeated. Gone was the strong presence she had been attracted to in his kitchen. In its place sat a lonely, desolate man. A man who had lived in darkness for far too long. She gently placed her palm on his shoulder.

"Get out."

"But I—"

"Now."

She opened her door and slid out quickly. Autumn sliced through her, and she wrapped her arms tightly against her ribs. The menacing intensity vibrating through his voice made her lungs feel squished within her rib cage. She'd barely made it to the front porch before his truck squealed, digging up dirt as it turned and bounced across the land, not headed toward his house, but somewhere else.

For a moment she held perfectly still, a deep pain spreading through her, immobilizing her. Would she ever say anything right? She drew a full breath, released it, then turned and went inside.

Mary stood in the hall, forehead puckered. "What's wrong with Trevor?"

"We were talking about God," Gracie murmured.

Her brow smoothed. "That explains it, it does. He doesn't like the mention of Him."

Gracie followed Mary into the dining room. "You've known Trevor a long time."

"Since I was a wee babe." Mary ran a dust rag over the rich-hued furniture. "His mama and mine shared a profession together, and he watched out for me. He's a good man, he is, just can't accept that God loves. He can't put it together in his head because of his upbringing, I expect."

"His upbringing?"

"Our mothers were prostitutes."

"Oh." Gracie winced. Trevor had been speaking from his own experiences. "What about your fathers?"

"Mine just wanted his whiskey. Don't look so sad, Gracie. Bad things happen in life. So do good. It's the way things work out."

"It's not right, Mary. I wish there was something I could do to change things. You don't seem bitter."

"God's helped me forgive."

"You're a Christian, then?" The heaviness in Gracie's chest lifted a little. "Trevor said churches here don't accept you."

"Some churches, unfortunately, are very prejudiced, but I do meet with a few Christian neighbors every other Sunday for our own version of a church service. There's no local church close by so we do our best."

"But you don't pray at meals."

Mary sighed. "Not out loud, no."

They walked upstairs, and Gracie felt her depression dissipating. Church! She bounced after Mary into the bedroom, forcing thoughts of Trevor and the life he'd endured to the back of her heart.

Mary wiped the window and Gracie wrinkled her nose at the stench of vinegar.

"I'd love to meet some of the neighbors."

"You can come." Mary smiled gently. "But please, leave me be so I can finish cleaning."

"I'll help."

"Absolutely not. This is my job. Maybe you need a rest?"

"I suppose." Gracie shrugged and left the bedroom. Despite the excitement tumbling through her at the prospect of attending church, thoughts of Trevor would not leave. Perhaps she had been hasty in her judgments of the people here. Perhaps she was not as modern, not as accepting, as she'd once thought.

Chapter Six

A great journalist must be bold and fearless.

Gracie set her shoulders and walked to where James stood against the wagon, eyes squinting against the morning light.

"Good morning, James."

He grunted in reply.

"Are you heading to Burns this morning? I've need of several things. Toiletries, chocolate…" Clues as to Striker's whereabouts. That letter on Trevor's counter had been quite interesting, though she hadn't seen enough to know what it meant, or if it had anything to do with Striker.

She knew only that the return address was from the Bureau of Investigation. Why would the government be writing to Trevor?

"I got no patience for your yapping. Git," James replied. The wagon creaked as he straightened and turned away from her, messing with something in the back.

"No talking…I promise," she said.

He shook his head and spit his tobacco to the side. "Nope. Stay here with Mary."

Taken aback, Gracie didn't know what to say. Sunshine rolled over her, bathing the wagon with light. James paid her no heed. He walked around the wagon and clomped up the front porch steps.

Drawing a deep, unsteady breath, Gracie glanced around. No one to see if she left. Would they worry? She gnawed her lower lip, then made her decision.

A quick dash through the kitchen door brought her to Mary, who was cleaning the stove.

"I'm going on a ride. I'll be home later," Gracie told her breathlessly.

"Do you need food?"

"No, thanks."

Biting her cheeks to keep from smiling, Gracie darted out the door and back to the wagon. With no one in sight, sneaking up under the covers in the bed of the wagon didn't pose a problem.

The rough wool contained a musty smell. Like hay and mold. Her nose twitched but she managed not to sneeze. Voices drew near. Low, male tones.

The wagon shuddered as the men climbed in. Gracie grimaced. Would it be more than just James going to Burns? She was counting on him not noticing her. But with two…well, maybe that would work out better. They'd be busy talking and might not notice if she needed to shift around the bed to get comfortable.

Something tickled her nose. A sneeze worked through her and exploded out, just as the wagon burst into action. The force of its movement rolled her into the wagon side. Sharp pain rocked through her scalp but she ignored it.

Focus, that's what she needed.

A journalist couldn't be a prissy socialite, but a daring adventurer who took risks others only dreamed of taking.

Besides, she needed something to take her mind off Trevor. Curiosity was no excuse for upsetting him the way she had.

She relaxed against the floor of the wagon bed. Perhaps this trip would be the only one she'd need to get the information she wanted. If she couldn't get an interview, she'd settle for an article. She frowned, remembering Mother's most recent letter. It had been a virtual tirade, accusing Gracie of being ridiculous for refusing marriage to an upstanding, socially appropriate man.

It didn't matter what Mother said. Love would be the foundation of Gracie's marriage someday. Not money or connections. This was the twentieth century, after all. The archaic system of arranged marriages was long dead, at least for Americans.

Closing her eyes, she waited for the wagon to reach its destination.

An hour or so later, judging by the position of the sun in the sky, the wagon rolled to a stop. Perspiration trickled down Gracie's neck as she peeked from her wool cover.

"You want flour?" James's voice crackled so close that Gracie almost shrieked. Instead she stiffened, holding perfectly still.

"Yep." Uncle Lou's voice floated over clear as a lake in summer. "I'll go check the telegraphs."

Sounds and smells inundated her, the pounding of feet against wooden sidewalks, the murmur of voices hurrying back and forth. Gracie tried to take deep, even breaths but her heart refused to quit knocking against her sternum and the blanket was about to suffocate her.

After minutes of dreadful heat, she could take no more. She flipped the blanket off and scooted up, carefully inching her way toward the edge of the wagon, hoping to slip off and question a few people before Uncle Lou or James came back.

Oh, this was a foolhardy plan. Spontaneity proved once again to be a foe. Stifling a groan, Gracie slid off the wagon and attempted to straighten her hair and skirts. She must look a fright, for a few people stared at her quite oddly.

She patted her pocket and felt the reassuring bulge of her notebook. If only she'd thought to bring some sort of disguise, a hat or a veil.

But no matter. She'd just avoid the dry goods store and the Post Office. It should be a simple feat.

She looked up, taking in her surroundings. There was more than she suspected. Buildings hugged each side of the road. Avoiding James and Uncle Lou might be harder than she'd thought. The mercantile stood directly across from her and the telegraph office appeared to be down the street.

Her shirt stuck to her skin and an itch crawled along her neck. She must hurry. She ducked to the other side of the wagon. Spotting a linen store, she dodged to the door frame. Surely the men wouldn't visit a store dealing in lady's clothing.

A little bell rang as she opened the door.

She stepped inside, observing the petite woman at the counter and a lone woman standing before daisy-bright bolts of cloth.

"Good morning," she said, moving into the store and giving both women her friendliest smile. "I'm looking for Striker."

Their brows went up in unison. Then a shuttered look seem to come over them. The woman at the counter turned her back and the lady at the bolt of cloth became preoccupied with a particular daisy.

So this was how it would be? Gracelyn set her shoulders. She would not back down from a challenge. Not when it came to her Striker.

* * *

"Went to Burns today," Uncle Lou announced over supper.

Gracie paused in eating. "I really need to get to town, if possible." Especially since today's trip had proven so unfruitful. She'd narrowly managed to return to the wagon before Uncle Lou and James.

A risky business, journalism.

"I don't know about a trip to town. Seems the influenza is all over the country. Military boys are dropping like flies, and the grippe's spread to civilians." He spooned mashed potatoes into his mouth, glancing around the table. His blue eyes weren't sparkling with mirth tonight, Gracie noticed.

"How severe is it?" she asked.

"Oregon doesn't have too many cases yet. It's bad by your parents, Gracie. Real bad." Uncle Lou looked at Trevor. "You're leaving in the morning for that business deal?"

Trevor nodded.

"Wear your mask. Keep safe."

He was leaving? A shiver of foreboding slithered down Gracie's spine. "How long can the influenza last?"

"This one's virulent, but I don't know how long it lasts. I've never had it before." Uncle Lou looked at Mary. "I want you to stay away from town for a while." He paused. "Mendez has been spotted skulking around."

Mary's eyes lowered.

Very strange. Uncle Lou seemed proprietary, almost. As if he had feelings for Mary. But more interesting were his words. Mendez usually kidnapped very young, blonde women.

"Why would Mendez care about Mary?" Gracie shot Trevor a look. He kept eating, head down. He hadn't spoken directly to her since he'd ordered her out of his truck the other day.

"Mendez is obsessed with her," Uncle Lou said slowly. "Years ago, before she came here, he kidnapped her and tried taking her down to Mexico."

Her attention shifted to Mary. "That's horrible. However did you escape?"

"Striker saved her and brought her here," Uncle Lou said.

"Striker," Gracie breathed. "Oh, Mary, what is he like? The papers are wrong, aren't they?"

Mary smiled a quiet smile. "He's wonderful."

"I knew it. A true hero." Gracie sighed and propped her elbow on the table, her cheek on her hand.

"He ain't a hero." Trevor frowned. "Eat your food."

Gracie flinched. His first words to her since their altercation in the truck sounded unbearably bossy.

James cackled around a mouth full of potatoes. "Don't listen to Trevor. We all admire Striker around here, girl."

"The point," Uncle Lou said briskly, "is that you women keep an eye out and if you see anything suspicious, let someone know. Mendez will stop at nothing to get Mary back."

"Why did Striker bring her here? Do you all know him? And how is it you've heard of Mendez being nearby?"

"Everyone knows about Striker." Mary grabbed a biscuit and didn't meet Gracie's eye.

Interesting. They must know the true identity of Striker. They had to. Why else would he have brought Mary to this forsaken place? How would he have even known where to find it?

"So, the rumors are true. Striker's in Oregon. Maybe even in Burns." Gracie speared a broccoli stem and plopped it in her mouth, plans barreling through her mind.

Hadn't the women in the shop ignored her question? Looking almost afraid to answer for fear of repercussions?

"What do you know about Mendez?" Uncle Lou leveled his gaze at her.

Her thoughts rolled to a stop as familiar outrage swelled in her chest. "He kidnaps women and sells them. The Mann Act of 1910 was created in order to stop criminals like him from taking women across state lines for immoral purposes, but he's changed the game because he carts them down to Mexico. And sells them to the highest bidder." Gracie could hear her voice quivering with rage but didn't care. "He's a villain of the lowest order." She cleared her throat, trying to shake the anger, trying not to remember the story Connie had told her about her cousin. The vile deeds that occurred. "I've heard Mendez recently escaped federal custody and is being pursued by Striker."

"You learned all that from the papers?"

She flushed, hating her wayward tongue. "Actually, I have a few additional sources."

"Sources?" Uncle Lou's gaze never wavered, and she had the uneasy feeling she was being interrogated. If her parents found out she'd retained a few contacts from the *Woman's Liberator,* she'd be banned from all sorts of social activities.

Even more reason to secure employment and become independent.

Trying to appear nonchalant, she poked more broccoli into her mouth.

Uncle Lou sighed. "Your sources are off, Gracie. Striker is not pursuing Mendez."

The food lodged in her throat. Uncle Lou had to be wrong. She swallowed hard. "He will. Striker never lets his quarry get away. And I plan to interview him to prove just that. It's time America understood he's not a cold-blooded assassin, but a warm, honorable man."

Uncle Lou shook his head and stood. "You be careful, Gracie. If Mendez is near, I'm starting to think you would've been safer in Boston."

During the following weeks the threat of Mendez and his men roused constant dinner conversation between Uncle Lou and James. It was a fear that loomed larger than the influenza. Gracie found the topic fascinating and it was a distraction from wondering how Trevor fared on his trip.

Late one evening in the bitter beginnings of October, she sat on the porch, stewing. Uncle Lou had returned from town this morning. Never even asked her to go. It seemed that despite Uncle Lou's curious quirks, there'd be no convincing him to traipse around Oregon in search of Striker. That plan needed revision. How could she convince him to help her? Perhaps he'd empathize with her need for independence? Her foot tapped against the porch floor.

She was beginning to suspect Uncle Lou's trips to town were purposefully secretive.

A frigid blast of wind hit her in the face. She wrapped her arms tight against her ribs and shivered. She had to get to Burns again. Surely the entire town wouldn't be as closemouthed as those women at the store.

The sound of hooves caught her attention. Her breath trembled as a lone horseman galloped up to the porch.

Mendez?

No, he wouldn't come by himself. The coward.

She stood, trepidation quivering through her. Uncle Lou had sent Trevor to Kansas three weeks ago. If this was a person up to no good, only Uncle Lou was home to defend her and Mary.

As soon as the rider dismounted and began walking to the porch, Gracie recognized the long, lazy stride. Her stiffness melted as she realized how much she'd missed him, and how happy she was that he'd come back. She couldn't have stopped herself any more than Noah could have stopped the flood. She flung herself off the porch into his surprised arms.

"Trevor!"

"Don't gotta yell in my ear, Gracie." His voice sounded gruff but he didn't let go, just held on as if they never parted in stony silence.

Finally she disengaged herself, straightening her thick wool skirt as if she cared about it being wrinkled.

Uncle Lou walked onto the porch, his shoes heavy on the wood. "Trevor. We worried when we didn't hear from you. C'mon in, tell us what's been happening."

Gracie followed the men, her whole body shaking. She'd hugged Trevor. How completely inappropriate. Yet she wasn't sorry.

She hung her coat on the rack by the door and floated into the sitting room. Trevor was home. She couldn't stop smiling. She'd known Trevor for very little time but her interest in him rivaled her obsession with Striker. In a way, he reminded her of the mysterious agent.

Perhaps it was the undercurrent of honor that dogged his every step.

She sank onto the couch opposite him. Uncle Lou sat like a king in his chair. The fire made the room bright and warm. Gracie hoped it hid the blush she was sure still stained her cheeks. Mary came in and set a tray of cookies and milk on the table between the couches.

"Business is well," Trevor was saying. "But the influenza in Kansas is out of control. I wore a mask the entire time I was there. This epidemic is killing the country."

Wood crackled in the fireplace. A log fell and Gracie jumped. Trevor's features turned her way. His face was craggier, his cheekbones more pronounced, his chin covered with shadow.

She felt as if he were slicing her open with his sharp gaze. A nervous smile trembled on her lips.

"You think it's funny? People are dying. You've probably never heard that word in polite conversation, have you?" His hands pushed through his thick hair before he shot off the couch and stalked out of the room.

Gracie's heart lurched painfully in her chest. Was that what he thought of her?

"I'll go talk to him," Mary said.

Gracie shook her head and stood. "Let me."

Uncle Lou looked at her kindly, for once appearing a benevolent uncle instead of an older brother. "He's tired. Don't take it personally."

Gracie slipped down the hallway. She grabbed two coats from the rack before heading into the starlit chill.

Trevor stood in the front yard, looking at the sky, his back to her. For a second she was struck by the solitary figure and deeply saddened. He was alone and without God.

She went to him and gave him the coat she knew he'd forgotten. Wordlessly he took it and put it on. She wanted to slide her fingers through his but didn't dare. They stared into the night together.

She wanted him to speak first.

"Didn't know you could go five minutes without talking," he said after quiet stargazing.

"I have my moments," she answered lightly, transfixed by the display above. The night sky stretched endlessly above her, stars flung across as if at whim. She knew better.

"You stop eating while I was gone?"

She felt him watching her, probing, and knew a hot flush was spreading across her cheeks. She wasn't sure how much weight she'd lost, wasn't in the habit of looking in the mirror, but Mary had taken in the waists of several garments and her blouses hung looser. The weight loss hadn't been intentional.

"Every meal," she joked.

"You looked fine the way you were," he said brusquely, as if she should stay overweight just to make him happy.

"It so happens that I've been helping Mary with chores. And because Uncle Lou carries less chocolate than to what I'm accustomed, I've become thinner. I don't know why you should care. I'm the same person." She struggled to control her emotions.

"You've been working?"

"I'm not a spoiled rich girl." She hated how her voice trembled. "I care about others…I promise you I do. So I'm learning to do chores and help Mary with whatever I can. Personally, I think I would do better in Uncle Lou's office. I saw his books and they're a mess. I know I could straighten them. I'm excellent at math, but he won't let me near them."

"Lou's books are the least of your concerns. Worry instead about Mendez and his men hiding in these hills." He scanned the horizon, searching, and goose bumps pebbled her arms.

"Surely Striker will stop him."

Trevor's gaze roved over her before he looked away. "He can't do everything, Gracie."

"Of course not. I have complete confidence in God."

"Good. You'll need it. Especially with this influenza going around." Moonlight fell against his face as he looked down at her, his eyes dark pools of mystery. His chin jerked in the direction of the house. "Let's go sit on the porch."

His hand reached up to rub the back of his neck as they walked. "People are dropping like flies all over the country. I've never seen anything like it. Some are saying this grippe is akin to the Black Plague." They lowered themselves into the rocking chairs.

"How horrible." Light from the windows washed over Gracie's face. She fiddled with her skirt. "You've been gone a long time."

"After I conducted business, by chance I discovered my father died. I—" He paused. "Stayed intoxicated for a week or two."

"Oh." Gracie looked away. As if she felt bad for him.

He didn't know how that made him feel. Strange. Angry. He didn't need pity.

Their rockers creaked on the wooden floorboards. Somewhere in the night an owl screeched.

"I'm sorry about your father, Trevor."

He laughed woodenly. If she only knew. When he spoke, his voice was flat. "I hate my father. I've hated him since I learned to speak. He was poison, hurt anything and everyone he ever got close to."

"Why do you seem so disturbed by his death, then?"

He turned to face her, and this time he could clearly see the depths of her irises, the line of her nose, the pity in the turn of her lips.

His chest constricted at the look on her face. When was the last time someone felt bad for him? No one did. He had a great life. Nothing to feel bad about. And yet the expression on her features moved him in some strange way. Prompted him to speak without knowing why she would care.

"My father was an evil man." He stopped rocking. "I

always hated him." A stretch of silence as he searched for words. "He died two weeks ago. I didn't know he was living in Kansas. He found out I was there somehow and sent for me."

"Was it the grippe?"

"No. Just too much whiskey, too much of everything. I went to see him. He was a shriveled husk of a man lying on a dirty cot and I felt like a little boy again."

Trevor cringed, remembering that dark room, the odor of coming death.

"I raised my voice, lost control. Somewhere deep down, I thought he might care. At the end of a life, looking back, most have regrets. But he was the same, Gracie." Trevor wiped his palms down his face, wishing he could wipe the memories just as easy. "He laughed at me, said he wanted to say good riddance before he left for good. I didn't stay. I got out of there fast, went back the next morning and was told he'd died the night before. I've hated him my entire life, and he didn't care a fig." He pinched the bridge of his nose. "My hate served nothing. It was useless and now that he's gone and I have no reason left to hate, my life feels purposeless."

"Oh, no." She twisted toward him. "That's not true. Mary adores you. She says you were always rescuing her from one thing or another. And Uncle Lou couldn't run the ranch without you." Her eyes were large, the light hitting her face and highlighting her earnestness. "Your life is not purposeless," she continued fiercely, gripping the arms of her rocking chair. "You have meaning. God made you for a reason."

"God again," he scoffed.

Gracie leaned closer, as if daring him to look at her. "What if you'd never been born? Who would have watched over Mary? The stars look random at first, don't you think?

But there are patterns to be found, pictures of a larger hand at work." She did touch him then, tenderly, on the shoulder, and the warmth of her fingers seemed to melt his scorn. "I realize I'm just a young woman who hasn't had to deal with much unpleasantness, but I believe with all my heart that God cares for you."

Trevor frowned and moved away from her touch. "I've heard religion before and it's a bunch of hogwash."

Gracie cocked her head.

"You don't think that, though, do you?" he asked.

"Sacrifice borne of passion is not 'hogwash,' in my opinion."

His fingers tapped against the rocking chair. Passion and sacrifice. That was a new thought. "You've got a strange way of looking at God."

Gracie smiled the softest smile he'd ever seen. "His love is life to me."

Feeling awkward, Trevor gave her a stiff nod. Wasn't much a guy could say to a sentiment like that. He didn't know anything about love. "Well, thanks for listening to me ramble," he said.

"You weren't rambling at all. You shared your thoughts and feelings with me. It's what friends do." She stood, tucking her hands into the folds of her coat, and inclined her head to Trevor. "I'll see you in the morning, then?"

"In the morning."

After she left, Trevor looked out over the land. The place he'd been raised, a place that had never had anything to do with God or love. Yet somehow Gracie's words found their way deep inside, slipping by the things his mother taught him, by the lessons of the past, to a place where Mary's soft voice sometimes resonated. Hadn't Mary said something similar to him before? He'd never listened, though.

Never needed to hear her.

But now his pa had passed. Trevor didn't want to end up like him, alone, purposeless, railing at a world that just didn't care. Maybe Mary and Gracie had a point about love. There was one way to find out.

Chapter Seven

Sunday dawned clear and crisp, perfect for fellowship with others of like faith. Gracie jumped out of bed, bounced to her closet, and removed one of the suits Mary had altered for her. The lilac print always made her feel pretty. She'd talked Mary into shortening the length so it skimmed below her knees, a change that bordered on scandalous.

How should she do her hair? She needed to borrow Mary's full-length mirror. Racing down the hall, she knocked on Mary's door and then opened it. "Mary, aren't you ready yet? We have to go."

"I only now finished the breakfast dishes." Mary turned from her closet, a frown on her lips. "What are you wearing?"

Gracie skipped to the mirror, examined her image and grinned. "My favorite suit. You did a wonderful job. I feel so chic, so completely modern."

Mary's eyes rounded in the mirror's reflection. "Gracie, that skirt is a wee bit short to wear to church, don't you think?"

"Nonsense. I'm wearing wool stockings. My legs will never get cold. Itchy, yes. Cold, no." She moved to the closet, admiring Mary's collection of clothes. A deep blue dress with lace embroidered sleeves and pale pink flowers etching the hem caught her attention. "This is lovely." She plucked it from the closet and held it out. With all the work Mary did, she deserved to dress up and feel pretty.

Mary's nose wrinkled but she took it. "Could you help me put it on?"

"Of course." Gracie hummed a hymn as she helped Mary. Today was going to be beautiful. She could feel it.

When Mary finished dressing, Gracie flung the door open and skipped down the hallway. She stopped at the stairs to wait for Mary, who walked at a more sedate pace.

It made her think of her parents, the way Mary walked straight and smooth, the way Gracie herself had been taught to walk. She missed her family, even if they were a little controlling. She missed Father's rough pats on her back, his proud smile when she finished his accounting and the books balanced to the penny. She missed shopping with Mother, who had a flair for picking flattering styles and colors for Gracie.

Gracie settled on the bench in the hallway while Mary went to get the keys to the automobile from Uncle Lou.

Boots echoed on the wooden floor, and Gracie looked up. Trevor stood in the doorway that led to the kitchen. He'd slicked his dark hair back, but he hadn't shaved and the deep shadow on his chin gave him a rugged edge. His dark blue jeans and hunter-green-plaid shirt melded tightly to his long form, emphasizing pantherlike strength. His eyes were haunted.

Her hands began to sweat. "Are you coming to church with us? We just read the Bible and talk. Well, Mr. Horn says a little something usually, but it only lasts about twenty minutes." Gracie clamped her mouth closed. Why did she always jabber on like this in front of him?

Her heart thumped painfully against her ribs. It was his wounded gaze that did this to her.

He walked closer and stood between her and the front door. "You look different."

What did he mean? Her throat suddenly dry, she swallowed, and then slowly patted her curls. "Yes, I know. Losing weight doesn't suit me. I can't help it. I have the face God gave me and less or more weight won't make me pretty." *Oh, no.* That had sounded much too snippy. And insecure.

Embarrassed, she looked past him to where Mary and Uncle Lou stood on the front porch, nose to nose, arguing. Perhaps escape would loosen the tension that suddenly seemed to weigh her down.

"I should go protect Mary from my ogre of an uncle. Honestly, whatever is the matter with him, yelling at her like that?" Uncle Lou must've tried to order Mary around again. At least she seemed to be sticking up for herself this time.

"They'll be at it for the next fifteen minutes. It's their bimonthly routine," Trevor said.

Gracie forced herself to look at him, despite her shame at revealing her insecurities. He studied her, his head cocked to the side.

Being so near to him was scattering her wits. The sooner she escaped the easier it would be to gather her thoughts. She stood. "I'm ready to leave."

"Gracie, you look very pretty. Have you looked in a mirror lately?"

"Actually, I studied myself for a bit in Mary's full-length one. Now, kindly let me pass." She gulped down the shock that tried to choke her. He thought her pretty?

He leaned against the wall, his eyes flicking over her

dress before meeting her gaze. "Thought I'd hear what your preacher has to say this morning."

Joy filled her as Trevor pushed away from the wall and reached out to push a curl from her forehead. His eyes had turned soft. Warm. Their intensity stirred something in her. And then his gaze dropped to her lips.

Was he going to kiss her? She sucked in a shallow breath.

He pulled away abruptly, a flush darkening the planes of his cheekbones.

Gracie swallowed hard, watching as his hand kneaded the back of his neck. Once again, she'd come up lacking.

Mary poked her head into the hallway. "Let's go, Gracie."

"I'm coming." She looked at Trevor. "Are you driving us?"

The scowl on his face looked darker than storm clouds on a horizon.

A bit of a nudge might be needed here. "Stiffen your spine, Trevor, and let's get on with it," she said, borrowing one of her mother's favorite phrases. His face grew darker, if that were possible.

Oh, well. She didn't have time to stand around and watch him scowl. She scurried out of the house to wait on the front porch while Mary pulled the vehicle around.

It was an expensive Ford, the latest model, Uncle Lou had told her one day, eyes shining. He normally kept it at the back of the house beneath a weathered lean-to. Riding in automobiles was exciting business, especially fast ones. It would've been nice if James picked her up from the train station in the beautiful automobile but apparently he refused to drive such a fancy vehicle.

Odd that a ranch owner could afford such a car as this, Gracie thought, opening the gleaming back door. Perhaps she should take a small look at Uncle Lou's ledgers one evening. Just a peek, really, to make sure he was not over-extending himself. She slid into the car, mind churning. The idea bore consideration.

Trevor slammed into the driver's seat as she closed her door. Neither Mary nor Trevor seemed inclined to speak, so Gracie kept up a steady discourse on the weather. She wanted them to relax before the service.

In fact, *she* wanted to relax. This would be Trevor's first time. What would he think? When the car thudded against the ground Gracie glanced at Trevor. He drove quite le-thally on the rough-hewn land.

It didn't take long to reach Mr. Horn's tiny homestead. Gracie had no clue how the man survived out in this desert. From what she'd seen at a past service, he owned a cow, a horse, three chickens and the little place where they came together to worship.

The church group consisted of six families and they filled the house. As far as she could tell, no one minded the close quarters.

Gracie sat on a wooden bench and Trevor settled next to her. Mr. Horn chose the worship songs and Mary sang, softly at first, then her soprano rose and others joined in. Gracie didn't know how she'd go back to her church in Boston. Not after the warmth she'd felt here. No instru-ments, nothing but the sound of human voices raised in praise.

As she sang, she was careful not to touch Trevor. Now was a time to sing to God, not think about how raw and vulnerable Trevor could be. When the music ended Mr. Horn stood and Mary came to sit on the other side of Trevor.

Mr. Horn began his sermon but Gracie had trouble concentrating. The faint exotic scent Trevor wore kept invading her senses. Leather and cologne?

She studied him covertly. His eyebrows were furrowed and though he held no Bible, he appeared engrossed by Mr. Horn's words.

To her horror he turned at the same moment and caught her staring like an enamored schoolgirl. He smirked.

Quickly she looked away. Prickly heat filled her body. Remembrance of that moment in the hallway swept through her, followed by the quick thought that she hoped Uncle Lou never found out about her foolish attraction to his friend.

Although surely he wouldn't disapprove. After all, it was obvious he couldn't keep his eyes off Mary. Personally, Gracie thought he was a little old for her quiet friend.

Then again, Mary was what Connie called an "old soul." Gracie leaned forward and squinted at Mary. Serenity marked her features as surely as her Indian heritage did. And she looked tidy as a pin.

Gracie self-consciously pushed a wayward curl behind her ear.

She sat back and forced herself to pull her errant thoughts together as Mr. Horn concluded his message on the importance of kindness. A few murmured amens swept the room, and then a couple across from Gracie rose and came to the middle of the circle. The woman wept silently, shoulders shaking, and her husband held her close to his side.

"We found out this week our eldest daughter died from the influenza. She was in California visiting Alice's sister." He swallowed, his Adam's apple moving painfully up and down. "Please pray for us in our time of grief." They shuffled back to their seats. A thick congestion filled the room.

Another man stood. "Lambert's daughter a few miles

down has gone missing. We followed a trail to the border and then lost it. We think she was kidnapped." He sat down with a thump.

Gasps cut through the air, followed by the low hum of voices.

Gracie's throat clogged. That poor girl. How could Striker have let this happen?

After the closing prayer, Gracie walked to Mr. Horn and complimented him on his sermon. She shook someone else's hand but couldn't concentrate on the socializing she'd intended to do. Not with the sorrow that draped the room like a heavy quilt. Someone tapped her shoulder and she spun around.

Trevor.

Facing him proved painful. It was quite embarrassing to have the man catch her ogling him during service. Though he didn't smile, she had the feeling he was laughing at her just the same.

"Mary wants to know if you're ready. A storm's brewing and she wants to get on," he said.

Gracie felt someone brush past her. Conversations around her muted as she struggled to voice an answer.

His eyes glinted. "Cat got your tongue, sweetheart?" His lazy drawl infuriated her and she struggled to control her temper, something she hadn't needed to do in years. He wanted to laugh in this sacred atmosphere?

She glowered at him. "My tongue is fine."

"Good." He jerked his chin in the direction of the door, and Gracie followed him, feeling like an irrational child.

They reached Uncle Lou's automobile and Trevor opened the door for her. She slid him a smile, feeling suddenly shy. Although the ride home was silent, Gracie's thoughts raced. Somehow, someway, she had to make it back to Burns.

If Mendez had been in this area, then surely so had Striker.

Chapter Eight

He almost had them now.

Trevor shifted in his saddle, scanning the musty interior of the cave he'd seen smoke rising from. They'd cleared out in a hurry, that much was obvious. He stooped down and picked up a coin. It felt cool between his fingers. Smooth. He bit it. Gold. The markings proclaimed it Spanish. He flipped the piece high, caught it and slid it in his pocket. Soon, very soon, Mendez would be taken care of.

And then he could be free.

The word rolled around on his tongue, as foreign and enticing as Gracelyn Riley.

Had he really almost kissed her? The unexpected impulse yesterday before church had rattled him and made him regret promising Lou he'd keep an eye out for Mendez by staying at the ranch. Keeping his real identity separate from the Striker persona was imperative. That meant maintaining his distance from the naive journalist determined to find him.

Lambert's daughter had been located. Turned out she'd run away with one of the hired hands and not been kidnapped. Good news, if not for this morning's news.

An agent had intercepted a telegram arriving in Los Angeles. According to the agent, who contacted Lou immediately, Mendez had found Mary in Burns and requested backup so that he could succeed in kidnapping her this time.

If he figured out Striker lived on the ranch, too, there'd be trouble. Mendez wouldn't hesitate to put every person on the ranch in danger if he thought it would bring him what he wanted.

The thought of another shoot-out prickled Trevor's skin and sent waves of dread through his gut.

He nudged Butch and the stallion burst into a gallop. Wind rushed past Trevor's face, cold and harsh, a reminder that the life he led wasn't a life suitable for a young woman like Gracie. She had dreams. An innocent belief in goodness that felt alien to everything he'd learned about life from the moment he realized what his mother did for a living, what his father encouraged and what his town judged him for.

Butch zigzagged across the land, aiming toward Lou's stables. He'd have his own homestead someday. He'd heard of a ranch for sale nearby. Maybe he'd write a letter offering terms of a sale. Or he could stop by. The place wasn't too far from Horn's spread.

Trevor's thoughts moved to the church service yesterday. He had expected to be annoyed by Gracie sitting so near, to be distracted by her scent, but instead it was Horn's message that moved him. And at the end, everyone drew together to pray. There'd been a sense of community he couldn't remember ever feeling with anyone but Lou and Mary.

Yep, church had been something more than what he'd expected and not the boring, senseless gathering his mother always claimed it to be.

He drew up to the stables, noting the open door. Butch

didn't make a sound as Trevor guided him to the side of the building and signaled for him to stay still. Silently he slid off his mount and crept to the edge of the stables.

Someone inside muttered. A thunk filled the air, followed by a squeal and then a definite groan. Trevor touched the gun at his hip and worked his way toward the stable's opening. With care, he peeked through the open door.

Gracie stood in the center of the aisle, hands on her hips and an unladylike scowl on her face. Messy curls lay pasted to her face and a pink ribbon hung around her ear. A streak of dirt darkened the tip of her nose.

At her feet lounged a displaced saddle, hay clinging to the blanket still stuck beneath the leather.

He felt a tugging at his lips but ignored it. Releasing the holster of his gun, he stepped into the entrance. "Having a little trouble?"

She looked up and the expression on her face almost made Trevor smile.

"Indeed I am. Is it too much to ask that Uncle Lou own an English saddle?" she huffed, blowing strands away from her face. Swiping a hand to clear the rest of her hair from her face, she left a dirt streak running from her eyebrow to her chin.

This time Trevor grinned. He took off his holster and laid it near a wall, and then strode the rest of the way to her. Honey snorted and stomped a hoof. Gracie edged away from the horse.

"Patience," he told the mare, running a hand over her nose. She nudged him. "No treats this time."

"You talk to her?"

He shrugged. He'd been talking to horses since he was a kid. They made better listeners than drunken parents. "There's dirt all over your face."

"That's quite an ungentlemanly thing for you to point out, Trevor."

The cutest little pout he'd ever seen curved her lips. He shook himself, forcing his gaze from her mouth to her big, brown eyes. A very unwelcome feeling was stealing over him, a feeling he recognized and didn't like one bit.

Fixing her with a pointed stare, he said, "I don't aim to be a gentleman."

Her eyes went wide at that but he ignored her and scooped the saddle off the ground.

"This is heavy compared to what you're used to, but you'll get the hang of it. Watch me closely." He patted Honey on the neck and made sure the blanket on her back was smooth before he set the saddle on her. "These saddles are made for comfort. Both for the rider and the horse."

"Because you're in them all day?"

"Exactly." He shifted so Gracie could watch him as he fixed the saddle onto Honey. He felt her near him, could even smell the scent of her perfume rising above the more familiar odors of horse and hay.

"You have to make sure the front cinch strap—you'd call it a girth—isn't twisted." He needed to concentrate on the task at hand, not on her. Using his fingers, he felt the strap. He moved his hand toward Honey's belly. "This rear cinch should be loose."

Satisfied with his work, he straightened and moved away from Gracie. "You see how I did that?"

"I believe so." She studied the saddle and its parts, forehead furrowed. "May I try?"

"Sure." He undid the saddle and laid it at her feet. "First you have to lift it."

She scrunched her dirt-streaked face at him but tried to do as he said. Air whooshed out of her and she staggered back beneath the weight of the saddle.

Something unfamiliar bubbled in Trevor's chest. He frowned at the sensation and focused on Gracie. "Hold it like this." He motioned to each end of the saddle. "Now make sure Honey is aware of what you're doing and slide it up onto her back."

Gracie groaned but Trevor didn't rush to help her. If she wanted to ride, she'd have to know how to do this on her own. Honey sidestepped when Gracie dragged the saddle near her.

"Careful," he cautioned.

She cast him a disgruntled look and somehow hoisted the saddle onto Honey without dropping it.

"Now saddle her up," he instructed.

Surprisingly, Gracie caught on real quick.

"Should I get on now?" she asked.

"Before you mount, make sure the strap is still tight because a horse'll blow out its belly and then suck in and you don't want your saddle slipping to the side."

She nodded and checked. "It feels right, but—"

"Good." He helped her mount. "Why don't we make a few circles in the yard?"

"If you think so…" She sounded strangely hesitant.

"Riding well takes practice. Comfort and knowledge is important." Before she could object, he led Honey out behind the stable and then circled her around the yard. Gracie didn't speak, just sat stiff, clenching the reins.

Strange.

After a few rounds, Trevor returned to the barn.

"Honey's a good horse to ride." He gestured for Gracie to dismount.

"She is." Gracie leaned forward to dismount but Honey lurched in response. She clutched the saddle horn, face contorted. "Could you help me?" Her voice came out breathless.

Trevor stepped forward. He didn't like the look on her face. "You're afraid," he stated.

Hair askew, knuckles white, she didn't look at him but rather down at his boots as she mumbled what sounded like a denial.

He really didn't want to touch her. Only yesterday he'd been tempted to kiss her and now the feeling was roaring back, unbidden. Mouth tight, he reached for her.

"Take my hand."

Honey snorted again and he reached for her neck. "Shh," he soothed, but he didn't take his eyes off Gracie. A pinched look had contorted her face.

"Could you just please get me down, Trevor?"

"You'll be fine."

He saw the way her hand trembled on the horn. He moved closer, sliding his palm down Honey's neck until he'd moved behind Gracie. "Slide your leg over Honey's flanks and step down."

She looked back at him, her gaze dark and worried. "What if she moves?"

"I'm right here."

Slowly she slid her right leg over Honey's rump. The saddle creaked with the action. Then somehow she misstepped and tipped backward. He grunted as she rammed into him. Honey startled, jerking away, and pulling Gracie with her.

Trevor's arms tightened around Gracie and he locked his knees, twisting so Gracie's foot, which had become entangled in the stirrup, slipped free. Honey whinnied and stomped back to her stall to reward herself with oats.

Gracie was still clinging to him.

Or was he clinging to her?

Releasing her, he stepped back, away from her fragrance.

She spun to face him. Hair clouded around her face, unkempt, falling from its bun to curl over her shoulders.

"Well," she said brightly, dusting at her skirt as if she could dislodge unseen debris. "That was a close call. Thank you for seeing to my dismount."

"I thought you said you could ride."

"Did I say such a thing?"

He crossed his arms.

"I've ridden before, just not often. I wanted to practice a bit. There are things I have planned to do but my uncle is being uncooperative so I'll just have to go it alone."

"It?"

"To Burns, if you must know."

Her chin jutted forward and he knew she expected him to argue with her. He didn't give her the satisfaction. Instead, he walked toward Honey's stall. "If you're going to ride anywhere, you need to overcome your fear of horses."

She dogged his heels. "I'm not afraid."

"Could've fooled me."

"I'm simply…cautious. Yes, very careful. Horses are large and unpredictable." She caught up to him and put a hand on his arm. He froze.

"If you could help me a few more times, I'm sure I could be more comfortable." She peered up at him, her big brown eyes earnest in the stable's dimness. "That is, if you have time. You don't have to, I mean…" She was stuttering now.

The muscles in his stomach contracted. Her hand still lay on his arms, small and warm. She looked up at him and suddenly he wasn't thinking clearly. A straw of hay clung to her hair. He bent forward, pulled it off and flicked it to the ground.

She was so very close to him.

"What made you scared of horses?" He looked her in the eyes, wanting her to face this truth.

She squirmed but didn't break his gaze. "My cousin's horse threw me when I was ten. I've ridden very few times since then." A faint blush suffused her cheeks, as though she was embarrassed to admit fear.

Something very tender moved through him, squeezing his chest, making his throat constrict. He leaned forward and brushed his lips against hers. Everything in him pushed for more but he ended the exchange, jerking back.

He hadn't been thinking. Not one little bit.

Her lips were parted, eyes wide.

Then she grinned. "That was wonderful."

"Won't be happening again." At least he hoped not. This was bad, real bad.

She stepped closer to him, her eyes alight.

"You're a nice girl, Gracie, but that was a mistake."

"A mistake?"

"I'll help you get comfortable with the horses but that won't be happening again." His eyes mocked her "You might want to go clean up—your cheeks are filthy."

There. He'd been rude again. Maybe she'd leave quickly. For a second he thought her face was going to pucker up and his chest tightened, but then her features smoothed out and she gave him a stiff nod.

"Thank you for your help. I certainly can't find Striker without a mode of transportation." With that parting comment, she flounced out of the stables.

Groaning, he turned to Honey in the stall and began unsaddling her. He hated to see someone afraid of horses, but helping Gracie was only going to make his life more difficult. In more ways than one.

"You and Trevor have been spending time together lately," Mary commented one afternoon while she and Gracie scrubbed the kitchen floor.

"He's teaching me to ride." Gracie leaned back on her heels and wiped the back of her hand across her forehead. Her knees ached from Uncle Lou's hard Italian tiles and her palms were raw from the soapy water.

Mary didn't stop her brisk movements. "You don't ride?"

"I ride English style. He says he's teaching me the real way. The Western way." Gracie smiled.

"Do you enjoy his company?" Mary asked.

Gracie chewed her lower lip, Trevor's quiet chuckles haunting her thoughts. "He's quite serious, but when we're out in the corral he manages to laugh a little. So yes, I suppose I do take pleasure in his lessons. Anyway, I'd like to ride into Burns today and I am going to talk him into it. A week in a corral is far too boring."

"That's a long ride for a beginner."

"I've been riding every day." Gracie sat back on her heels and observed the woman scour a spot with vigorous determination. She grinned. "If I didn't know better, I'd think you enjoy cleaning. How is that possible?"

"You've only been scrubbing for twenty minutes." Mary sounded amused, despite the accusation in her words.

"It feels like days."

Mary laughed. "So," she murmured. "Trevor seems more open about God now."

Gracie leaned forward and began swiping the floor with broad, wet strokes. "Did he tell you that?"

"It's the little things I've noticed. The way he doesn't smirk when we pray at dinner. How he's taken to looking at my Bible in the mornings."

Warmth surged through Gracie. "We talk a bit."

"You two are close, then?"

"I don't know about that," she muttered, suddenly unnerved at the studied casualness of Mary's questions. "I'm leaving after winter to go home. My parents and I will be traveling to Europe in the summer, assuming the war is over. My ex-beau, Hugh, just returned home and told my friend Connie the war is close to finished."

Mary glanced up. "You are no longer courting?"

"No. My parents arranged an engagement without my consent, and I refused."

"I see." Mary's pretty lips twisted into a frown.

Gracie saw the expression and tried to shove down her worry. Mary didn't sound as if she saw at all. She sounded doubtful and that bothered Gracie. Surely Mary didn't think she was leading Trevor on while being engaged to another man?

She swirled her brush in the pail of water. Then she bent and continued at her chore. Water slopped over tile and the scratch of their brushes was the only sound in the otherwise silent kitchen.

As they worked Gracie couldn't help but think of Trevor. She really would like for him to kiss her again. What would he do if she just grabbed his face and planted a smooch on those serious lips?

She really shouldn't. After all, she had a life in Boston. Plays, shopping and friends. A budding journalism career. Now that she'd lost a little weight she even felt more confident. Trevor had said she was pretty, hadn't he?

Gracie stopped scrubbing for a second to rest her fingers.

If only Uncle Lou owned a telephone. It would be comforting to call Connie and chat, or to phone her parents. Despite missing them, Gracie supposed it wasn't so bad here. She enjoyed the wide spaces and endless sky, the jagged mountains and all the adventure they represented. She just missed human contact.

Yes…it would be better to keep her distance from

Trevor. After she finished her lessons. She glanced at the clock. Close to three. Trevor would be waiting for her.

She gave one last scrub to the floor and then sat back on her heels. "I'm done," she announced, stretching her hands above her head. "Time for a trip to town." She winked at the other woman.

Mary shook her head, a smile softening her features as she stood and toted her dirty bucket to the kitchen's side door. She stepped outside and Gracie heard the muffled splash of water hitting the fine layer of snow that had fallen last night.

Gracie followed her. "What are you going to do now?"

"Oh, I have a baby blanket I'm knitting for the Dunways a few miles over."

"Ugh, knitting." Gracie wrinkled her nose. "Have fun. I am off to explore Burns."

She traipsed across the acres that led to the stables. It was mid-October and last night's snow had been the first of the season. Not much, just a dusting across the dry land, but old James kept predicting an ice storm. She sincerely hoped he was wrong because being stuck inside for days on end made her feel like choking.

The rich scent of hay, leather and horse greeted her as soon as she entered the stables. Trevor stood in the center aisle, readying the horses. Her wool skirt swished between her legs as she ground to a halt. Something hitched in her chest, making it hard to breathe.

His dark hair hung around his face and his hands moved with graceful purpose as he cinched the stirrups on the mare. Gracie closed her eyes briefly, then opened them and prayed the soft fluttering in her belly would go away. She didn't need this now. What did it matter if he was funny and thoughtful, overly solemn sometimes? She did not want feelings for him. This experience was only high-spirited fun. An exciting episode to share with Connie someday.

She needed to find Striker. Needed to do something with her life other than live on her parents' by-your-leave.

She must focus on her only opportunity for freedom. An article with her name in the byline. She forced her booted feet forward and Trevor looked up at her approach, patting Honey's caramel rump.

"She's ready to go," he said, gaze locked on her. "It's cold so we'll make this lesson quick. You've pretty much got it down anyway."

Gracie let her hand slide over Honey's nose, down her sleek neck. The horse whickered, pressing her mouth against Gracie's jacket. She couldn't help smiling. What a relief to no longer be afraid.

"Sorry, Trevor." She offered Honey her palm. "I had to bring her something."

"Sugar's not good for their teeth."

"It's just a little," she crooned, enjoying the tickle of Honey's lips against the base of her fingers.

Hat tipped forward, he left her to ready his stallion.

"That's all, dear Honey." The horse nuzzled Gracie and she patted her strong jaws with empty hands. "Maybe later I'll sneak you a carrot."

Moving away from Honey's front, she looked for Trevor and found him closer than she'd expected. His horse's mighty hooves moved restlessly against the floor and a quiver ran through her. Remnants of a silly fear. She straightened and suppressed the urge to back away from Trevor's beast of a horse.

Honey nudged Gracie again and she smiled. Not all horses were beasts. She rested her face against Honey's neck for a moment.

"Stiffen that spine and let's get on with it," she called to Trevor as he finished saddling Butch.

He glower at her. "Gracelyn, if you say that one more time I'll inform Lou you regularly fix his account ledgers, do you understand?"

"How do you know about that?" She bristled beneath his parental tone.

"It's not hard to figure out when numbers start slanting right instead of Lou's hard left. No one but me and Lou go near those books."

"Threatening exposure is quite rude, Mr. Cruz. And I do not care for your tone at all. I'm not your daughter."

"That's a blessing."

Gracie glared at him. He was far too arrogant for her liking. Before coming here, she'd always thought of herself as someone who avoided conflict as much as possible without compromising her standards. Trevor seemed to bring out an aggressive streak she did not care for.

She gritted her teeth and tried to speak calmly. "Will you please help me up? You know I can't mount in these clothes. I don't understand why Uncle Lou won't let me wear trousers. Dozens of girls are wearing them. They're a perfectly acceptable form of attire."

Trevor stalked toward her, long legs eating up the ground between them. "Do your parents let you wear them?"

"Well, no, but my parents are old-fashioned. Connie wears them all the time."

"I'm real tired of hearing about this Connie girl." Trevor hovered over her and she couldn't stop the little thrill that trickled down her spine. "Seems to me she's a bad influence. Trousers," he said with disgust. "It's not right."

"Help me up," Gracie said stiffly, ignoring his comment. Trevor hid his amusement beneath a cool smirk. He'd tossed out the trousers comment to rile her. Truth was, his version of right and wrong didn't seem so clear cut anymore. He'd been reading the Bible a bit and found it hard to believe he'd persisted in hating God for so long.

His daddy had done him wrong. Lots of folks had done him wrong, but now he saw that blaming God for actions people took made no logical sense at all. The perky woman in front of him inspired him, though he was reluctant to admit it.

Mary told him she worked hard. In fact, Mary had a high opinion of Gracie overall, but cautioned him not to get too close since she was leaving after winter. An unnecessary warning. Gracie acted like a young girl most of the time, not a woman.

He studied her closely. Her cheeks radiated health and the weight loss had only succeeded in emphasizing her heart-shaped face, lips the color of a rosebud and doe eyes.

Okay, maybe he did react to her as a woman, even if he thought of her as a girl. Twenty was awfully young, he reminded himself as his hands settled on her hips. Too young for an almost-thirty-year-old man who'd seen and done things she couldn't imagine. Besides, he didn't want some debutante who missed the glamour of the big city. He was going to settle here, own a ranch, raise a family.

A city girl wasn't part of the plan.

"Are you going to put me on that horse or stand there dillydallying all day?" Impatience and a hint of breathlessness tinged her voice.

She grabbed the reins as he lifted her up.

"I'd like to ride into Burns today," she informed him from her lofty position. She sounded like the pampered socialite she was.

"Absolutely not." He met her eyes and hoped his expression was as forbidding as he wanted it to be.

"Don't be so stodgy," she said. "Do you have a good reason for saying no?"

Apparently he'd lost his ability to intimidate. He sighed and tightened the stirrups for good measure. "Two words— *thirty degrees.*"

"I need to go to town before James's ice storm rears its ugly head. Please?"

"It's too cold."

"I'm perfectly warm."

"It's not safe." Trevor threw on his heavy scarf and tossed Gracie an extra one from the coat rack. She caught it and wound it around her neck, covering her chin and nose. A mulish jut to the folds of cloth around her chin gave Trevor pause.

As he watched, she nudged Honey to the door. "I'll see you this evening." With a shriek of glee she dug her heels into Honey's flanks. He heard her gasp as the icy air ripped the laugh from her throat and flung it behind her.

Biting back a curse, Trevor mounted Butch and spurred him forward. Wind whipped past as Trevor gained ground. She didn't get far from the stables before he grabbed her reins and pulled Honey to a stop.

"Keep it up and you'll break your neck." His heart knocked against his rib cage, warning him of the dangers this foolish girl put herself in just to find a man who didn't deserve to be found.

Gracie visibly stiffened in her saddle. "Yelling will not solve anything." Snow softly fell, landing like powdered ice on her nose and eyelashes.

"You're crazy trying to go to Burns in this weather," he said flatly.

"I've waited long enough."

"We'll go when it's safe."

"Are you always this domineering?" she asked.

"Common sense."

"Are you implying I have none?" Her eyes flashed. "I'm tired of your insinuations," she snapped. "Your overbearing attitude toward me is wearying."

He started to speak but she interrupted. "The kiss you gave me does not give you the right to order me about. It was a mere brushing of the lips."

His scar thrummed with the beat of his pulse.

"Mere?" he said softly, intently studying her.

"Yes, nothing special."

They were nose to nose now, the horses standing patiently beneath them.

"Let's race," Gracie suddenly blurted. "I've a need to expend energy."

"We're not racing, got it?"

Her chin lifted in that same stubborn way. "Don't be a spoilsport!"

Trevor's heart almost stopped when she impulsively heeled Honey forward. He sprang into action but she was well ahead of him. Pounding hooves muffled his shout. Or maybe she ignored him.

Hunkering down, he signaled Butch to surge forward. Ahead of him, Gracie's horse slipped, then righted herself. The ice had shown up, earlier than James said it would. Growling, Trevor urged Butch faster.

He blinked snow from his eyes, and in that second, a shrill scream bit through the air.

Chapter Nine

Trevor bolted off Butch and rushed to where Gracie lay crumpled on the ground. Honey had scrambled up and galloped toward the stables, appearing unhurt. Snowflakes floated over Gracie's body, settling and melting against her pale skin. Throat so tight he could barely draw a breath, Trevor knelt near her still form. He reached for her neck, checked her pulse.

He was so tired of death, of watching the soul drain right out of a body.

But Gracie's lifeblood beat steadily against his fingers. He leaned back on his heels, finally gulping an icy, ragged breath as the muscles in his throat unclenched. White coatings of snow blanketed Gracie's heavy jacket as he sucked in lungfuls of air. He brushed the flakes from her cheek, grateful for the warm breath whispering from her lips.

He felt the back of her neck, touching each vertebra. Nothing seemed out of place there, but she could've hurt her back. He measured the distance between them and the house. It would be unwise to leave her out here just to get a solid surface for her back. Better to carry her in and hope for the best.

Very carefully he tucked his arms beneath her, shifting

until her neck lay against his biceps so he could cradle her body against his chest. The stillness of her face was eerie. Despite its waxen paleness, he felt her body heat seeping out and that reassured him.

As smoothly as possible, he stood and walked toward the house.

Images from the past bombarded him. Wounded men he'd carried to a waiting vehicle. The stink of blood and excrement. The heavy burden of guilt that shrouded his life now.

Somehow he kept one foot in front of the other, reminding himself that this was Gracie. She'd fallen from a horse. She hadn't been shot.

This wasn't Council Bluff.

"Gracie, can you hear me?"

Mary's voice drifted to Gracie from far away, but in the end its sound wasn't what coerced her eyes to fly open. Hot irons of pain branded her leg. With a strangled moan, she jerked her eyes open and pointed to her knee, or at least where she thought her knee might be. Mary's face wavered in front of her like a flag billowing in the wind.

"My knee," she managed to croak, and then grimaced when gentle hands began probing her leg.

"It's sprained." James's gravelly voice came from the foot of the bed. Gracie didn't bother to look anymore. Her head had started pounding the moment her eyes opened, so she closed them and kept as still as possible.

She cleared her throat. "How long have I been lying here?"

"'Bout half an hour," James grunted. "Trevor carried you in, then left to get the doctor."

"Where's Uncle Lou?"

"He's coming."

"Quit your wiggling, missy," James barked.

Fire ripped across her leg. "That hurts! Can't we wait for the doctor?"

"You let old James wrap it for you. Trevor won't make it to the doc's. Fixin' to blizzard out."

Gracie groaned.

"Have a drink, Gracie, because fixing your knee is going to hurt like the dickens."

She cocked an eye open, then recoiled when James thrust an evil-smelling brew under her nose. "Is that whiskey?" Horror made her words come out in a squeak.

"You're going to need it," Mary said.

The door to the bedroom slammed open and Trevor staggered in, shaking snow from his shoulders. "It's freezing out there. Too cold to get the doctor." His eyes met Gracie's and she managed a faint smile.

"I guess it's up to you, James. But I'm not drinking whiskey. I'm a teetotaler."

"Have it your way, missy."

Mary pulled Gracie's arms above her head and Trevor pressed her ankles against the mattress.

"What are you doing?" She began to squirm, alarmed by their forceful pressure. Were they insane?

"Gotta hold you down so you don't mess me up while I wrap it. Need to get the swelling down. Trevor, Mary, hold tight."

Before Gracie could react, James pulled out a length of cloth and reached for her leg. A shrill scream splintered through the room. Her scream, she realized, just before her vision turned black.

Trevor heard the moan first. He looked to where Gracie lay limp on the bed. Her lashes fluttered as she struggled to escape the faint that had overcome her when James bound her knee. She resembled a fragile porcelain doll, her hair dark against pale skin. Fingers clenching, he looked away. If she drank the whiskey she could've numbed the pain, but not Gracie. Obstinate about her beliefs, as usual.

"Do you think we should tell her?" Lou asked beside him.

"No." Mary's voice quivered. "James said she has a small concussion, and I think we should wait until she's stronger before we break this to her."

Trevor was about to warn them to be quiet, but the rustle of the bedsheets caught his attention, followed by another moan. They turned toward Gracie, conversation halting. She stared at them, face white, a weak smile trembling on her lips. He strode to her and took her hand. It felt like ice.

"How are you feeling?" His voice came out more tender than he would've liked, and he quickly swallowed his embarrassment. He didn't know how he could have compared her to the other women he'd known. Lying there so small and vulnerable, she seemed sweet and mellow, far from the vibrant socialite she usually appeared to be.

"What happened?" she asked.

"Honey slipped."

"No, what were you whispering about? Just now."

Trevor glanced at Lou. He wasn't sure if he wanted to stay while Lou broke the news. Who knew how Gracie would react? He had a hunch her life had been fairly easy up until now and could be she'd easily break.

Or she might stand strong as an oak. It would largely depend on how deep her roots were. Still, if she cried, he wasn't sure how he'd handle it. He'd come to care for her as a person. She was witty, sweet and kind. And he found her incredibly attractive. He'd almost kissed her again today.

As he held her fragile hand, he forgot why that would be so wrong.

Lou and Mary moved from the doorway and walked to Gracie. Trevor's warmth seeped into the skin of Gracie's right hand. Mary rounded the bed and took her left. Gracie's lungs constricted. Uncle Lou looked worried, and he never looked that way, at least not in the month she'd known him. The characteristically carefree smile he usually sported didn't grace his even features as he knelt beside her.

"I picked up the mail in town earlier today, and I got a telegram from your father. Influenza is all over Boston. He thought it would be better if I told you in person than him through a letter."

"Mother?" She felt the blood draining from her face and thought she might throw up.

"No." Uncle Lou shook his head and Gracie closed her eyes too soon in relief. "Constance died yesterday."

The words hit her, a sledgehammer that knocked the breath from her chest. It wasn't true. Connie was strong. She'd had the grippe before. There had to have been a mistake, but one look at the somber faces around her confirmed Uncle Lou's words.

"Leave me alone," she said quietly. The bruises on her body, the aches in her bones, couldn't compare to the pain ripping through her chest. Her eyes burned. She waited. Slowly they filed out of the room, Mary weeping softly for someone she didn't know. The door whispered shut and Gracie closed her eyes.

Alone.

Trevor stood on the porch outside the kitchen two days later when Gracie came down. He heard the shuffle of her crutches first, then the scrape of a chair as she sat.

"Hey there." Lou's voice floated past the door. "How're you feeling?"

"Lousy."

Trevor paused in cleaning snowy sludge off his boots. He'd barely heard Gracie's answer, her pitch was so low.

"Those crutches working okay for you?" Lou asked.

"If I had trousers I could walk easier." Gracie sounded mighty grumpy.

"My brother specifically told me no pants for you, young lady. Do you want some eggs? Oatmeal? Mary put raisins and sugar in it."

Trevor stepped into the kitchen, and caught Gracie staring out the kitchen window, shaking her head no. Crushed by the grief on her face, he almost stumbled. Turning away, he plucked a plate from the cupboard and moved to the oven. The warmth emanating from the stove immediately crept into his bones and relaxed his muscles. He scooped up some of Mary's spiced oatmeal.

Lou sent Trevor a helpless look before turning back to Gracie. "Mary tells me you haven't been eating normal. I know Constance was your best friend, but starving yourself sure won't help matters. Now, you eat this bowl of oatmeal." He slid it to her and she looked at it with distaste. She ate slowly, paying no attention to the food. When she finished she continued looking out the window, unaware of Lou's sympathetic gaze.

She looked like death. Her skin stretched haggard and dry, purple shadows hung beneath her eyes, and her usually mobile mouth was listless.

Had she broken, then?

Trevor couldn't blame her. He'd lost friends, too many to count. The pain that came could destroy a man, jade an idealistic young woman.

She'd survive the numbness, whether she realized it or not. The question was how the pain would change her. Would she let life slap the spirit out of her? She claimed her God was kind and good. Now she knew what it felt like to be struck down.

Trevor didn't find the thought comforting. If anything, he'd wish for her to never experience this. Even if it meant staying locked up in her little world of optimism. He liked her spirit, had thought it strong. He studied her while eating. Maybe he ought to talk to her, but he couldn't help but recall the comment he'd made about Connie before Gracie raced off.

He hoped she didn't remember.

She must've noticed his perusal because she turned to him, dragging her weary eyes to his face.

"You don't need to look so concerned. I'll be okay. I need time."

Gracie wasn't sure if it was true, but it sounded like the right thing to say. It had only been two days, after all, since learning her most precious friend was gone from this world. She cast a last glance at the window. The world outside was cold and desolate.

She reached for her crutches. Grasping the rough wood, she hopped out of the kitchen and toward the stairs.

She sensed Trevor before she heard him, felt his strong arms around her waist before he spoke.

"I'm going to help you," he said, in the tone she usually chafed at. Now it comforted. She gave her crutches to Mary, who'd followed Trevor. Turning into his soft flannel shirt she let him pick her up and cradle her like a baby as he mounted the steps. Her head rested against his warm shoulder. His scent surrounded her.

"I'm sorry I tried to race," she murmured. His arms tightened around her as they moved into her bedroom. She didn't want to let go of him, felt so needy, so unlike her normal self.

"I should've mentioned ice beneath the snow."

They entered the room. Mary waited by the bed, covers pulled back. Trevor set Gracie down gently and she was stunned by the comfort she felt at his touch, when her best friend in the world was dead.

But not dead really, she reminded herself fiercely. Connie was with God, and she would do well to remember it. "Trevor, could you bring me my Bible? And when Uncle Lou has time I'd like to speak with him."

"Lou has to travel on business for a few days." He handed her the large King James she kept on her dresser. Her name, embossed in gold, scrawled across the bottom of the leather cover.

She didn't really want to read the Bible. Right now God seemed neither loving nor kind. But she would have it near, just in case. Sleepiness stole through her, and she yawned.

"I want to go to Connie's funeral." She covered her mouth when she yawned again. Trevor stared down at her, his handsome mouth twisting into a frown. He looked like he wanted to say something but then he stopped and, leaning forward, let his fingers graze her hair. His touch was sweetness and warmth.

"Sleep now," he advised gently. In that moment, with his hand on her, Gracie felt treasured. Her eyes drifted shut and she never heard Trevor and Mary leave.

She woke hours later when Mary whipped the covers off her.

"Up you go, girlie," Mary said, brogue thicker than usual.

Gracie ignored her. She turned away, favoring her knee. But when Mary began pulling her clothes off, she was forced to react.

"What are you doing?" She yanked the sheets up to her chin, but Mary snatched them away.

"You need a bath. Now."

"But my knee…"

"Hibernating in here willna bring Constance back, so get up."

"It's only been two days." Gracie wrested the sheets from Mary.

"Four."

"What?"

"You've been lying in here going on four days. It's time to get up and get moving. Into the washroom you go."

Gracie dropped the sheets. She'd been lying here for days? Feeling defeated, Gracie let Mary help her to the washroom.

"Thank you, Mary," she said, ashamed. She removed her clothes and, with Mary's help, stepped into the tub. For the first time she found herself focusing on the bindings around her leg. Her knee still hurt, but by no means with the same excruciating pain that first accompanied the twist. If only her heart would heal so quickly.

Hot water and scented bubbles should have felt like bliss. Instead, they only reminded her of the time Connie had given an entire basketful of Parisian soap to her female servants. The gesture caused quite the stir amongst the older ladies of their mothers' circle.

Mary gently propped Gracie's leg on the edge of the tub.

She eyed the bandages, banishing her memories to a dark place inside. "I hope James knew what he was doing."

"Oh, he does." Mary nodded at her from where she sat on the shiny white toilet. "He used to be a doctor, studied in one of the greatest schools in Britain, Cambridge."

"That's difficult to imagine. He doesn't even speak proper English."

"Don't let him fool you."

Gracie trailed her fingers through the bubbles. So James

had been a doctor. It did not fit with the man she knew. "Why is he no longer in the profession?"

Mary stood and reached for a washcloth. "You should probably ask him. It's not my place to say."

"I suppose that's why he had crutches available."

"No, we keep crutches and other first-aid items stored in a closet. Accidents happen easily on a ranch and we like to be prepared."

Gracie smiled faintly. At least the ranch was well stocked. She soaped herself and let Mary wash her hair, glad to be clean again. Scrubbing off the grime went far in lifting her mood. Mary reached for her arm with firm fingers and Gracie gingerly stepped out of the tub, careful not to wet the bindings.

"Trevor seems besotted with you." Mary rubbed a towel through her hair without pausing, as if her strange comment fit right in with their conversation.

"*Besotted* is a strong word," Gracie muttered, letting Mary help her finish dressing. She limped to her bed and sat down. Weariness spread through her, sucked the energy from her marrow until even the thought of waiting for tomorrow filled her with dread.

"You make him smile." Mary said it as though it were a miracle. "Just be careful. Don't hurt him."

An image of Trevor's chiseled features and hard eyes flashed into Gracie's mind. "I think you're mistaken." She shifted on the bed, uncomfortable beneath Mary's scrutiny. If only Mary would let her sleep. "We get along well. How could I possibly hurt him?"

"You're awfully interested in Striker."

"He's my ticket to a profession. Independence."

"He seemed like more to me, when you first spoke of him."

"He's more than just a special agent to me," Gracie answered truthfully. "But what does that have to do with Trevor?"

Her mouth pursed. "I'll be back in a bit to check on you."

After Mary left the room, Gracie used her crutches to hoist herself to the window. She watched as the heavens wept and her own eyes remained dry.

Chapter Ten

Winter brought harsh flurries of snow and dusky clouds. By the end of October, the sky wore a permanent pallor.

Trevor's boots crunched ahead of Gracie. "Hurry up."

"I am. My crutches only go so fast."

"I should pick you up and carry you."

"Don't you dare," Gracie warned. For two weeks she'd managed to stay away from Trevor and the feelings he roused within her, but today he'd dragged her out of bed and announced she was going to his house. She'd tried to say no but Mary had sided against her, claiming she needed to air out the house.

Who was Mary fooling? The weather hovered above zero. Just walking from the house to Trevor's Ford created icicles out of Gracie's eyelashes. Trevor opened the side door for her and she slid in, adjusting the crutches with cold-stiffened fingers.

Once they headed out, the ride was slow going. She felt his glances but didn't dare look at him. Not with the fire that burned inside, a nice healthy dose of rage that had kept her sleepless for the past two weeks. It had also given her a break from her depression.

"I'm still angry with you," she said, unable to contain the fury.

"For what?"

"For what?" she repeated incredulously. "You kept me from Connie's funeral."

"I told you it wasn't my call. Lou said no, your parents said no. I just agreed."

Her fingers curled into fists. "If you would have taken me, they'd have said yes. I know they asked your opinion."

Trevor glanced at her, and then focused on the road. His profile formed a sharp, unyielding line. "I don't think it's safe for you. The influenza is still raging and your knee has a while longer before you can put weight on it."

"You know, this is why I am a suffragist. You're not my father."

He braked slowly in front of his house, and then turned to her, his eyes so dark she could barely see the pupils. "Like I said before, that's a blessing. Now, are you coming in or are you going to sit here and pout?"

Gracie ground her teeth and swung the door open. Trevor came to help her but she jerked from his grasp. He grunted and grabbed her arm.

"Whether you like it or not, I'm helping you in."

"You overbearing—" Her angry words halted when her foot slipped forward on the icy edge of his truck.

"You need me," Trevor said in a low voice as his imposing form stopped her descent.

The knowledge he was right curdled her stomach. How she hated being needy and dependent. Concentrating, she pushed her crutches into the snow and shifted to the edge of the seat until she could safely slide out. Once she stood firm, Trevor slammed the door shut.

As they picked their way to his door, her anger calmed beneath cool reason.

Trevor had a point. Traveling during this pandemic would be tantamount to suicide. Her rage was unreasonable. Knowing this didn't make her feel better.

Only alive.

He opened the door for her, a bit of chivalry that knocked a hole through her resolve to stay upset. She clumped into his house. A squeak made her pause at the entry. A calico kitten the size of a ball of yarn ran in front of her, followed shortly by a black-and-white kitten.

"Oh, how beautiful." Surprise circumvented the bitterness that still raged in her chest.

She shut the door and then pulled off her jacket and boots. After several clumsy attempts, she managed to sit down. Trevor had walked to the kitchen, sober-faced as he watched.

The calico jumped into her lap while the black-and-white hung back, tail tucked between its spindly legs. She stroked the calico's soft fur, marveling at the loud rumbling vibrating its tiny ribs.

As a child she'd longed for a kitten but her parents refused. Her mother, actually. It was one reason Gracie never wanted to marry the wrong man. Growing up, she'd watched Mother constantly controlling her father and she vowed she'd never be controlled that way. She pressed her face against the silky fur and smiled.

"They're so lovely, Trevor. Connie had kittens." Sadness welled up. If only she could have gone to the funeral. Realistically, she knew it wasn't Trevor's fault. Even if there were no influenza outbreak, the traveling took too long. She would have missed the funeral if she'd left the day she found out.

She held out her hand to the black kitten. "Where did you get them?"

"Horn had extras he couldn't deal with. They'll eat rodents in the barn."

The black kitten edged toward her, his little whiskers quivering. For some reason, she wanted to cry. She forced the tears back. Men were uncomfortable with a woman's tears, she'd heard. "Have you named the kittens?" She glanced up at him.

His eyebrow performed its telltale quirk. A definite no. He stood in the kitchen, tall and strong, light flooding over him. Gracie looked away.

"I'll name this one Connie, if you don't mind." She stroked the rumbling calico curled in her lap.

Trevor cleared his throat. "Not at all. I'm going outside for a few minutes. If you need anything, just holler."

She looked up. Trevor sounded forlorn. He turned, but not before she caught a wisp of something pass over his face. Sadness?

He disappeared through the kitchen and she heard the door click when he went outside.

The black kitten retreated behind the couch but Connie plastered herself against Gracie, her gravelly purr filling the silence of the room. Eventually, the kitten jumped off Gracie's lap to explore the kitchen.

She grabbed her crutches and struggled to her feet. Trevor's home appeared small and cozy, if a little sparse. No hint of femininity here, but an artistic and sensitive mind could be seen at work in the little touches. A faded photograph stood alone on a table by the couch. A patterned wool blanket draped the couch. Thick oak floors adorned by nothing but spit-clean polish.

The fireplace was the only ornate fixture. Large and bordered with multicolored stones, Gracie could imagine sitting in front of it on a snowy evening talking or playing chess.

She limped over to Trevor's bookshelf. Every book was neatly placed and not a speck of dust marred the wood. In fact—Gracie squinted—his books were arranged alphabetically. She couldn't help but contrast his home with hers. The only things she kept orderly were the account ledgers, which would have to be straightened when she returned. Neither Father nor Mother had a head for figures.

She moved on to Trevor's photos. There weren't many. One in particular stood out from the rest and she picked up the burnished frame. Trevor and a woman posed against the backdrop of mountains. He wore his familiar scowl, his scar a crooked line on the faded picture.

It wasn't often he looked happy. Not then, not now. She remembered his pronouncement of atheism.

With the loss of Connie, she could see where he might find belief in a loving God difficult. Perhaps the denial of a creator stemmed from his wounded soul. She understood a reaction like that, especially with her own soul in such torment.

She focused on the frame in her hand, taking in the blonde's delicate bone structure and tall, willowy form. Trevor looked achingly young in the photograph. Next to him the woman looked like an innocent. Her prim beauty accentuated Trevor's dark glower and Gracie hoped she was a sister.

She didn't like the churning in her gut, the insecurity rising to the surface, and quickly set the picture down just as a door slammed. She heard Trevor's boots against the kitchen floor. Then a soft scuff as he stepped into the living room.

She turned to him. "How's your garden?"

"Dead."

"Only for now, right?"

"Yep. It's just waiting for spring." Trevor set his hat on

the small table in front of his couch. Then he moved in front of her, his stare strangely intense. "You looking at my pictures?"

"There are not many," she remarked, her gaze roving his lined face.

The scar on his cheekbone gleamed and before she could stop herself, Gracie reached up to touch the broken flesh. Gently, with her forefinger, she traced its jagged edge. "Did you really get that from barbed wire?"

His eyes were stricken. He grabbed her wrist and pulled her close, black orbs glinting. "My father gave it to me with the bottom of a liquor bottle."

Later, Gracie would blame her actions on her vulnerable state. She might even blame them on *his* vulnerable state, but in the second before she kissed him, her feelings overcame her practicality.

She leaned forward, on tiptoes, and pressed her lips against his ferocious anger. At first he was unyielding, but she didn't give up. She needed the contact, and if she was being too bold, she didn't care.

Death did not wait, it came when it pleased, and she would have this kiss.

She moved her lips against his, needing him to respond. When he did, it was as though she'd unleashed something she couldn't control. She kissed him for herself, but also to soothe the monsters within him.

And then, amidst the emotions racking her, she felt wetness on her cheeks.

Salt mingled with the taste of Trevor's lips. His mouth released hers and his thumbs moved from the small of her back to lightly smooth the tears from her face. His head bent and he whispered in her ear, "Don't cry."

Strange how two little words could affect her so profoundly. They unlocked a flood that had been dammed for more than two weeks and she drenched the front of his shirt. Even through her sobs, she could smell the sweetness of him, the musky scent of earth and man. When her tears slowed, he backed up a step, wary.

"You need some water?"

Gracie shook her head, hunched against the wall, and when she realized she couldn't stop the weeping, she began to laugh. Through a haze of tears, she saw Trevor's eyes widen.

Steering her to the couch, he gently pushed her down as she simultaneously wiped away tears and chuckles.

"I'm so sorry." She sniffled. He handed her a hanky and kept his distance. He probably thought her insane. Connie would've held her, not looked at her as if she were a strange creature.

A harsh sob ripped from her throat.

No more phone calls, no more long walks to the harbor to watch fishermen preparing for their day. No more trips to the fish market and no more laughing at the vendors hawking their wares. Why had God allowed this?

Trevor was going nuts.

He gripped the steering wheel and kept his eyes on the road back to Lou's. He'd spoken to Gracie once and been silent ever since. What would he tell her? That her kissing awakened some long-dead emotion in his heart? That she belonged here in the desert. That she fit?

Well, she didn't.

The sooner she knew it, the better. He had problems to deal with, a life to live, and her impetuous kiss was messing everything up.

Scowling, he glanced over at his silent passenger. She stared unseeingly out her window. Her hair had come undone, falling along her jaw in shiny waves.

As if sensing his gaze, she looked at him. "You must think I'm horrible. Brazen."

The thought hadn't crossed his mind. Sad, yes. Desperate even. But never horrible.

"There can be no more kissing," she said. "It's my thorn in the flesh."

Trevor almost ran over a shrub. He swerved, working hard to hide his smile. There were worse things than a kiss in time of need, however inconvenient. She looked awfully guilty over something so slight.

"Are you smiling?"

"Just relieved." Too late he realized how that sounded.

Gracie's face fell. "There's something you should probably know, Trevor."

Her tone pricked his ears. Years of honed instinct bludgeoned him. Whatever she had to say, it wouldn't be good. Unbidden, his thoughts turned to Eunice. The girl he thought he'd be with forever.

Money had been more important to her than love, though. Good thing he'd found out sooner rather than later.

"It's about the kiss," Gracie continued. Her voice shook, sounding raw from her weeping earlier.

Thinking about how she'd felt in his arms, how his heart had splintered at the sound of her sobs, made him feel crazy again. There was no room in his life for a woman. His jaw tightened.

He darted a quick glance toward her. She wasn't looking at him, but at her hands as they twisted in her lap.

"I shouldn't be kissing anyone," she said in a dull tone. "My parents announced a betrothal for me in the papers, and though I rejected the proposal, my parents are complicating matters. According to them, I have a fiancé."

His head jerked her way and the truck shook as the

wheel slid through his fingers and caused him to run over a rock. Quickly he turned his attention back to the crude road. His pulse twitched through him.

"I thought you had a thing for your Striker," he said carefully.

"I adore Striker and I *will* find him. This thing with the fiancé is a big mistake. It is only on paper and I meant to send a correction—"

"Then what's been stopping you?"

Gracie cringed and Trevor knew his voice had come out harsher than he'd intended. He pulled up in front of Lou's house. Turned off the truck and looked at her.

She gnawed on her lower lip, looking flustered and guilty. Swallowing a growl, Trevor grabbed his hat off the seat, jammed it on his head and got out of the truck.

He helped Gracie into the house without saying another word. He stomped the snow from his boots before turning to slide the bulky coat from Gracie's shoulders. When he hung up the coat, he caught sight of Mary near the sitting room doors. Her eyes were wide and her skin unnaturally pale.

"There's someone who came to see you." Mary's gaze flickered to Gracie. "Could you come with me to the kitchen?"

An uneasy feeling crept through him. "Who's in that room?"

Mary's hands twisted together, and she moved from the entrance of the sitting room as if to escape the inhabitant.

"Is it her?" he asked coldly.

Mary squeaked as he strode toward the sitting room. He ignored her and pushed the doors open and then stopped when the woman he despised almost as much as his father rose from the couch like a coiled cobra to a song.

She held out a hand. "My love, how are you?"

* * *

"What's going on?" Gracie whispered. Mary had practically pulled her into the kitchen and now paced the floor, muttering to herself, skirts swishing angrily around her ankles.

Gracie worried about Mary's reaction to the visitor, and it was not in her nature to worry. She hobbled to the high-backed wooden chair near the round oak table and sat down, awash with nerves and curiosity.

"Mary, who is she? Why are you agitated? Things can't be so bad." When Mary didn't respond, impatience began to prick at Gracie's fingers, making them itch.

Mary stopped suddenly. "I have to breathe. If Lou were here, he'd know what to do. I'm going outside." She rushed to the side door and, with a blast of cold air, Gracie was left alone in the kitchen.

She shrugged. Well, there was nothing for it. She'd have to eavesdrop if she was going to have information. A small niggling of guilt edged her conscience as she crept into the hallway, but she suppressed the feeling. This couldn't be worse than the blank look that had washed Trevor's face when she'd told him about that ridiculous engagement. Surely it couldn't be legal without her consent.

Her crutch scuffed the wall and she paused, but the arguing voices kept up their relentless tirade. With determination, she continued until she had reached the base of the stairs.

Now if she heard anyone about to open the door, she could be in the process of going to her room and thus guilty of nothing.

"You used us," Trevor shouted.

Gracie grimaced. Doors could shake off their hinges with that roar. The woman's reply was too soft for Gracie to hear so she shuffled nearer to the door. The voices were muffled, then she heard the woman say clearly, "I've always loved you, darling. I know I made my mistakes but…"

The rest of her words became lost behind the door. Gracie pressed her head against it, propping the crutches beside her so she could get a good angle with her ear.

"Don't touch me, Julia. You don't deserve to be forgiven." Trevor's voice was cold. He spoke emotionlessly, as if long past caring. The sound of a woman's copious weeping filled the room and Gracie froze.

Should she go in there? No, it wasn't her business. But Trevor had made Julia cry, and she sounded devastated. Was she an old flame, someone who'd left him and now wanted him back?

If Julia was that woman, she sure didn't want to comfort her. Mind made up, she stepped away from the door. Julia was Trevor's issue. As much as she wanted to get involved, she needed to stand aside and mind her own business.

Besides, she had a secret agent to track down.

But Trevor was being so cruel. Could she really leave the poor woman in tears? She was sure to have a fascinating story on why she'd come back and Gracie hadn't seen a new face in weeks.

Unquestionably, it was her Christian duty to comfort others. She turned and using her crutches for support, whipped the door to the sitting room wide open.

Trevor brooded near the fireplace, hands clasped behind his back and posture rigid. He appeared to be staring into the flames and made no indication he'd heard her entry. Julia sat on the sofa, dabbing at the corners of her eyes with a white linen hankie and sniffling softly. She must have felt the draft because she looked up in surprise.

Gracie's heart dropped to the pit of her stomach. The woman was gorgeous in a delicate flower kind of way.

"Oh, dear," Julia murmured in a slight Southern accent. "How do you do?" Her affected tone oozed insincerity.

Squinting, Gracie stepped forward and saw Julia much clearer. Something in her faded cornflower-blue eyes gave her away as being older than she looked at first glance. Certainly older than Trevor, who Gracie had been told turned twenty-nine in July. As she neared, she caught a glimpse of several grays artfully disguised within the full head of blond strands. Fine lines webbed the corners of the woman's full lips.

So this was the woman in Trevor's picture.

"Hello, I'm Gracelyn Riley," Gracie said, spontaneously using her full name. She wanted to be formal with Trevor's possible ex-fiancée, ex-love, whatever she might be.

Trevor turned from the fireplace, a formidable expression crossing his face. "What are you doing in here?"

"Well, I heard weeping and thought I could possibly help," she answered brightly, fully mindful that he was coming at her like a train rushing into a depot. She braced herself for the blast, but it didn't come. He stopped an inch away, the firelight flickering over his chiseled features.

"I'm probably not needed after all." She backed up awkwardly with her crutches. "It was a pleasure to meet you, Julia."

Trevor grabbed her sleeve. "Do you usually make a habit of eavesdropping?" He watched her closely.

Too late, Gracie realized she'd been caught. Julia hadn't introduced herself. Foolish tongue. "Uh, yes, I mean no. I heard you yelling in the hall, and then I heard this awful crying." She cleared her throat. "Perhaps I should go now."

"I'm betting it's not Christian to eavesdrop." He fixed her with a hard stare before relenting and gesturing to the woman near the couch. "Gracie, this is Julia Williams. Julia, Gracelyn Riley."

Julia inclined her head. Gracie reciprocated. The woman stood quietly but Gracie had the feeling Julia was no mouse. In fact, she looked distinctly feline. Gracie shuddered at the thought of being within reach of the woman's sharpened claws. She no longer felt intimidated by Julia's surreal beauty, but rather by the gleaming awareness that lit her feral eyes.

Gracie's hands balled. She was not accustomed to feeling intimidated. She resented the intrusion on her self-esteem.

Trevor turned to her, his lips quirking in a most suspicious manner. "Now that you two have been properly introduced, why don't we enjoy coffee and cookies. Gracie, you know where Mary keeps those things?"

She flinched. Have coffee with Julia? She couldn't. Absolutely not. "I need to rest. I'll leave you with your ex-fiancée or lady friend, or whoever," she stuttered.

Trevor recoiled, his mouth flattening. Julia grinned, baring perfectly white pointed little teeth. Gracie desperately wanted to escape. How could he love this woman?

"Julia is not my ex anything." Trevor looked Gracie square in the eye. "She's my mother."

Chapter Eleven

Buried secrets rotted slowly.

That's why tonight Gracie would get some answers. She stared at her plate of mashed potatoes, willing them to disappear. The past few days had been interminable. She'd spent most of her time with Mary, cleaning, ironing and performing other tedious tasks. Uncle Lou was scheduled to come home tomorrow and though Mary hid her feelings well, Gracie detected a quiet excitement in Mary's movements.

The only interesting happening this week involved a tiny snippet of information in today's paper. She'd seen it this morning and with Mary's permission, cut it out and slid it in her pocket to look at later.

She'd tried to stay away from Julia. She wasn't one to take instant dislikings, but in this case, her hackles rose at the thought of the woman. It wasn't just the way she had exposed her son to the harsh elements of life, but a cockiness in her demeanor, a calculating gleam in her eye. Consequently, Julia had been left to herself much of the time, roaming Lou's house at will. She didn't offer to help with chores.

Despite her antipathy for the woman, Gracie could not

quell her curiosity. Trying to get information out of Mary, however, was like trying to eat one of Mother's muffins.

Impossible.

Mary's reticence regarding Julia frustrated Gracie. How could she know the proper way to act when she had no information to go by?

She glanced up from her potatoes and stole a peek at Trevor's dark head. She'd missed seeing him, talking. It seemed he didn't want to be around his mother any more than she did. There was the sneaking suspicion he might be avoiding her, as well. He could still be angry about that kiss, she acknowledged to herself. It really hadn't been fair of her to take advantage of him that way. Perhaps she could corner him and explain.

After dinner and clean-up, Gracie left in search of Trevor. The past few nights he and Julia had gone to his house immediately following dinner but tonight his mother announced she wanted to stay awhile for conversation. When Gracie slipped from the sitting room, however, she left behind only Julia's dry monologue and a stone-faced Mary.

Gracie crutched her way down the hall, careful not to slip on the freshly waxed wood floor. After poking her head into the kitchen and Uncle Lou's office, she concluded Trevor must be on the porch. Freezing, no doubt. She headed back down the hall and braced herself for the biting wind that would steal the warmth from her bones.

As she neared the front of the house, Trevor let himself in, shutting the door against a chilly gust. Gracie couldn't help the smile that slid so easily across her face at the sight of his frown. He shrugged the leather coat off and hung it on the rack.

"Trevor, I've been looking for you. We've matters to discuss."

"Don't talk so loud." He steered her to Uncle Lou's office. She shoved down her impatience and waited until she was seated in a chair before she pounced.

"I'm awash with curiosity. Could you enlighten me as to why your mother is here?"

"You think it's your business?" His face remained impassive and she wanted to jump from her seat and wring his neck until he showed some kind of emotion. She clasped her hands together tightly.

"No," she answered frankly. "But if I had some information to go on, I could establish a proper relationship with that woman."

"My mother."

"As it stands now, I'm not sure how to behave. You and Mary both seem to hate her." That wasn't a very tactful thing to say but it was out now. "Anyhow, I'd like to develop a plan of action for dealing with her."

"That's very prudent of you."

"I have my moments. We've never played chess, have we? I believe I could show you some excellent strategies for taking out the king within six moves."

Trevor studied her from where he sat across the desk. It was nice to see her thinking about something besides Connie or Striker. He wished he could see the familiar bounce in her step but figured that might be a long time coming. Her cheeks had filled out some and there was a rosy glow to her skin.

She was an oak.

It heartened him. Her dark hair gleamed in the lamplight and suddenly he wanted to touch it again. But she was untouchable, he reminded himself fiercely. She belonged in the city, not in the desert.

Not with a man weighed down by his past.

He remembered how she'd looked in his house, how he'd

savored the view. As if she belonged there. In his home. The realization brought a pain to his chest, a yearning he couldn't put a name to.

Tapping his fingers against Lou's desk, he forced his thoughts to the matter at hand. Hashing out his life history wasn't easy for him, but it would help for Gracie to know a little bit about Julia. It was always safer to keep the enemy close.

"Julia managed a gentleman's club," he began, noting the surprised curiosity that crept across Gracie's face. "She just discovered my father died and that the brothel was in his name only."

"She lost her business," Gracie said, cupping her cheeks.

The movement startled Trevor. He jerked his gaze away, ignoring the tenderness surging through him at her innocent expression.

"She came here to get a loan to start another one in Burns."

Gracie shot upward. "Oh, you can't, Trevor. Please do not have any part in that."

"Sit down. There's no need to preach at me."

She sat, twisting the folds of her skirt with vigor.

"I'm not giving her money, so you can relax. You're not the only one who believes in right and wrong, Gracie."

She blinked. "I know that. I only thought you might want her away and giving her money is the quickest means to accomplish that."

"She'll leave." He hesitated, then plunged on. "You should probably know Julia is the one who arranged for Mendez to kidnap Mary."

"What? And she's not been jailed?" Her eyes rounded, shocked.

Because there'd been no proof, only suspicion. Trevor frowned. "Stay away from her."

"But why would she do such a thing?"

"Money." And envy. It had occurred to him years later that maybe his mother envied the closeness he'd shared with Mary, the deep love he held for her as if she were his own sister. He caught Gracie's gaze. "I'm thinking of sending Julia to Spain to visit relatives."

"That's so expensive. How will you buy your new ranch?"

Trevor's jaw tightened. She was too nosy for her own good. "Who said I'm buying a ranch?"

Gracie rolled her eyes. "Uncle Lou notated your bonus earnings. I assumed you've put quite a bit of those earnings into savings. When James mentioned the other day that there is a ranch for sale nearby, I came to the conclusion you might want to purchase it."

"That's an odd way to come up with such a conclusion."

"You are not a man to stay beneath the shadow of another for long," she reassured him. "I took that into consideration, as well."

He frowned. Despite her assertions, there was only one way she could have known. "Did you see a copy of my letter to the ranch owner?"

"No, I just told you how I reached this assumption. You sent a letter?"

Actually, he'd left it on Lou's desk. He'd wanted to talk with Lou first but had been putting it off. "There's no way you didn't see my letter."

"Are you calling me a liar?"

"Are you one?" he challenged softly. "You never said one word about a sort of fiancé. Seems to me this could be a pattern."

Gracie blinked quickly, distress evident in her eyes. "I am not a liar," she said quietly.

"You're the nosiest person I've ever met." So he was still

in a bad mood about her relationship with a former beau, and he couldn't quite figure out why. Maybe because she'd kissed him as though he were the only man in the world.

He'd never had that feeling before.

"Perhaps I'm nosy, but it's only because I was bored. Numbers busy my mind, as does conjecture, which, I assure you, is the extent of my knowledge regarding your financial transactions."

Numbness spread through Trevor. Up until a few days ago, he'd begun to trust Gracie, to respect her and enjoy her company. That she would sit there and lie to him point-blank made him more angry than he could remember being in a very long time. Her denial stank like betrayal. It cut more deeply than her insults. His fingers curled into fists.

"From now on you don't come into this office, understood?"

Gracie shoved to her feet. "Of all the nerve! No one has ever called me a liar." She pointed a long finger his way. "Uncle Lou's in charge here."

"When he's gone, I'm in charge."

She snatched her crutches up.

"We'll see about that," she shot out. Hobbling to the door, she turned back to Trevor, who remained at the desk, unwilling to move. "I never saw any silly letter so you can stop looking at me as if I've sprouted a beard. It may be hard to believe, but I do have a brain and I know you want your own place. You should inform Uncle Lou."

"Is that all, Gracelyn?"

"You may call me Miss Riley. Yes, that is all, Mr. Cruz."

She stepped into the hallway and clicked the door closed. What she really wanted to do was slam it until the roof shook. Fury made her limbs tremble. He thought her a liar. She gripped her crutches until her knuckles ached. The man did not even blink an eye. For the first time she wondered if he felt things as others did. One could not guess it by the remoteness of his features.

Mary moved out of the darkened corner of the hallway and held out an envelope. "It's for you."

Gracie struggled to control her temper, calling on years of social etiquette to force a small smile to her face. But her pulse still thundered as she took the envelope from Mary. "It's wet." She ripped it open, scanning the smeared contents.

"Lou came in and handed it to me before heading to his room." Apology filled Mary's tone.

"I cannot read most of it, although I believe it's from my parents. I hope nothing untoward has happened." She looked up at Mary, whose eyes widened with concern.

"If there were bad news I'm sure they would've sent a telegram."

"I suppose you're correct." Gracie balled the illegible paper in her hand, listening to the rustle and wishing it were Trevor's face crumpling beneath her fingers.

"I'll throw the paper away for you." Mary's gaze skittered to the office door behind Gracie. "Were you and Trevor yelling at each other?"

"He barely raised his voice." Yet his words had spoken volumes. Her spine tightened at his nerve. She met Mary's eyes. "Does Trevor always leap to wrong conclusions and think he's right?"

"He's strong willed, that he is. But he's usually right." Mary glanced at the still-closed office door.

"Not this time." Gracie's lips pursed. She moved away from the door, toward the staircase. "You can tell him not to bother talking to me until he apologizes."

The office door swung open.

"You can tell me yourself, Miss Riley."

The nerve of the man! She glared at him. "Don't bother

talking to me until you apologize!" She was alarmed to hear her voice rise an octave and clamped her mouth shut. *In your anger do not sin.* She groaned silently. Too late for that. Not only had she lost her temper, but now she was behaving like a child.

"I'm going to bed now," she snapped. She turned around and pushed past Julia, who had at some point slithered unnoticed into the hallway. Trevor didn't resemble her in the least. The woman bothered her immensely but she squelched her growing sympathy for Trevor beneath her indignation at being labeled a liar.

It was time he realized he was not right about everything. She itched to teach him a lesson. Looking at his papers, indeed. As if she would fib about something so inane.

Before bed she looked over her articles on Striker again. She pulled out the one she'd clipped from the newspaper this morning.

Engineer's daughter rescued near the border in Texas last month now claims Striker helped her. After killing her kidnappers, Striker returned her home, the girl states. The daughter, whose name is withheld for privacy purposes, says the government agent wishes to remain anonymous. The daughter also says Striker is younger than she expected.

Frowning, Gracie placed the article with the others and slid her box back into her closet. A good thing she hadn't wasted time in Burns these last weeks since apparently Striker had been cavorting about somewhere else.

But that meant he should be returning to Burns soon. All the more reason to ramp up her efforts to find him.

She went to bed hoping for dreams of the heroic agent.

Instead, nightmares in which Trevor pointed his finger at her and called her a liar over and over again invaded her sleep. Then she turned into Julia and had to watch him begin to loathe her.

It was a strange night. When she finally made her way into the kitchen the next morning, bleary eyed and vexed, she found Mary mixing up pancakes and Trevor sitting at the table sipping coffee. She deliberately ignored him and hobbled to the counter to pour herself coffee. Bitter and black, it fit her mood and she sipped it with relish. She couldn't carry it to the table while holding her crutches, so she leaned against the stone counter and watched Mary rhythmically stir the batter.

"Did you sleep well, then?" Mary's brogue seemed thicker in the mornings.

"Not really. I had bad dreams. I keep thinking about Connie and her family. I don't know how I'll ever be able to be happy when I go home."

Mary kept stirring and did not reply. Gracie could feel Trevor's gaze on her. Let him stare. She had not called him a liar, undermining his character and everything he stood for.

Even still, it was hard for Gracie to hold on to her anger. It had always been hard for her to stay cross. Not her nature. And to be fair, he really didn't know her well. Could she blame him for leaping to the obvious conclusion? Not everyone was trustworthy.

Gracie's stomach growled loudly. She sipped her coffee, hoping no one had heard the rumbling. "Are we going to church again?" she asked.

Mary flipped the pancakes. "Too cold today."

"Went to the neighbor's this morning." Uncle Lou slid into the room, silent as a shadow. When Trevor turned to look at him, Gracie studied Trevor beneath her lashes.

Freshly shaven and with his hair slicked back, he looked strong and in control. Her lips tingled as she remembered his kisses, the way his fingers had cupped her cheeks so gently. The way he'd pulled her to him as though he never planned on letting go.

"War's over," Uncle Lou announced, a broad grin spreading across his tan features. "It's all over the papers. Our boys are coming home in droves."

Gracie set her cup down and faced her uncle. "When did it end?"

"The eleventh." He looked over her shoulder at Mary, who had gone back to finishing up the pancakes and turning the bacon on the back burner. Clearly a man in love. Did Mary know how Lou felt? Did he, even?

Would Trevor mention to Uncle Lou their little altercation last night? Her uncle appeared dense where love was concerned.

A movement caught her attention.

Julia flounced in, wearing a high-fashion, icy-blue dress. She stopped short when she saw Uncle Lou. There was an awkward silence in which the only sound was the pop of bacon sizzling in its pan.

Something quite murderous shadowed Uncle Lou's features. Gracie shivered in response.

"What is she doing here?" His jaw seemed carved from stone, except for the small rhythmic twitching at its base. "Get her out before I shoot her between the eyes."

Chapter Twelve

Uncle Lou didn't shoot Julia between the eyes.

Instead, Trevor ushered her to the front door. Gracie followed the strange little procession. Tears streamed down Julia's cheeks as she clung to Trevor's arm. An unexpected sympathy welled inside Gracie's chest.

"Please don't make me leave," Julia sobbed. "I have nowhere to go, no one to turn to. Please, son."

Julia sunk to the floor.

This was too much. Gracie rushed over to the crumpled woman, sending Trevor what she hoped was a scathing look before bending toward his mother. Trevor's face remained composed as he watched. Mary stood beside him, just as expressionless, arms folded tightly against herself.

Gracie held out her hand, giving Julia a small smile. Truth be told, Julia deserved their animosity. She certainly wasn't an easy woman to get along with, or to like, for that matter. And she had sold Mary for money, a loathsome act worthy of judgment. Still, as an objective watcher, it was Gracie's Christian duty to help the woman.

The love of God was not only for righteous people.

Waiting, she kept her palm out but Julia snatched her

long-nailed fingers from Gracie's reach as a sneer disfigured her pretty face.

"Leave me alone," she snarled like a wounded animal prepared to attack. "I know how you hoity-toity people back east look down on women like me. Don't you try to touch me with those pristine hands. I know your type." Julia made a sound in her throat. Then she spat at Gracie.

Gracie recoiled, trying to force down the bile rising up her throat.

At that moment, the love of God seemed to desert her and unexpectedly the urge to slap sense into the other woman clawed through her. She closed her eyes and tried not to gag as she stepped away. It wasn't her business, she reminded herself sharply as she limped to a far wall, out of reach in case Julia should decide to continue her unladylike behavior.

Uncle Lou appeared at the other end of the hall, a silent specter hovering near his office and the kitchen entrance. His legs spread as if going into battle. He must have heard the commotion.

Stalking toward them with the grace of a tiger hunting prey, he scowled fiercely, and for a second it flashed through Gracie's mind that her uncle might be as dangerous as Trevor.

She shook her head.

That was ridiculous. Nobody here was dangerous except Julia, who was now scrambling to her feet with a panicky look on her face. Her long blond hair tangled around her shoulders, giving her a youthful air and lending to her an innocence Gracie was sure she didn't possess.

Gracie shrank back farther against the wall but luckily Julia's attention stayed riveted to the man in front of her. When Uncle Lou spoke, he directed his comments to Trevor.

"She stays at your place. I don't want her in this house again. She's to keep away from Gracie and Mary." Then he pushed past Trevor and went outside.

Julia, of course, had not finished with the dramatics. She fell into a silken-skirted heap, weeping loudly. The only thing that kept Gracie from rushing to her again were the obvious theatrics. The woman never could have succeeded on stage.

Still, her heart went out to Trevor's mother. Surely, despite the obvious masquerade, Julia was sad. Perhaps lonely. She had nowhere to go but here, and it was here where her presence was not wanted. After being spit on, however, Gracie was reluctant to get any closer to this family quarrel. She would not be here much longer, anyhow.

Past Christmas, and into early spring perhaps. And then she'd leave and go back to a house that no longer felt like home, back to her golden cage. Unless she found Striker—and quick.

Trevor leaned forward and gently pulled his mother to her feet, his response clashing with the rock-hard expression on his face. Gracie thought he might hate his mother, and yet his touch appeared to be soft. He murmured something in her ear and she went out the front door, still sobbing but saying nothing more.

Mary hovered near the steps, statue still, her skin dusky.

Trevor walked past Gracie, who felt as frozen as Mary looked, then paused and turned back to her. "I apologize for Julia." He cleared his throat. "Do you need help getting upstairs?"

She shook her head, loosening her death grip on the crutches. Mary followed Trevor down the hall and into the kitchen.

Shuddering, Gracie let out a deep breath. She was not

used to such emotional outbursts. False or not, the scene left an ache in her heart.

She decided to relax in the sitting room for a while. Perhaps the crackling fire would ease her throbbing knee and tense nerves. Taking out her hankie, she dried Julia's spittle from her skirt and then propped her crutches beside one of the plump scarlet chairs near the fireplace. She sank into one and sighed as the soft fabric embraced her. She couldn't remember feeling so stressed in her entire life. Of course, she'd experienced bumps in life and there were times she felt suffocated by the restrictions of society and the unrealistic expectations of her parents. But no one had ever believed her to be a liar, to her knowledge, and certainly no one had ever looked at her with such undiluted hatred as Julia had.

It was unsettling, she admitted. Her honor meant much to her. If she didn't have these crutches she would go outside and race Honey as far as she could, shedding her worries in the wind. But she was stuck here, forced to endure the endless cycle of thoughts spiraling through her head. There was always her notebook, which patiently waited in the closet, stashed away when Gracie had heard about Connie.

She watched the small flames flicking back and forth, devouring wood. Crackling in their greedy hunger.

Trevor's disbelief hurt. She sighed again. Quite possibly she might be getting her first gray hair over the entire matter. If only there were some way she could convince him of her innocence. But there was nothing she could do, no way she could prove the truth.

Why did it matter anyhow? She would find Striker, establish a career and never see him again. Life would continue and soon he might become only the faint memory of a man she once kissed.

Right.

Gracie closed her eyes, feeling warmth from the fire on her face. When she went home, Boston would be different. She was used to doing everything with Connie, from jazz halls to church luncheons to secret writers' meetings. How would she be able to go back and not be reminded every day? Suddenly the quietness of Oregon seemed much more appealing than the bustle of Boston's social life.

God, I know Connie is up there with You, but I miss her so much. My soul is heavy from her loss. Please help me, Lord. And Trevor's accusation haunts me. Forgive me for losing my temper, for my rudeness to him. Please show me Your goodness and give me peace. Please make me more like You. Thank You, Father.

She continued to pray for a few minutes, the quiet room lending to her heart the solitude she needed. Gradually, peace calmed her nerves and stole her worries.

Chapter Thirteen

Later that evening, after the others had retired to their own activities, Trevor joined Gracie in the parlor. She didn't hear him come in, only the soft slide of his clothes against the couch when he sat. She looked up and the flickering shadows against his face did funny things to her insides. Her gaze shifted to his hands. Strong and calloused. The hands of a man who'd worked hard to make a life in this desert. He held a green leather-bound book.

After trying to read the spine of it she gave up and settled back into her own novel, a rousing reread of Tom Sawyer.

Pages whispered as they turned. This was ridiculous. She set her story down, marking her spot with a bit of ribbon. She couldn't concentrate with Trevor so near. "I'd like to go to town soon."

"Uh-huh."

"Really, Trevor. Uncle Lou always goes without telling me. I've Christmas presents to buy."

He looked up from his book. "In a few days we're going. I'll give Lou a heads-up." He went back to his story.

Gracie snatched her book up, feeling triumphant. At last. She could shop, talk with others and perhaps glean information on Striker's whereabouts. Even if he hadn't returned, surely he owned a home somewhere. Knew people. Perhaps even had family nearby. She grinned and opened her book.

A sound at the doorway pulled her gaze upward. Uncle Lou poked his head into the room. "Trevor, have you been looking for a letter?"

Out of the corner of her eye, Gracie saw Trevor's head snap up. "Yes," he said.

"Let's go to my office and discuss it."

Both men glanced Gracie's way and she tried to keep her face blank, pushing down her disappointment at missing out on what might be an extremely enlightening conversation. She couldn't help but admire Trevor's long, confident stride as he left the room. She finished a chapter, and then reached for her crutches.

She thought she understood why Trevor was reluctant to discuss striking out on his own with Uncle Lou. From what she knew, they had been friends for more than ten years, before they'd ever owned a ranch. Trevor probably didn't want to hurt her uncle by going into business himself.

She put the fire out, casting the room into a soft darkness. Loyalty was hard to come by nowadays. Trevor had risen above adversity, become an honorable human being. This was just one more example of his thoughtfulness to those he loved.

But he didn't trust easily. Only time and a healing God could change his heart. She picked her way laboriously up the steps.

She could not forget how gentle he'd been with his mother earlier, even though she saw the disgust practically steaming off him. He was a man of great self-control.

His image didn't fade as she readied for bed. His black eyes, intelligent and perceptive, his confident walk, his protective and loyal character. Gracie's heart thumped. Nine years wasn't such a great difference in age.

Drawing back the covers, she dragged herself into bed, amazed her energy had fled so quickly. Her flannel nightgown billowed around her and she pulled her knees up against her stomach. The deep feelings Trevor inspired posed a problem.

Striker was supposed to be the one she longed for. She frowned. Was she so shallow, then? Perhaps Striker merely represented what she admired in a man. After all, she had never met him. Didn't know his weaknesses or fears. Could she truly love someone she did not know?

Of course not.

Trevor, on the other hand…

She had never wanted to marry, hadn't wanted to place herself in a position to be controlled. No. There was no room in her life for a man like Trevor.

In the morning she'd develop a plan of action for when she arrived in Burns. Questions to ask, a way to snare the townspeople into revealing more about Striker.

"So you want out." Lou tapped the letter against his desk.

"It was a temporary thing."

"I know." Lou's eyes appraised Trevor.

He shifted, wishing he didn't feel like he was letting down his best friend, his country, by his distaste for what he'd become. "It's time to move on."

"You think you'll like ranching?"

"I like honest work."

"Killing wasn't in the plan, you know."

Trevor nodded. "But it happened." Sure, he'd only killed criminals, most of the time in self-defense, but he didn't like how killing numbed him. Made him react without heart. If he would have slowed down at Council Bluff, given the lawbreaker in his sights time to put his weapon down, maybe the child who appeared out of nowhere would have run past unscathed. Shoving down the deep remorse that plagued him, he met Lou's gaze. "I'm done now. The neighbor's spread will make money. They've got good land, steady stock. They're moving to Arizona to be with their oldest son so I figure I can buy their property and move in within the year."

"You've done good things for your country, Trevor. For Mary. If you hadn't found her…"

They both fell silent, knowing full well the evil that would've befallen her at the hands of Mendez so many years ago. Thanks to one of his mother's Paiute "friends," Trevor had learned at a young age the art of tracking in the desert. The skill served him well after Julia's betrayal, helping him find Mary and then making him specialized enough the government had enlisted him as a spy. He'd met Lou that way, quickly working his way up the ranks until his last job….

Even now, his chest burned at the memory of so many lost lives.

"We've been through a lot," he said finally, meeting Lou's gaze. "But I need to do this."

Lou's fingers tapped against the desk. He glanced at the letter again then slapped it down and leaned back, hands resting behind his head. "You set on this particular property?"

"Seems like a good choice."

"'Cause I've got a proposal for you."

Trevor leaned forward, intrigued. "I'm listening."

The following morning slithered by slowly, despite Gracie's many tasks. She helped Mary dust, mop and do laundry. Then she snuck into Uncle Lou's office to discreetly check his account books while he and the other men were out on the ranch, doing whatever they did in winter.

She found the extra money during a calculation. Or rather, the record of money. The ledger in her hand confirmed a payment of fifty dollars for which there was no designation and, though it was not the first such payment, it was most definitely the largest. And most obviously the reason why her figures would not calculate.

Feet scuffled outside the office door. She stuffed the ledger back and shut the drawer. She was on the floor, but because of her knee could not stand quickly. She popped her head up just in time to see the door swing open. Then it slammed shut.

Trevor stood there, hands behind his back and a bemused twist to his mouth. Gracie groaned. She could tell by his lips that inwardly he was laughing at her, and when a stray hair floated in front of her face she blew it away impatiently. It was no mystery what he found amusing. No doubt she looked a mess.

Pressing her left hand against Uncle Lou's heavy leather chair and her right on his teak desk, she managed to push herself into a somewhat standing position.

"Does Lou know you're in here?" Trevor walked to the other side of the desk and lazily sat down, the chair creaking in protest.

"I think you're too big for that chair," she pointed out, desperately racking her brain for a plausible excuse for being where she was. She sat down, relieved to get the pressure off her weak knee. "I'm helping Mary clean today."

"It's obvious you're fiddling with Lou's account books again, but I've decided to let it go. Lou probably needs the help, anyway." He leaned forward. "I've been looking for you."

She felt heat rise in her cheeks. She liked the way Trevor was studying her, even if there did seem to be a spark of humor in his eyes. She resisted the urge to shove her hair back where it belonged and instead focused on smoothing her paisley skirt.

Trevor seemed to be taking a moment to collect his thoughts, so Gracie figured she would help him along. There really was only one reason she could think of that he'd be looking for her.

"Thank you, Trevor, for coming to apologize. That takes true honor and I find your action admirable." She rested her hands on the desk, hoping to radiate composed benevolence.

With difficulty, Trevor swallowed his snort of laughter.

Gracie wondered why he was choking but he recovered so quickly she didn't feel the need to rush over. She was willing to forgive him his distrust, especially in light of his painful past. Thank goodness things had been solved so neatly.

"What did Uncle Lou say happened?" she inquired serenely.

"Found the letter on his desk and looked it over."

The crinkles around his eyes when he smiled grabbed Gracie's attention. She let her gaze linger. "I suppose he had good advice?"

"Yeah, he wants me to buy this ranch. Seems he wants to travel for a spell."

"He wants to sell? But it's so beautiful and peaceful. How could he?"

"He's like you, Gracie, doesn't want to be stuck in the desert."

"I like it here," she said stiffly. "It bothers me that it will no longer be in the family."

Trevor met her gaze, deliberately challenging her.

She flushed. "I've become more attached to Oregon than I realized." She cleared her throat. "I'll be quite sad if he sells the ranch. The land—" her lashes fanned across her cheeks "—does something to me. It makes me yearn."

The huskiness of her voice pulled at Trevor. He tapped his feet, figuring she probably didn't see the shock she'd given him. He'd thought she couldn't wait to get away. He'd assumed she hankered after city life, but now he saw that Harney County had worked itself into her heart, just as it had him so many years ago. His chest tightened.

Her eyes opened and she pinned him with her amber gaze. "When are you going to buy the land?"

"We didn't get that far. Just discussed it, is all." She looked so distressed that he added, "Don't worry. I'd rather be an equal partner in the ranch."

"Oh." He heard the relief conveyed in that single utterance. "James said I can remove my bindings permanently today."

"That's good news."

"Yes. And you're to break a wild horse this afternoon?"

He nodded.

"Mary says the horses listen when you speak to them. Is that true?"

"I guess." He shifted, embarrassed. "Are you coming to watch?"

"I'd like to very much." He saw her glance at the little clock sitting on the corner of Lou's desk. She made a tiny noise, a little catch of breath he found strangely endearing. "Oh, goodness. I'm to help Mary with laundry." She pushed her chair back, lifted the crutches and stood. "I want you to know I completely forgive you." She paused, head tilted to the side. "And thank you for coming to apologize."

Trevor tensed. "That wasn't why I came."

"Didn't you say Uncle Lou had your letter the whole time?"

"That's right."

"So you know I never saw it."

"Yeah. Look, Gracie…it was a logical assumption that you saw my letter. I'm not sorry for that."

"But you called me a liar," she said, her words whispery thin.

"Not important." Trevor rose, shoulders stiff. He was annoyed at the way the conversation was getting away from him. He didn't need to explain himself. Not to her. Not to anyone. "I came in here to say thank you for not lying to me. I appreciate your honesty on that matter."

Gracie blinked. "Thank you? You called me a liar, hurt me with your unreasonable distrust, and now you do not even have the courtesy to apologize? Your thanks is terribly insulting."

She hobbled past him, holding her head high.

"Now, Gracie, you're being silly."

"Don't you talk to me like you're my father," she shouted, obviously past her limit of endurance. "I am not being silly! My honor, my very character, was besmirched by your accusations. And now you wish to treat me as a silly girl so you won't feel guilty."

Trevor cringed. An uncomfortable feeling was spreading through him, some emotion he couldn't identify that cramped his gut and coated his palms with sweat.

Gracie pursed her lips, blinking quickly. "You have too much pride, Trevor Cruz. I forgave you anyway, before an apology, but you ought to be ashamed of yourself. How hard is it to say you're sorry?"

The door cracked shut behind her, sounding very much like the splintering pieces of Trevor's ego.

Chapter Fourteen

"I found out it was Julia who sold you to Mendez," Gracie told Mary as they stood in the kitchen rinsing vegetables for dinner.

Mary's face paled a bit but then she shrugged as though coming to an internal decision. "Julia isn't a good person. She gave Trevor's fiancée money to run off to New York City with some high-and-mighty businessman from Chicago before the Mendez business."

Fiancée? Gracie's hands stilled, then continued the rhythmic rinsing. When she could trust herself to speak she said, "I didn't know Trevor had a fiancée."

"It was before I lived here. He must have been, oh, eighteen or nineteen. I only met her once, but it was enough to know she wasn't for him. She was a young girl, and I could see in her eyes she liked to have fun. But he trusted her, despite her light ways."

"She left him, then?" Gracie dried the squash and set it on the counter.

"Two weeks before their wedding. He was always serious, but after that he changed." Mary frowned. "Lost his trust in women. I told him he only needed a solemn woman who was content to live in the country, raise children and not give him any trouble."

"How tedious." Gracie picked at a speck on the squash with her fingernail. The residue crumbled off and she brushed it into the sink. She could never be a "solemn" woman. Was that what Trevor wanted?

She'd watched him today with a wild horse. His voice had been nothing but a whisper, yet the mare responded. He'd held out his hand and the horse had inched forward, its hooves crunching in the brittle snow.

She wanted Trevor to have a woman who would see him as more than a rancher. Who would see his generous soul. The sensitivity he hid beneath his expressionless mask.

Mary went to the small porch right outside the kitchen and came back with chicken from the refrigerator. She coated a piece thickly with homemade batter, swirling it in the batter bowl before setting it on a plate. Her movements were brisk, smooth and spoke of inner passion. Her heart was in her cooking.

As Trevor's was in the calming of Oregon's wild horses.

Gracie observed Mary's movements and tried to push down the irritation rising inside. Normally Mary hovered on the reticent side when it came to personal information, so why had she shared Trevor's past with Gracie, making it sound as if being lighthearted was akin to being evil incarnate? Was she warning Gracie? Telling her she wasn't good enough for Trevor?

Gracie dumped the rest of the rinsed vegetables on the counter and began to slice them.

"A fiancée," she whispered.

True to Trevor's word, Uncle Lou took everyone into Burns. The day dawned crisp and bright, the fifteen-degree breeze carrying sweet scents of juniper and sage upon her airy breath. Although the drive into Burns took almost an hour, Gracie enjoyed every moment of it.

She pressed her face against the window, enchanted.

The Oregon land, vast and untamed, loomed before her. Rocks the color of a burning sunset jutted against the horizon. Some lightly dusted with snow, others drenched in glittering whiteness. Harney County was majestic in its wild splendor, captivating her interest and leaving her speechless almost the entire trip. Out of the corner of her eye she saw Uncle Lou, Mary and Trevor exchanging glances, and knew they were secretly amused at her lack of chattering.

Let them laugh. A strange love for her surroundings rose in her breast. She hadn't realized it before but now she knew nothing in Boston could equal this place. Nothing.

They pulled into Burns just past ten in the morning. People lined the streets, going about ordinary errands and chores. Any one of them could be Striker.

To Gracie's amazement, quite a few Indians walked through town. Some dressed in what she guessed was traditional Indian garb, others dressed like any other man or woman on the street. All possessed eyes black as night, shining at her as the car passed. In addition to pedestrians, horses and cars crowded the streets, horses outnumbering the cars by far.

That was different. Her upscale Boston neighborhood consisted mainly of automobiles, though at the harbor there were more horse-and-buggies.

The common denominator amongst the pedestrians were the masks covering their faces. Gracie hadn't wanted to wear one as they were large, bulky triangles of gauze, but she'd do what proved necessary to stay in good health.

Uncle Lou pulled into a parking space and proudly showed her the Ford dealership where he'd gotten his

Model T a few years ago. It stood shiny and new, a tes-
tament to the growing prosperity of the town. The men
helped each woman out of the car, careful not to muss their
skirts.

Gracie wore a deep blue suit beneath her coat, the fan-
ciest she'd brought, with shiny black shoes. It fit her form
beautifully, thanks to Mary's needle, and Gracie preened
with delight when Trevor's eyes kept flicking back to her.

Mary looked stunning in a sleek suede skirt and a
simple coat the color of a spring rose. The men had slicked
up, too, each wearing neatly pressed trousers and shirts beneath their leather coats.

James stayed home, expressing no interest in shopping
and eager to make sure "that woman," meaning Julia,
stayed out of trouble.

Gracie and Mary soon split from the men to go shopping for presents and left them to do more manly things,
like discussing the cars displayed at the Ford dealership.

Gracie looked up and down the street, wondering where
to start. "Do you suppose we'll see Striker today?"

"Really, Gracie, you're obsessed with the man."

"He rescues women," she blurted.

"And he's an assassin."

"That's a rumor." Gracie chewed her lower lip.

They walked the sidewalk, glancing into windows.

"You met him, Mary. What did you think of him?"

"This is what I think." She stopped walking and faced
Gracie. "He doesn't want to be found. He doesn't care what
people think of him. Rescuing women…and taking care of
criminals is what he does with whatever means necessary."

Gracie shook her head and turned away. She wouldn't
believe that of Striker. After the interview even Mary

would know Striker could not possibly be so cold. So brutal.

The rest of the morning passed amiably enough. She found things sure to please her family and friends, candies and delightful knickknacks Mother could display in her china cabinet. For her father she spotted leather slippers lined with rabbit fur, and after stroking the soft insides, she found his size and paid for them.

She bought gardening tools for Trevor and a huge book that categorized native Oregonian plants, illustrated with detailed drawings. She had the tools engraved with his name and when the shopkeeper showed her the case designed for the tools, she bought it, as well, ignoring Mary's groan at the exorbitant price.

When she brought up the topic of Striker with the clerk, Mary practically dragged her from the store. Gracie shrugged out of her grip at the door and made her way back to the counter.

"I simply want to know if he's passed this way," she told the gentleman. His thick eyebrows drew together, wrinkling weathered skin he hadn't bothered protecting with a face mask.

"Well, now." He chomped his tobacco. "Last week he rode through town but I ain't seen him since."

Thrilled beyond belief, she leaned over the counter. "How did you know it was him? Does he live nearby?"

The clerk scratched his head.

"We're sorry for bothering you." Mary tugged on Gracie's sleeve. "We've more shopping to do."

"Now, hold on a minute, Miss Mary. I gots something to say to this young woman."

"Yes, sir?"

"We don't talk about Striker here. We protect him." The

clerk spit into a can on the counter, then fixed her with a grizzled look that was obviously designed to intimidate her.

As if that could work.

She met his look head-on. "You protect him because he's a good man."

"He's been known to kill folks."

"I don't believe that." Not innocent ones, leastwise.

"Believe what you want, girlie. I'll tell you one thing. There's been journalists come up here before, flashing their money, but we keep our mouths closed. Now get on and leave the man alone."

He turned his back to them.

Frowning, Gracie let Mary guide her out of the store.

"I tried to warn you, Gracie."

"Does this mean Striker's nearby? That if I look closely, I'll find him?"

"No."

Mary refused to say more and Gracie let the matter rest. They did a little more shopping and though Gracie asked more questions, they remained unanswered. Disappointed, she followed Mary back to the car.

Gracie's step faltered when they passed shops closed for business, signs posted in the windows stating they would not reopen until the influenza pandemic waned.

She was watching Uncle Lou and Trevor cross the street when another sign caught her attention. Big, bold lettering stated "Infectious, Influenza Outbreak." The store was dark and the sign stood out like a proclamation of future evil.

She tried to tamp the fear coiling in her stomach, but in her mind she kept hearing Uncle Lou's quiet voice. "Constance died yesterday." Kept seeing the lines around his eyes, the concern tilting his lips.

Her fingers went to her mouth but touched fabric instead. She felt faint but didn't realize she was weaving un-steadily until Trevor's strong hand cupped her elbow. Her gaze cleared, focusing on his features.

"I'm fine," she said, pulling her arm from him and ad-dressing the question in Mary and Uncle Lou's eyes. She blinked fiercely as they returned to the car.

"Dance halls are closed," Trevor said, tone low.

"The pandemic is all over the country, hasn't hit us as hard, but it could." Lou fingered the newly grown mus-tache that peeked out from beneath his mask. "Best bet is to go home, lie low until this thing blows over."

Gracie trudged behind the group, forcing one foot in front of the other. Going out no longer excited her. The heavy bags in her hands no longer warmed her.

Here in Oregon, living life without Connie was easy. But in Boston? They shared the same friends, hobbies, church. Had grown up together.

She swallowed the lump in her throat and hoped no one would see the lonely tear sliding down her cheek. No one but God, who promised to put all her tears in a bottle. The day darkened as the soft sun slid behind thick gray clouds.

"Sorry, ladies," Uncle Lou said once they were situated in the car and he was pulling onto the street. "We wanted to take you out to eat but now isn't a good time."

"I'll make something special," Mary said.

Gracie gazed out the window, watching the townspeople and wondering which ones carried the fatal virus.

And who would die next.

After dinner, chores, and an hour of restless tossing and turning in her bedroom, Gracie cautiously slipped down to the sitting room with the hopes the fireplace still crackled. As she neared the base of the steps she saw with relief the flickering shadows coming from the room.

Good. She needed warmth. Something to chase the chills from her soul.

When she walked into the room, she stopped short. Trevor sat in a chair, head bent over a Bible, shadows of flames dancing across his dark hair. One of his arms draped the side of the chair, the other steadied the book on his lap. A peculiar warmth crept through her.

"Hello, Gracie." His head did not move as she continued to move into the room, her night robe making small whisking sounds as it brushed against the oak floor.

She settled onto the couch nearest the fireplace. The room was set up so the furniture grouped around the hearth. The big cushioned chair sat directly across from the fireplace with two scarlet couches flanking it and placed vertical to the fireplace to face each other. The overall design of the furniture and fireplace created a large rectangle. Between each couch and the chair Uncle Lou had strategically placed his antique tables. The arrangement evoked a cozy, inviting atmosphere.

Trevor closed the Bible and placed it on the table to his left, then faced her. She put her back to the fire in order to see him fully, casting her own face into shadows, but for once his was covered in light. He looked peaceful.

"Couldn't sleep?"

"No." Her fingers plucked at her robe. "What were you reading?"

"Romans."

"I love that book. If it was the only book of the Bible I had, there would be enough in there for me to live out a successful Christian life. How do you like it?"

"It's interesting." The flickering fire reflected in his eyes, making them gleam. His craggy features stopped short of handsomeness, yet they tugged at her, made her want to explore the depths of Trevor Cruz.

"Are you feeling better now?"

She blinked. "What do you mean?"

"In town, you seemed woozy for a few seconds. Everything fine now?"

"Yes, I'm fine."

"You didn't look fine," he persisted.

She didn't want to talk about it, so she changed the subject. "Have you decided to buy the ranch?"

"I'm not sure. Being half owner appeals more."

"Oh." She sighed, letting her lips curve into a smile. There would be more vacations here. She'd insist on it. "Thank you for the trip into town. I found a huge assortment of goods and believe I've finished my Christmas shopping. The shops were wonderful. I've never seen so many Indian artifacts or specially hand-crafted items."

"How'd your knee do?"

"Wonderful." James had removed the bandages like the professional he used to be. "Why is James no longer a doctor?"

Trevor grimaced. "He drank too much. Mary found him on the streets and brought him here."

Gracie gazed sightlessly into the fire. She could learn much from Mary. How many times had she snuck into the poorer areas of Boston for adventure's sake, only to ignore the needy of its streets?

"Are you still searching for your Striker?" Trevor asked.

"Of course."

"Why, Gracie?"

"I want to prove he's honorable."

Trevor shook his head. "That's not enough. What's in it for you?"

She turned to him, debating. What would he think of a woman in journalism? "Who's to say I have ulterior motives?"

"Everyone does."

"I suppose that's true. The fact is…I want to be independent."

His brow traveled upward, a familiar movement she was beginning to associate with him.

Could she explain what she wanted? Odd how her stomach clenched at sharing such a deep-seated need. She found herself longing for his approval. "If I find Striker, I'll accomplish what no other journalist has been able to do. I'd make a name for myself as an investigative reporter. I'd procure a career."

"I see." He linked his fingers and rested them against his ribs. "And you think the answer lies in Burns?"

"I know it does. I won't stop exploring until I find him."

"Speaking of exploration, you're not to go on the porch at night anymore."

Gracie's head jerked up at his abrupt words. He had seen her?

"If you keep up that reckless habit," he continued. "I'll have to let Lou know."

"Don't be so stuffy." Gracie strove to inject lightness into her tone, although anger and embarrassment battled for control. "It's only the front porch. And how is it you've seen me? Shouldn't you be asleep?"

"What I'm doing is none of your business, Gracelyn. Stay in your bed at night. There are dangerous animals roaming."

"I could say the same for you. If I choose to go on the porch, with all due respect, I fail to see how it is any business of yours." Her foot twitched beneath her robe.

In the hall, the grandfather clock chimed ten times, ten seconds' worth of Trevor staring at her with a hard edge to his features. He went too far with his insane rules.

"Lou will know," he threatened.

She crossed her arms and turned her head toward the fire, foot swinging with indignation. What could she say to that? It was Uncle Lou's home; she would do as he said. She fought the urge to grind her teeth together. "Do you always fall back on threats to get your way?"

"There are things you don't know." She felt his perusal. "Harney County has its share of nefarious men. Lou likes the house locked up tight at night and when you go outside you're endangering yourself, as well as the others."

"You mean Mendez." She heaved a deep sigh. "I didn't consider the night dangerous. I'll do as you say. But you'll not stop my midnight ramblings in the house."

"Fair enough," he answered, and she knew he was amused because he had won this clash of wills.

A log splintered, cracking loudly in the silent room, sending sparks up like fireflies dancing on a breeze. The scent of pine flavored the atmosphere.

What would Mother and Father think of her sitting alone at night with a man? They would not approve. Life here was different. The restrictions of high-society Boston seemed absurd in the quiet comfort she shared with Trevor.

He'd had a fiancée. Did he still love her? Mary had said it was years ago.

That must have been how she had hurt him when she first arrived, asking why he wasn't married yet. She cringed at the memory.

"I was talking to Mary today," she began, then stopped. Maybe bringing Mary into it wasn't a good idea. "She said the weather could warm up."

"Sometimes reaches as high as the thirties," he muttered, eyes never leaving the fire. His long legs stretched in front of him with lazy elegance.

"How is Julia?"

"Sleeping, I hope."

She racked her brain for anything more she could say to distract him so when she brought up the subject of his former love, he would not suspect Mary had told her. No great ideas came to her. She pushed her hair behind her ear, thinking she might as well just jump in.

"You had a fiancée, I heard." She peeked at his features. They remained impassive. "Was she beautiful?" *Did that just come out?* "I mean, uh, how long ago was that?"

"Years and years."

"What was her name? I bet it was pretty."

He sniggered. "Eunice."

"The poor girl." Gracie wrinkled her nose. "Children should be given beautiful names."

"You like kids?"

"Of course. They're wonderful, precious gifts of God. Why do you look so surprised?"

"Just thought you were more like Eunice," he admitted.

"Really, Trevor, I hope you've not been comparing me to that woman."

His annoying eyebrow arched in the flickering light from the fire. "That woman?"

"You know what I mean! She left you. How could she be so cruel? I would never do that to someone I loved."

"I'm glad to know that about you," he said quietly. His fingers drummed against his thighs. "I owe you an apology." His eyes met hers, seared through her, and all the indignation she felt at being compared to that faithless Eunice fled.

"I'm sorry for calling you a liar. That was wrong of me." The words sounded as though they stuck in his throat a little but she was thankful he forced them out.

"Thank you so much. I cannot tell you how much your apology means to me. I am so sorry that woman left you, Trevor. You didn't deserve it. You're a wonderful man."

Disbelief flitted across his face, but she launched on. "You're compassionate and kind. Gentle. But strong and forceful. You have that dangerous edge, as well."

"Dangerous?"

"But in a good way." She nodded forcefully to drive the point home. "You've a wonderful gift with the horses. I have never heard of breaking a horse by simply speaking to it. Surely a man who deals with animals in such a way must be good at heart."

A rare smile curved his lips. Gracie drew her legs up beneath her skirt as they lapsed into comfortable conversation, the glow of the fire their companion. Time passed, and before Gracie expected it, the clock sounded eleven times. She should go to bed. It wasn't proper to be up this late with a man who was not her husband, and although she loved to stretch boundaries, perhaps this one was better left in place.

She yawned, hand covering her mouth in an attempt to look ladylike, but Trevor laughed at her anyhow.

She loved his laugh.

"You seem like you're ready for bed, little Gracie."

"Don't call me that. I'm a woman."

His grin widened. "Yes, ma'am. Just meant you look tired."

"I am. Trevor, I…" Standing up, she tugged at her robe. "Thank you. I couldn't sleep and you were the perfect company."

"And you, Gracie."

He wanted to kiss her; she recognized the look in his eyes. If they were married they could kiss anytime they wanted. *But we're not,* she reprimanded herself sharply and moved to the door.

Marriage to anyone at this time was out of the question.

Chapter Fifteen

Spinsterhood had its benefits.

The next morning after breakfast Gracie decided it was time she tried her hand at making herself trousers. It couldn't be too difficult, could it? And really, who would stop her? Not a husband and certainly not her parents, who sent her off without any thought to what she wanted.

She locked the door to her bedroom, then selected an old wool skirt from the closet to be her first pair of pants. As an afterthought, she checked to make sure her jewels were still down in the bottom of the closet where she'd nudged the bulky box months ago. They were. She closed the door. The dark corner made a perfect hiding spot. No one would see the box unless they looked there specifically.

Not that she feared a thief in this desert place.

She dragged skirt, scissors, needle and gray thread she had grabbed from Mary's sewing box over to the window seat. Frosty sunlight streamed in, the day bright despite its chill. Perfect for sewing.

For the next hour Gracie cut and stitched, and by ten o'clock she had a ragged pair of trousers and sore fingertips. She frowned as she twisted the pants one way, then the other. One side appeared to be shorter than the other. And the seams zigzagged crookedly up the sides. She groaned and threw the mangled skirt on her bed.

How was she supposed to join the modern world when she couldn't even make a pair of pants? It was a good thing God had put her in a wealthy family because she seemed to lack the necessary skills to make it as any kind of specialized laborer.

She pressed her nose against the cold window. In the far distance a herd of cattle ambled across the sagebrush desert, thick flanks urged along every so often by a nudge from Trevor's horse. Even from this distance she could read the confidence in his posture, the control in his hand. He sat on his mount tall and proud, sunlight streaming over him in graceful lines.

Her door shook slightly, followed by a brisk tapping. She rose and unlocked the door. She pulled it open.

Mary held out frothy pink material. "Here's the night-gown I altered." Her eyes lighted on the crumpled trousers Gracie had tossed on the bed. She smiled. "Are those your pants?"

Gracie opened the door wider so Mary could step into the room. "They more resemble a mutilated skirt."

Mary clucked her tongue, picking them up so she could inspect them. "They're not too bad. I could fix them for you, if you'd like."

"Really? But I don't want you to get in trouble with Uncle Lou." She slanted her eyes to Mary. "Trousers would be much more convenient, however, and I could make it worth your time."

"Are you trying to bribe me?" Mary continued to hold up the pants, turning them around, feeling the seams. "We're going to have to take these stitches out," she muttered, expression distracted.

"Thank you, thank you!" She launched herself at Mary and squeezed the smaller woman, careful to be gentle.

"Don't tell Lou," Mary cautioned, and Gracie found herself wagging her head in agreement like an eager puppy. Trousers of her very own. She was suddenly overcome with the urge to jump on the bed like she had as a child and crow with delight.

Mary left with promises to have the pants done by evening. She already had Gracie's measurements from earlier alterations, relieving her from having to be measured, poked and prodded again.

The sun had not yet reached its zenith. Gracie checked the time. Ten-thirty and nothing to do. Saturdays usually moved slow but today Gracie almost wished she had a list of chores to accomplish. Perhaps Uncle Lou would let her look at his accounts, though she had just snuck in the other night and fixed his arithmetic. She still needed to broach the subject of the unlabeled profits but in the meantime perhaps she could ride into Burns again.

If only she could go alone, she was certain she'd discover something intriguing. She needed to get there without having someone looking over her shoulder constantly. Mind made up, she skipped downstairs, marveling every few steps on the strength of her knee.

Thank you, Jesus.

Bursting into the brittle sunlight, still pulling on her wool coat, she had to squint before she located Trevor. That could be him, galloping her way. She kept her eyes on him as she leaped down the porch stairs.

Suddenly Trevor's horse stumbled. Shrieking, it began to buck. Gracie started running. If she could grab the reins… The horse threw Trevor. He landed in a sickening heap, his hat fluttering down beside him. The horse galloped away but her attention was focused on Trevor's still form. Her chest ached, unbearably tight.

If anything happened to him…

She heard shouts just as she reached his prone body. Ignoring them, she bent down and pressed her face close to Trevor's mouth, but felt no warm breath upon her cheek. Her fingers shook as she stroked his shadowed cheek, feeling the stubble beneath her fingertips. She traced his scar, so much softer than the rest of him.

"Trevor," she whispered. "Please don't die." He appeared small and vulnerable at that moment, a strange paradox considering his hands were at least twice the size of hers.

The wind lifted her hair, whipping tendrils across her face.

"Oh, God, please make him okay." She touched his cheek. "He's special, Lord. Uncle Lou needs him, and Mary. Don't let him die." She leaned closer to his ear. "Trevor, you are needed here. Open your eyes. Wake up!"

What if he did die? Hadn't she learned life's cruelest lesson of all? In the space of a second, breath had fled Connie's vulnerable vessel and she'd left this world. In only a moment.

She shook Trevor's shoulder vigorously. Only feet away, Uncle Lou dismounted his horse.

"Trevor," she said more urgently. "Open your eyes. You're fine. A little bump is all you have, you're fine."

"Gracelyn."

She hitched back.

"If you yell any louder in my ear, I'm going to strangle you." Trevor's eye cocked open. Grimacing, he grabbed Uncle Lou's outstretched hand and shakily pulled himself up.

He was alive! She jumped to her feet and, not caring that

Uncle Lou stood inches away, tiptoed up to kiss Trevor's cheek. She loved the scrape of his roughened jaw against her chin. She wrapped her arms around his body. The steady beat of his heart calmed her nerves. Surely nothing was wrong with his head when his heart pounded so steadily against her ear.

"Gracie, you can let go now. C'mon."

Vaguely she felt his hands gently pulling on her arms.

"I'm so glad you're alive," she babbled into his shirt, tightening her grip.

"What's this?" Surprise caught Uncle Lou's words and snapped them up into the breeze. "Is Gracie smitten with you, Trevor?"

"She might be," he acknowledged grimly.

She pushed away from him. "Might? You know I feel more for you than a mere schoolgirl crush, Mr. Cruz."

His mouth twisted. "No, I didn't. Thought you were having fun with a cowboy, passing time until spring."

"That is the most ridiculous thing." She poked his chest. Hard. "Perhaps at first it was all an adventure but you know perfectly well you're the first man I've ever kissed. Of course I would not deliberately tamper with your feelings. What kind of person do you think I am?"

"Someone who's got other interests," he said, face dark.

"Kissed?" Uncle Lou's voice rose a notch.

Gracie took no notice of him. She focused solely on the exasperating man in front of her and stepped forward, into his heat. She went to poke him again, but Trevor grabbed her finger and somehow twined his fingers through hers so they were holding hands. His grip was firm and strong.

She frowned. "You've misunderstood my situation. You think I'm like that woman, that Eunice."

"Gracie." He lowered his voice. "Can we do this inside?"

"No. I'm quite done explaining my circumstance to

you." She squared her shoulders and marched back to the house.

Trevor watched her, knowing a scowl twisted his mouth.

"You kissed her?" Lou demanded, his scowl darker and meaner. "I've enough problems with my brother without you flirting with his daughter! You're ten years older than her. What were you thinking?"

Trevor looked down at his hand, the one she'd stroked. It still felt warm. Sagebrush whispered around them, and Lou's horse nickered softly as he tried to formulate an answer.

What could he say? That she'd gotten under his skin the moment he met her? That she was different, more vibrant and alive, than any other woman he'd ever known? And since when had he started thinking of her as a woman?

He bent and picked his hat up, brushed the dirt off, then placed it back where it belonged. "She's not ten years younger than me."

Thoughts of Gracie plagued Trevor the rest of the day, during round up, while he stabled the horses, as he washed and prepared for supper. He found himself snapping at Julia when he spilled her bottles of herbs and castor beans on the kitchen floor.

So Gracie had feelings for him. He might've guessed but it was hard to tell with someone like her. The jaunty girl she'd been on the train appeared less and less. Had the death of her friend changed her? Or was he beginning to know the woman beneath the light-hearted exterior?

Whatever kind of person Gracie was, he sure wasn't looking forward to supper. Lou acted madder than a nest full of disturbed snakes and Gracie had left just as angry. Kept comparing herself to Eunice. He didn't want to talk about Eunice with her. That relationship ended a long time ago and dredging the whole thing up again irked him. Why did she need to know anyway? Her parents should've made sure someone had a better handle on her curiosity.

Trevor trekked to Lou's for supper, even though snow had started falling and the temperature had dropped at least ten degrees. As he walked, he thought of Gracie. Last night her eyes glowed when they talked, her cheeks had pinked with excitement, her lips had softened with pleasure. He couldn't remember being so relaxed and stimulated by a member of the opposite gender before.

And she was smart. She didn't realize it, but he knew intelligence. Had been taught to recognize and use it.

He opened the door and, after stomping his feet on the rug, strode to the dining room. Maybe he could trust Gracie with his past, but maybe not. Lou was right in pointing out her youth. She might not understand who he was, who he could be again so easily. No, telling her was just too risky. Better to leave the past where it belonged, dead and buried.

Mary and Gracie were carrying in the food when Trevor stepped into the dining room. Mary looked lovely, as always, but it was Gracie who held his gaze. She wore a soft green blouse and a velvety skirt that hugged her hips before flowing to her knees. The color of the blouse did something to her skin, made it rosy. And her hair was down, soft waves framing her face.

Trevor swallowed. Lou should tell her to change that skirt, he thought as she turned and left the room again, Mary in tow. The way it fit her was indecent. But he couldn't swallow the lump in his throat and when his knee knocked against a chair he almost cursed.

He sat down, not meeting anyone's eyes.

"Ya got it bad, boy?" James chuckled. "Which one is

it? Not that hoyden, I hope." He laughed again, grating on Trevor's already raw nerves.

"Nobody's got anything bad around here James, so shut your mouth." Lou glared at him, and Trevor looked up just in time to see James's smirk.

"You ain't got nothin' to say yourself, Mr. Fancy Pants. I see the way you look at that girl, too. Sure 'nough, we'll have babies here 'fore long."

"That is disgusting." Lou lowered his brows. "She's my niece."

James snorted. "Ain't the one I mean, boy."

"You aren't fighting in here, are you?" Mary walked in and set the roasted chicken on the table, then sat next to Trevor. That left Gracie beside Lou, directly across from Trevor, with James at the head.

"Shall we say grace," Gracie offered, a perky smile flashing across her face.

"Do what you want." Lou spooned mashed potatoes onto his plate.

"Very well. Lord, we thank You for this food and the wonderful day we've had. In Jesus's name, amen."

Silverware clinked as everyone ate. Gracie looked like she was trying to keep her thoughts to herself. No such luck.

"Isn't it wonderful the war is over?" She flashed him a bright smile. "Now all our boys will come home and life can go back to normal."

"They'll be coming home to disease," he muttered.

"A virus really," Gracie chirped, earning a scathing glare from James. She smiled at him. "How's your reading coming along?"

"Fair enough," he grumbled.

"Are you on *Walden* now? Or have you not finished Poe?"

James grunted.

"When we went to town the other day the baker said she knew of Trevor." Her fork swished through the air. "Said he was a mischievous boy and made some trouble back in the day. What did you do? Rob a bank?" She chuckled, then seemed to notice the suddenly frozen atmosphere. "You didn't, did you?"

"No," Trevor scoffed as relief coursed through him. Townspeople knew enough about him and Lou and their odd circumstances that they'd probably guessed who Striker was. Strangely enough, no one had leaked it yet.

"That's too bad. It would be rather exciting to know a reformed bank robber." Gracie propped her chin on her hand. "I did learn some intriguing news about Striker."

"Missy, you gotta learn to mind your own business here."

"That's what the clerk told me." Her eyes sparkled. "That the town is protecting Striker."

An unnatural stillness fell over the table. James broke it by coughing and starting a conversation about cows. Gracelyn, mercifully, let the subject of Striker drop and became immersed in a discussion with James about the details of ranching.

Protecting him?

Trevor ate quickly, trying to digest her words. It just didn't sound right. More than likely townspeople feared exposing him because they weren't sure what he might do about it. That made more sense.

Thirty minutes later, the ladies excused themselves from the table to go wash dishes.

"I thought that girl's prattling would never stop," James commented as soon as they left. He shoved his chair back and stood, stretching his arms high and groaning before leaving the room.

Trevor kind of liked the babbling, but figured he'd keep his mouth shut.

Lou knew him too well. "She's young. I don't like it, Trev. Not at all."

"She'll go home to Boston and be happy there come spring."

"You kissed her." Lou's tone was accusing.

Trevor ran his fingers through his hair. "It was an accident. A lousy thing to do."

"You've satisfied your curiosity, now stay away from my niece."

He ignored that, got up and started for the door.

"By the way, Trev, she'll be going home after Christmas. I got a letter the other day. Her parents will be here tomorrow, so don't get too close."

"Fine," he said, then stepped into the hallway and took a deep breath. He felt like he'd been socked in the gut. This was where curiosity had brought him. To feeling vulnerable and stupid.

So her parents were coming. It meant she'd be leaving and all that would be left of her was a memory.

At least Mary could do things right.

"Beautiful." Gracie stood in front of Mary's full-length mirror the day after her horrendously botched sewing attempt. She turned to one side and studied her figure. "They fit perfectly."

Mary sat on the bed, feet tapping as she hummed.

Gracie twirled one more time and sighed with pleasure. "Thank you so much for making these for me. I have longed to wear trousers since I was eight years old and mother told me I could not climb trees in a dress." She smiled. "Are you making yourself some?"

Mary stopped humming and looked up. "I'll keep my skirts, thank you."

"Very well. I think I'll head down to clean up the dishes from breakfast so you can rest."

"Oh, I slept fine. I'll be right behind you."

She left Mary and skipped down the narrow hallway toward the stairs. She was halfway down before she stopped abruptly. Voices floated up, male and female, tinged with the sharp diction of Boston's higher society.

Her parents.

"Gracelyn, is that you, dear?" Mother moved to the foot of the stairs and gasped. Her jewel bandeaux glittered in her dark hair. "William, come here at once. Look at your daughter." Her strident tones rang through the hallway, and then the quieter creak of Father's wheelchair as he reached his wife.

Gracie felt frozen beneath her mother's withering gaze, but as soon as she saw her father's warm smile, hesitance melted into an answering grin.

"Daddy!" She hopped down the rest of the stairs and bent over her father to kiss his cheeks.

"Gracelyn, upstairs—immediately."

"Now, hold on, Edith. Let me get a look at our girl. Trousers, eh?" William's perceptive gaze floated over Gracie. She kept her eyes down, glad only Uncle Lou witnessed this spectacle.

"I knew that girl was trouble, I did." James popped into the hallway, followed by Trevor. They stood near Uncle Lou, whose arms were crossed tightly against his chest. Trevor lounged against the wall, hands tucked lazily into his pockets.

Gracie held her tongue, just as she'd been taught.

Father touched her arm. "My dear, why are you wearing pants when you know your mother and I disapprove?"

Edith's mouth set as she took in her daughter's attire, but good manners prevented her from interrupting her husband in the presence of strangers. Gracie glanced at her mother, then at Trevor. Despite his relaxed stance, his face was devoid of emotion and he looked as cold as a block of ice. She shuddered and faced her mother.

"Well, my legs chill wearing these silly skirts and you really haven't forbidden homemade trousers. I thought it might not be an issue if there was no one to see me."

Edith's lips flattened even more, if possible, but William smiled. "Your trousers are flattering, my dear, a little too much so. I take it you did not make them yourself?"

She shook her head slightly.

"Well then, why don't you change into a dress to make your mother more comfortable and we can discuss this later."

"Yes, Daddy." Gracie leaned over again and brushed her lips against his pale forehead. "I've missed you," she whispered against his ear. He took her hand and squeezed it.

The men began making introductions as she trudged up the stairs, her mother close behind. As soon as they went into the bedroom, Edith closed the door and turned to her, a frown marring her patrician features.

"Gracelyn, I cannot believe you would wear something like that. Whatever were you thinking?"

She sighed and sat on the bed. "Today's the first day I wore them, Mother. This is not Boston. There are no society ladies here to gossip on my deplorable manners." She moved off the bed, restless. "I'm surprised you and Daddy risked traveling with all the grippe outbreaks. How was your trip?"

"Tedious." She sniffed. "We wrote to inform you we were on our way."

"That must've been the letter I threw away. It had gotten wet, you see, and I could not read it." Gracie walked to the window seat, needing a fresh view before her nerves exploded.

Mother followed her. "You must be ready to leave. I had no idea Lou's place was so remote."

An odd disquiet carved a hollow place in Gracie's chest. "At first I grew bored here, but now I find plenty to do. The land has grown on me. This place seems to have caught God's special attention. As if He spent special time crafting these hills."

"Really, Gracelyn." Edith's nose lifted. "As if the Lord cares. We'll leave within the week."

She stiffened. "I have heard the influenza is still spreading," she said slowly.

"Oh, posh, you will be perfectly safe with your father and me. We do not feel comfortable with you so far away, and with Lou, no less."

"I would feel uncomfortable being in Boston at this time, Mother. Even if there were no influenza, the fact that Connie is dead is difficult to deal with in a place filled with memories. I would rather stay here."

Remorse flickered across Edith's face. "I did not think." She lightly touched Gracie's cheek. "I will speak with your father."

"It was dangerous for you to come here."

"In what way?"

"The influenza, Mother." And Mendez, but her mother needn't be bothered with that.

Edith laced her fingers together. "We simply had to come. Sending you here was a mistake."

"Because of Uncle Lou?" She picked at an invisible speck on her skirt. "Daddy practically forced me into this trip. And now you're changing your minds?"

"Your father's tiff with Lou is their business, and I have told you to refer to William as *Father*." Edith stood and patted her stylish chestnut hair. "I must freshen up and then find somewhere for your father to sleep. He cannot make it up these stairs." Her skirts moved silently about her ankles as she stepped into the bathroom. "Does your uncle have a bedroom downstairs?"

"Yes," Gracie answered, trying to keep sullenness from her voice. How was she supposed to search for Striker when her mother would be watching her every move?

Edith emerged from the bathroom and picked out a dress from the closet for Gracie to change into. It was one Mary had altered. She yanked it on, trying to pull it down so Edith would not notice the shorter length.

"You've lost weight. It has made your eyes stand out." Edith appraised her carefully before adding, "Are there any others here besides that scarred worker and old man?"

Gracie had to work very hard to keep from bristling at her mother's descriptive. "Mary, the housekeeper, and Julia, Mr. Cruz's mother."

"Very good." Mother marched out of the room, and Gracie followed.

Life was about to become very dull, indeed. Down the stairs they went, Edith's perfectly erect posture reminding her to straighten her own shoulders.

Flickering lights crept out of the study and she trailed in after Mother, hands clasped and head bowed.

"We do ranching, a little bit of business here and there. Trevor here is in the process of becoming part owner of the ranch," Uncle Lou was saying.

"It seems like a nice little spread. I would love for you to show me around sometime."

Gracie's head whipped up at the familiar voice.

The gentleman who had spoken stood, firelight glinting

off his fair head, and stepped forward to reach for Gracie's stiff fingers.

"Gracelyn, my dear, you look lovely," said Hugh.

Chapter Sixteen

Hugh's gaze lingered on Gracie's face before she dropped her head in a demure gesture and gently removed her hand from his sweaty grasp. "How nice to see you. I did not realize my parents had brought a guest."

"Come now, Gracelyn. Your fiancé is not just any guest." Edith clucked her tongue and moved to an empty spot on the couch opposite Trevor.

Her fiancé? Gracie reluctantly followed her mother. She'd been quite clear about this engagement.

Uncle Lou sat in his customary chair, with William to the right of him and Hugh to the left. She settled between her mother and Hugh while Trevor lounged alone on the couch across from them. She did not look at him.

"It's been a long time since we saw each other," she said to Hugh. "Do you plan to stay long?" She smiled tightly, teeth grinding together. Manners dictated she remain calm and polite when what she really wanted to do was throw something.

"I plan to stay as long as your parents do." He grinned. "I've needed a vacation since I came back from overseas and this was the perfect opportunity." He glanced at Lou. "I really look forward to seeing how your ranch operates.

I've had enough of war and hope to invest in some property of my own."

The conversation turned to politics but Gracie didn't hear a thing. Her parents obviously planned to push an engagement between her and Hugh. There could be no other explanation for his presence, despite his supposed interest in owning land.

Well, he wouldn't own her.

She glanced at Trevor, whose face looked hewn of granite. She remembered his distrust over the letter he'd written. Would he believe her now despite her mother's words?

Gracie struggled to keep her face impassive as the men spoke of President Wilson and the influenza. Mother did not speak, and for once Gracie had no desire to, either. After fifteen minutes of interminable conversation she asked to be excused.

Father appeared surprised at her request but he assented and she left the room. Once in the hall, she heaved a huge sigh and rested her head against the wall. Christmas was so close and now she would have to share it with Hugh, a man intent on taking what her parents offered. She groaned and straightened. Plucking Trevor's leather jacket from the coat rack, she let herself outside into the bright winter sun and plopped down on a rocking chair.

She closed her eyes against the sharp wind and rocked for several minutes. Back and forth, the soothing cadence of the chair against the porch floor creating its own song. Trevor's scent surrounded her and she inhaled deeply.

The door opened behind her, and then the chair beside her creaked as someone sat down.

"Gracelyn, I have raised you better. Please come back inside before Hugh thinks you are avoiding him."

She opened her eyes. "I am, Mother. Why did you bring him here? There's nothing between us."

"He is perfect for you. Calm, dependable. He is what you need in a husband."

"He doesn't believe women should vote." She shivered.

"Come inside, out of the cold. What does it matter what he thinks?"

It mattered, but her mother wouldn't appreciate her opinion. They rose and went back into the too-warm study. Conversation still flowed smoothly and no one looked up as they reentered. This time Gracie sat next to Trevor, ignoring her mother's startled look in favor of straightening her skirt.

"Would anyone care for coffee?" she asked when there was an opening.

"Mary is getting it," Uncle Lou said, then continued his discourse on the government's economic policies. Gracie shifted in her couch, snuck a peek at Trevor. He appeared engrossed in conversation and his eyes did not once stray her way. Hugh, on the other hand, ogled. She scowled.

If her parents were not here she could speak freely, but now she was bound by propriety and manners. She had missed her parents but she would never miss the strict regulations they imposed.

"I've heard scientists are working on a motorized wheelchair," Trevor said to William. His gaze looked past her as though she did not exist.

"I believe some have sold in London, though I've heard they're unreliable contraptions."

"The technological advances are incredible," Gracie put in. "And now that the war is over, I think opportunities are going to arise for women like never before."

"Are you still on that soapbox?" Hugh flashed a patronizing smile at Gracie before winking at Trevor. "Gracelyn is out to save women from the big, bad world."

A scalding burn prickled through her body. "Only because women have been treated deplorably since the beginning of this nation. To think our gender should prevent us from the vote, or even from earning a decent wage, is reprehensible."

Father's hand gently touched her fingers, which had curled around the side of the couch. She swallowed the rest of her words, though they almost choked her going down.

"Before you know it, we'll be getting a woman president," Uncle Lou joked as the study door swung open. Mary appeared, carrying a tray laden with cups and a kettle of coffee.

Gracie jumped up. "Let me help you."

Edith cleared her throat softly. "I am quite certain Mary can handle serving us. Sit down, Gracelyn."

She obeyed, feeling the noose around her neck tightening. How could she have forgotten what living in a house with her mother was like? These last few months of freedom had been bliss.

And now they were over.

"Thank you, Mary." Gracie tasted her coffee.

"Are you restless, Gracie?" William peered at her over the top of his spectacles.

"It is impolite and unthankful to be restless," she said by rote.

Uncle Lou chuckled. "Then why is your foot tapping so loudly?"

She looked down. He was right. Her left foot seemed to have a life of its own and with a force of will she crossed it behind her right ankle. She sipped the bitter brew and began silently counting to one hundred in French.

"Hugh, I'd love to hear about your travels while in Europe. Why don't you join me in my office?" Uncle Lou set his cup down with a sharp click and from the shadows Mary retrieved it.

"Excellent idea."

"Mary, show William and Edith to the guest quarters beside the office. We'll be back by dinner." Uncle Lou rose and gave William a stiff hug, then nodded to Edith.

At the door, Hugh stopped and flashed Gracie a dimpled smile. "I will see you this evening, my darling."

Gracie wanted to throw her cup at him but managed a genteel grimace instead. She turned to Trevor. "Perhaps we should check on Honey. I've not ridden since my fall and I'd love to try the Western saddle again. I promise I'll obey all orders."

Mother brushed past. "Do you not have sewing to work on?"

She wet her lips. "I'm sure you and Father need to get settled in first, and I am positively bursting to get back in the saddle. Mr. Cruz, I'll need your help, of course."

Out of the corner of her eye she saw Mother's eyes narrow but thank goodness Mary stepped forward, still carrying the coffee-laden tray. "If you wish, I can show you your room now."

"Very well," Edith said briskly. She helped William maneuver his chair back so he could turn around.

"Have fun, Gracie," her father said.

"I will. And Mother, Mary is an excellent seamstress. You two would probably enjoy knitting together."

But Edith was already following Mary out the door.

She turned to Trevor. "Let us leave quickly, before Mother has a chance to stop me. I'll meet you in the stables. I only need to pull on some winter clothes."

She ignored his cold expression and leaped up the stairs, two at a time.

She had to explain one more time about Hugh. Perhaps

now that Trevor knew she'd told the truth about the letter, he might believe her over her mother. She might not get another chance to talk privately with Trevor.

If she didn't find Striker soon, she would have no choice but to go back to Boston with her parents. Regardless, she wanted nothing to do with Hugh, especially after his degrading comment about her being out to save the world. What a heel.

The thick scent of hay, leather and manure permeated the stables. Gracie stopped at the entrance, instantly transported to the last time she'd been in here. The way she'd felt when she watched Trevor saddling the horses. She breathed deep and trailed her fingers along the door of each stall, pausing to say hello to a horse when it nickered.

She stopped at Honey's stall. The mare watched her casually, tossing her long, black mane.

"Hello, Honey." Gracie leaned against the stall and reached to stroke the soft jaw. "I've missed you. Are you ready to go for a small ride? How are you doing since your fall? I am sorry for that. I did not intend to hurt you." The horse nudged Gracie's jacket and she smiled ruefully. "Sorry, girl, I forgot the sugar."

"Carrots are better for their teeth."

A smooth voice intruded and Gracie grudgingly turned around. "Hello, Julia. Out for a ride?"

"That's why I'm wearing a riding habit. And you?"

"I'm continuing my riding lessons now that my knee is stronger."

Julia moved forward and held out a carrot to Honey. The mare grabbed it, tossing her mane appreciatively. "Honey and I have become good friends these past few weeks."

Gracie sidestepped Julia as the woman led Honey out. She swallowed the lump of disappointment in her throat.

Julia readied Honey for a ride, her movements meticulous and efficient.

Gracie watched from her place near the saddles. "You're very good at saddling a horse. Have you been riding long?"

"Since I was a little girl."

The image of Julia as a little girl was so incongruous that Gracie didn't bother with tact. She said the first thing that popped into her head. "You're so good with horses. Why didn't you choose a career in ranching?"

Julia's sharp movements paused briefly, and then resumed. Her face was hidden on the other side of Honey's long neck.

"Ranching's difficult. Backbreaking. The profession I chose offers good money, interesting people to meet. What's not to like?" Her leg swung up over the saddle, and a stocking clad knee peeked out for a second.

"I do not believe you've been happy."

"Believe it, little rich girl. Believe it. Some people like to do bad things. Any man will tell you that." She nudged Honey sharply and the horse cantered down the stable aisle and into the blinding sun.

Gracie stared after the slender form. The poor woman.

Trevor came in through a side door and, stepping in front of her, grabbed a saddle. "You ready to ride?"

"Your mother took Honey. I'm not certain which horse to ride now."

"We'll find you one." He tugged at his hat. "Julia was here, huh? I'm not surprised. She loves horses."

"She doesn't seem so evil now, just someone who's bitter and selfish."

Trevor opened a stall door, led out a tall black horse and threw a blanket on her, then started the saddling. "Don't let her fool you, Gracie. Selfish and bitter is its own brand of evil."

"I suppose so." The horse pawed at the ground, jerking her massive head when he looped the reins over her neck. "Trevor, I really do not care to ride that horse. Look how nervous she seems."

"She's just ready to run."

"What if I fall again? And isn't it too cold for a good gallop?"

"You can't be afraid forever."

"I'm not," she answered stiffly, unnerved by how the memory of being thrown still filled her with fear.

He slanted her a look, for a moment appearing empathetic before disinterest masked the emotion. "Falls are always tough to get over. The ground's covered by snow, though. There shouldn't be any ice around."

"But I thought you didn't want me to race the horses." She stepped up to the big black and forced herself to stroke the soft neck. The mare stopped prancing as she absorbed the gentle touch.

"After this morning, I figured you might want to feel the wind on your face." He adjusted the stirrups on the other side of the horse. Finishing, he came around to Gracie's side and she caught a glimpse of his face, still set like stone. But his voice had sounded tender. She wanted to hug him but that would make things more difficult between them. Why was she fooling herself?

Until she found Striker and became independent of her parents, a relationship between them would be impossible. Things were not looking good and she almost wished she had never kissed him.

Almost.

She watched as his busy fingers straightened and adjusted, all the while her own fingers stroked the mare's neck and mane.

"I would like to run far away," she finally admitted in

a low tone. Trevor's head turned toward her briefly, and then he continued his tasks.

"Is Butch waiting outside?" she asked.

"Yes."

She swallowed hard. "Trevor, I want you to know that I am *not* engaged to Hugh regardless of what my mother said. My parents arranged a betrothal without my consent. I refused the engagement, yet they brought him and continue to insist on a relationship."

"You already told me this, Gracelyn."

"I want you to believe me. A future between Hugh and me is ridiculous. It won't happen."

"You'd go against your parents' wishes? Because it's clear to me they're set on you marrying him."

"For love, yes, I would defy my parents."

"Doesn't the Bible teach you to honor and obey them?" He glanced down at her, mouth grim.

She crossed her arms. Was he baiting her? "I would, in a very honoring way, let them know again that marriage to Hugh is out of the question."

"Let me help you up." Trevor reached for Gracie and she grasped his shoulders as he lifted her onto the mare. He led them to the main doors of the barn and Gracie took in a deep lungful of fresh, winter air. Besides footprints, the world looked pristine. Clean. A few plant skeletons dotted the landscape, not dead, but waiting for the right time to bloom.

Trevor mounted Butch and they set off at a leisurely pace for the mountains.

"I've never seen where you keep the livestock. Would you show me?" She pulled on the reins to quiet her horse, who kept edging past a trot toward a canter.

"Not much to show. Cattle sales have been steadily decreasing so we don't raise much now. Just keep a small herd going in case the industry picks up."

Gracie grimaced. "That does not bode well for your dreams of running a ranch. What is this mare's name? She's wanting to gallop."

"Name's Velvet."

"Because her coat is so smooth. I noticed that."

"I don't care about running a ranch," Trevor said. "I'm more interested in settling down, raising a family in a steady environment."

A man like Trevor would want a family. Something solid and secure. "And ranching will allow you to do that?"

"Maybe. Maybe not. Ranching isn't as lucrative as it once was. But there are other ways to make a living." He sounded pensive.

His words explained the lack of ranch workers. But not other things. Wind bit at Gracie's nose and she pulled up her red scarf from the neckline of her jacket. Her voice was muffled when she spoke next.

"Tell me this, Trevor. If sales are declining, how is it both you and Uncle Lou are making so much money?"

Chapter Seventeen

There was a drawn-out silence as Trevor formulated an answer.

"We hire ourselves out for different services," he said slowly. "Can't really explain them to you."

"Hmm. Are these services the reason my parents disapprove of Uncle Lou?"

"Their differences are no business of mine. Let's race."

He broke into a gallop and Gracie followed suit, laughing as wind whipped through her hair and pummeled her coat.

She must've needed this, the escape from the confining study and the rigid life her parents offered. Didn't take much to tell how the wind blew with Gracie's pinch-faced mother. Trevor pointed to a tree some distance away and Gracie nodded her head, then urged Velvet to go faster.

"You beat me," Gracie said, laughing several minutes later as she drew up next to Trevor. "But only by mere seconds. If I rode Honey I would've trounced you." Her cheeks were pink from the wind. Her eyes sparkled in the sunlight. And her laughter filled Trevor with warmth.

She brought to the surface yearnings he'd put away while still a boy. Filled him with hope for a future he couldn't quite see clearly yet. It would be without her, though. Whether or not she married Hugh, her fascination for Striker was misplaced. She'd see that someday and any respect she had for him would disappear.

He cleared his throat. "You do fine in the saddle. I think you're done with lessons now. We'd better get back before your mother begins to worry."

"I don't really understand why they came. Do you think Uncle Lou will take me to town again? I did not get a present for Mary."

They ambled toward the house, a small speck in the distance.

"I think we can arrange another trip into Burns. Mary has a few more items to pick up and Julia says she has errands, too."

"You know," Gracie slanted a glance at Trevor. "I could always drive us."

"No."

"I thought you might say that. I'd like to hear more about your and Uncle Lou's business. Perhaps it will help me reconcile the figures in his books."

Trevor frowned. "I should've never let you get away with that."

"Will Uncle Lou be very angry if he finds out?"

"You never know."

They rode in easy silence after that, content to listen to the swish of the horses' hooves against the powdery snow. When they reached the stables, Gracie sighed mournfully.

"I can take care of Velvet from here, Trevor. I am sure you have plenty of chores to do."

"I do. Gotta find James and see about fixing more of our fence line." Trevor tipped his hat to her and she gave him a wobbly smile.

Before he could turn away she stopped him with a touch.

"Thank you."

Why did her gratitude surprise him? He nodded stiffly and prodded Butch into a gallop, away from sparkling eyes and tender touches. Away from a woman whose words kept taking root down in his heart, making it impossible to forget her.

Three days.

Three weary days of mind-numbing needlework. Had her mother found out somehow that she'd spoken to Hugh? Was this punishment?

After her ride yesterday, Gracie had cornered Hugh and let him know in the kindest way possible that there'd been a misunderstanding with her parents. Months ago, before he left for service, she'd told him she could not marry him. He'd been quite mannerly about the whole thing then, and he remained so now. Disaffected, almost.

She glanced up from her needle-pricked fingers and crooked stitches to see her mother's needle flying steadily across the fabric. She sighed.

"Gracelyn, that is the third groan you have uttered in the last five minutes. Do concentrate."

"This is pointless." She sighed again. "I don't need any more new clothes and no one is going to want this mangled skirt for a present. May I please be excused?"

"For what?"

"I owe Uncle Lou a game of chess."

"That is not a suitable pastime for a young woman," her mother admonished. "Finish your skirt, Gracelyn."

She lowered her eyes to the skirt but her hands remained still. If only the weather would clear up. This snowstorm ruined all her plans.

"Where is Father?"

"He's resting."

"I hope he's feeling well." She fiddled with the skirt.

"He just needs rest."

Silence, but Gracie could not bring herself to continue sewing. "Why don't you sew with Mary? She loves needlework."

"I do not associate with people like her."

She took the skirt off her lap and set it on the couch. "People like her? Do you mean because she is Indian? Or because she is Irish? You must be clear, Mother."

Edith looked up from her stitches, hands pausing. "I do hope you are not being impertinent. You know exactly what I mean. She is a servant, as well as being of a different race."

Gracie's mouth tightened and she looked away. Thank goodness the door opened at that moment or she might have said something to later be repented of.

"Good morning, ladies." Hugh stepped into the bright study and closed the door behind him. "I hoped to find you in here. May I join you?"

"Of course." Edith shot him a radiant smile as he made himself comfortable in Uncle Lou's chair. "Why don't you two talk and I will have Mary bring some coffee and cake in." She rose like a queen from her throne and allowed Hugh to escort her to the door.

Scowling, Gracie picked up her skirt and pretended to be absorbed in the uneven stitches.

"How are you enjoying your stay?" Hugh asked, settling back in his chair.

She forced a rigid smile to her lips and looked up. "It's much different than Boston, but wonderful in every way. I particularly love the scenery and the wildlife. Did you know there are wild horses roaming about?"

"You don't say? I miss Boston myself."

Less than a week and he was ready to go back. She'd been the same way. "Are you happy to be out of the navy?"

"Absolutely." For once his features shone with sincerity. "The military life isn't for me. I prefer business. Your father was speaking with me about possible business opportunities."

"Really? I didn't know you enjoyed trade."

"It is a solid and stable way to earn a living." His fingers drummed the arms of the chair. "I understand your quest to establish the vote for women is nearing an end."

"President Wilson has been fairly supportive."

Hugh grimaced. "What do you plan to work on when you return to Boston, then?"

"Oh, I have other interests."

He leaned forward and his hand snaked out to touch her shoulder. "Gracelyn, I have had enough of the small talk. You say you never wanted to marry me. I've thought about it and I don't believe that."

She shifted away, but kept her eyes on his face. "I don't understand why you're here. We spoke very clearly months ago, before you were ever drafted."

He leaned back and studied her intensely. "I would not bore you, Gracelyn."

Exasperation rushed through her. She tried to speak calmly. "You're very kind but boredom is not the case here. We are incompatible."

Just then Mary swung into the room with the coffee tray. She placed everything on the table between the couch and the chair.

"Can I get you anything else?" Her eyes lowered in a subservient manner.

Gracie hated it. "This is wonderful. Thank you, Mary. I'll bring these to the kitchen when we're finished."

"That won't be necessary, ma'am." She swished out of the room and Gracie fought down an overwhelming sense of annoyance. So she would no longer help Mary with the chores? Absurd. She reached for her coffee, and then plucked a piece of cake off the tray, placing it on her plate.

"Do you think you should eat that?" Concern etched Hugh's brow. In his hand he held a plate covered with two huge pieces of cake.

Gracie looked down at the sliver of cake on her plate, then up again. "My cake?"

"After all the weight you've lost, you don't want to fill up on sweets, my love." He gently reached for her plate but she moved it out of his grasp and with as much dignity as she could muster, set it on the table beside her coffee.

Spine rigid, she stood. "That is highly insulting. And since you feel at liberty to be so rude, I will reciprocate. I am not your love, nor shall I ever be. Excuse me." She marched to the door. Stopping, she turned to face his bewildered expression once more. "I'll have you know, Hugh Jeffers, most of my weight loss came from long walks and hard work, not a lack of food."

She stalked out the door, heading for the stairs. How discourteous could someone possibly be? She no longer worried for his heart. The hall echoed with the force of her heels slamming up the steps.

After pacing her room to work out her frustration, Gracie turned to leave but her closet caught her attention. The position of the cracked door struck her as odd. She was tempted to close it but a premonition took hold of her.

The closet always remained shut because of her jewels hidden in its depths. Bending down on her knees, she pulled out the box and, with bated breath, opened it.

A sapphire necklace and ruby pendant glittered up at her and her eyes closed briefly in relief. She moved her fingers through the jewels. Diamond earrings, pearl rings, all accounted for.

And her notebook.

She fingered the bent pages, debating. Drawing a deep breath, she plucked it from the box and slid it into her pocket. She closed the box and shoved it to the back of the closet, then stood and shut the door firmly. Perhaps she should see if Uncle Lou owned a safe.

She shrugged the thought away.

Who here would paw through her room and then steal her jewels? She could not think it of Mary, Uncle Lou or James. Julia was another matter, but she wouldn't dare step foot in this house again.

She wandered downstairs, worry hovering at the back of her mind. Maybe she'd forgotten to close the closet earlier. She peeked into the sitting room. Empty, so she followed the sound of conversation drifting down the hall.

Raised voices came from the office. Uncle Lou…and Daddy? She inched closer, then with a quick look around her, pressed her ear against the door. Before she could hear any interesting details, however, a chuckle snapped her attention.

Trevor had come around the corner from the kitchen and now lazed against the wall, a partial smile on his face.

"Eavesdropping again?"

She straightened abruptly. "Possibly. And what are you up to, Mr. Cruz? I'm surprised you are not occupied elsewhere, as you've conveniently been the last three days."

"I've been busy."

"I thought perhaps you were avoiding me."

"That, too."

"Why?" She lifted her chin. "I'm leaving soon. There's no need."

"You might want to lower your voice, Gracie."

Unfortunately, he was right. She resisted the pout that trembled on her lips. "We had a lovely ride together. If you don't believe me about my engagement, then say so."

"I don't know what to think."

"Believe me," she said stiffly. "Hugh is no longer a burden on my conscience."

Trevor's lips twitched. "Now you can stop feeling guilty about those kisses."

"If my mother finds out about those, there is no telling how fast I'll be whisked away." She sighed. "At the moment, I've a mystery to clear up."

Amusement lit his face and she moved closer, just to catch a whiff of his spicy cologne.

"I do. There is discord between Daddy and Uncle Lou, and I'm sure it has to do with his 'other' employment. The extra income you refuse to acknowledge," she said pointedly. "I'm not ready for Boston, not when there's so much to discover here."

"Like the whereabouts of Striker?" Trevor moved away from the wall and eyed her. With a quick movement, he pulled the ribbon hanging askew over her eye and sent her embarrassingly untidy curls tumbling over a shoulder. He smiled and handed her the blue ribbon.

"I think the first mystery that needs solving is how to keep your hair in order."

She flushed as he moved curls off her shoulder. This was much different than when Hugh had touched her. Warmth corkscrewed through her and for a moment she wished to move closer, to feel his arms around her once again.

She swallowed, throat tight, watching as emotion flickered across his face and his hand dropped to his side. Would she abandon her desire to meet Striker, her need for independence, in order to have a future with Trevor? She didn't know.

At that moment her mother rounded the corner and Gracie hastily stepped back. Mother's eyes widened before quickly cutting into slits.

"Mr. Cruz." She nodded to him and grabbed Gracie's arm. "Come with me, please."

"Yes, Mother. Goodbye, Mr. Cruz. Perhaps we may continue our discussion later?" But he did not answer, only watched silently as Edith pulled her down the hall and into the sitting room.

She stepped in, cringing as the door shut behind her. She turned to face her mother.

Edith looked at her daughter for a moment, then expelled a heavy sigh. "What is going on between you and that man?"

She tried to keep her face blank though shock rippled through her. "What do you mean?"

"You went riding with him the other day and now I've walked into the hall and seen you two staring at each other like crazed lovebirds."

"I can assure you, Mother, Trevor would never gaze at me like a lovebird."

"And I can assure you, Daughter, he did."

Gracie spun around and went to sit in Uncle Lou's chair. She had to breathe.

"You are saying Trevor looks at me like a man in love?" she asked when she could speak again.

"What I am asking—" Edith moved to the left-hand couch and sat, face pinched "—is *why* would he be looking at you like that?"

She shifted in her seat. She hated the look Mother wore, hated the tight lips and hurt eyes. "I was under the impression that I'm an annoyance to Mr. Cruz. I think you've misinterpreted his look."

"We need to speak with your father about this."

Gracie caught her eyes midroll and directed them to her mother. "Very well. I still need to raise the issue of pants. It's terribly cold and they would do much to protect my poor legs. Have you ever worn trousers, Mother? I believe you would enjoy them."

"The very idea!" Edith sniffed. "Pants are completely unsuitable for women of our station. You would do well to remember that you come from a long line of revered ancestors, the oldest of which sailed over on the *Mayflower*, and through wars, famines and disease, brought forth strong descendants."

Gracie recited the litany in her head along with her mother. This was not the first time she'd heard this insipid speech.

"My point," Edith said when she'd finished her monologue, "is you must marry someone of similar background. Like Hugh. Which is why I've come to see you. He's informed me that you're *confused*."

Gracie licked her lips, which had dried suddenly. "Mother, I told you I'd never marry him."

"When?" Her mother had the audacity to feign ignorance.

"Recently, in letters, but also the very night he proposed. You requested I wait and think on it. Three days later he showed up waving his draft orders. That wasn't fair to me." She swallowed hard. "But I spoke with him then, and he has been aware of my decision from the very first."

"Dear, you're not yourself. You're overwrought."

"Because you and Daddy completely ignore my wishes." She huffed. "I have no voice with you two!"

"Your emotions are skewed."

Her fingers curled around the arms of the chair. "Mother, may I be more direct with you?"

A finely drawn brow curved. "Of course."

"I will not marry Hugh."

"It is out of your hands."

Did nothing she said get through? "I wish to honor you, however, I cannot marry that man."

"We'll see what your father says." Mother's chin lifted.

Panic fluttered in Gracie's chest. They could not force her to wed. This was not the nineteenth century. She rose and turned toward the door, because she could no longer look her mother in the eyes for fear of what she might say.

Edith placed a soft, well-manicured hand on her shoulder. "We love you very much, my dear, and only want what is best for you. Please remember that."

She closed her eyes briefly, then opened them. "I thought society had moved past the barbarity of selling off their daughters to the highest bidder."

Her mother recoiled as if she'd been slapped. "Is that how you see us?"

"I will not marry Hugh, and that is my final say."

"Gracelyn, you have always been passionate and strong-willed. You have also bored easily. Marrying for love or excitement is not a good foundation for marriage. You must let us, as your God-appointed guardians, guide you in this decision." Edith offered a smile that didn't reach her eyes.

Gracie ducked her mother's hand. How much clearer could she be? "This isn't like the sewing society you commanded me to join, which I did, though you know I hate needlework. Or when Daddy told me to stop playing chess with the fishermen down at the docks. Or when you both ordered me to stop writing a regular column for the *Woman's Liberator*. This is the rest of my life. I cannot be relegated to misery simply because you and Daddy do not see the flaws in this courtship." She took a deep breath. "Let's find Daddy…then you can send Hugh home. He is becoming tiresome."

Edith's full lips puckered in a most unbecoming way. "You are defiant, Gracelyn. I did not raise you to behave in this manner. Hugh will stay."

Chapter Eighteen

Who said women spoke more than men?

Dinner that evening remained the same as every night since her parents had arrived. Male dominated. Neither Mary nor Mother seemed inclined to give political opinions, but Gracelyn was full of them. Unfortunately, they stayed bottled inside, corked tight by her mother's continuous look of disapproval.

The scent of steamed broccoli hung heavy in the room, combining with the sweetness of Mary's homemade fudge cooling in the kitchen. The soothing smells, however, did not make for a soothing atmosphere. Mother refused to speak to Mary and it appeared Mary felt likewise. Gracie was forced to have two conversations at a time, when either woman chose to speak.

Of course, Mother had approached Uncle Lou about servants eating with employers, but he had put her quite firmly in her place. Gracie had heard the exchange from the other side of the office door.

Still deeply offended, Mother kept shooting venomous glances toward Uncle Lou.

"This is a wonderful steak, Mary." Gracie shifted so

that Hugh, who had been strategically placed next to her, would no longer be able to touch her calf with his foot.

She chewed a tender piece, savoring its tangy flavor. "I wish I could cook like you. Have you always been so proficient in the kitchen?"

Mary smiled serenely. "It was a job at first, but now I enjoy cooking."

"Enjoying it is a must, I suppose." Gracie moved a little to the left. Hugh's arm kept caressing her elbow.

"You do not need to cook, Gracelyn. We have servants for that." Edith forked a small broccoli floret into her mouth.

"Of course," Mary continued, as if she had not heard Edith, "it is every woman's privilege to excel in the art of cooking, which is a branch of homemaking. Men enjoy their woman's touch in the meals. I do feel sorry for those unfortunate enough to have never learned this necessary skill." She cut herself a piece of steak and bit it with a triumphant flourish.

Edith's cheeks flushed. "Such servitude will never be expected of you, Gracelyn dear. We are above menial labor."

"The twentieth century is so liberating. Most of America is slowly but surely leaving its snobbery behind." Mary's fork clattered against her plate.

Neither woman looked at Gracie; they were glaring at each other.

She hid a smile behind her hand. It would not do to divulge the fact that Mother was always trying to bake something but nothing ever turned out right. Poor Mother. Gracie would keep her secret.

While the two women seethed, she glanced down the table at Trevor. He ate with careful precision, cutting his steak perfectly, eating it, then moving to his mashed potatoes. She looked down at her own plate. She had mixed the broccoli and potatoes together and a few pieces of steak topped the mound haphazardly.

They were entirely different. Even the way she and Trevor ate their food was different.

A nudge against her knee caught her attention. Hugh appeared enthralled with his food but she was sure the contact had been purposeful.

Connie had thought him handsome. Gracie had also, at first. But now his skin stretched too smoothly across his face, lacking the character lines that distinguished Trevor's features.

Hugh's foot covered hers. She yanked her toes out, causing her knee to bump the bottom of the table. Dishes clattered.

She ducked her head, spooning food into her mouth until the men's voices rose again and the silent war between the women waged on.

When she was sure no one would notice she leaned over and whispered into Hugh's ear, "Stop pawing me."

He didn't even look at her. His ears must be filled with wax, the knave.

"Pass the butter, please," Hugh said. His finger gently touched her hand. She grabbed the butter and shoved it to him, silently groaning.

During their courtship in Boston he'd been nothing like this. They attended church and other events together and he was always charming and gracious, if a tad boring. But even then she'd been aware they did not suit one another. For one thing, there was his stance on the vote and music. His family disapproved of jazz, therefore, so did he. Surely music with such a fast pace must be wrong, Hugh had pointed out once.

Gracie scooted to the left of her chair and wished someone else would finish eating so she might leave the table.

Her parents wanted her to marry Hugh, and she wanted freedom. Perhaps she should go home immediately. But then she might never have the chance to be so close to Striker's territory again. She would never see Trevor again. The realization filled her with unease. Her entire purpose here was to seek out Striker, not worry about Trevor. She frowned. This was a wonderful opportunity, and she couldn't afford to let sentiment keep her from her goals. She'd lose her chance at the interview of a lifetime and possibly a career.

Gracie escaped to her room later that night when Mother pulled out her sewing needles.

Once there she realized with surprise that she felt quite tired. The day had been stressful. Hugh had found every opportunity to touch her, Trevor had kept her at arm's length, and Mother watched on like a hawk. Then Daddy forbade her from wearing trousers, citing propriety.

She reached under her pillow and pulled out the faded clippings she always kept nearby. Finding Striker was proving impossible. How could she look when she barely left the ranch? And now that her parents had arrived... She groaned and leaned against the pillows.

Did finding him really matter? There were other articles she could write, other ways to earn money and live independently. How silly to search for a secret agent, even if all accounts made him sound terribly exciting. And what if he did carry out assassinations? What if the Council Bluff rumors were true? What if he'd really killed a child?

Striker didn't care to defend his honor. Why should she? Whether or not she made a name for herself from his interview, something had still compelled her to seek him. The meager information about him had piqued her interest and the tidbits she'd gleaned convinced her that there was more to Striker than what the papers printed.

Rising, she went to the closet, pulled out her jewel box and stashed the papers in the hidden compartment at the bottom.

Then she readied for bed and, despite the tensions of the day, passed easily into sleep.

Perhaps it was the distant rumbling of thunder that roused her from dreams, but she awoke suddenly and jerked up, every hair on her neck raised. She shoved curls from her face and studied her moonlit room before determining everything was as it should be.

Out of the corner of her eye, she saw lights flickering outside. She slid out of bed, some instinct warning her to stay to the side of the window to remain unnoticed. From this view she could see the darkened silhouette of Trevor's house. Across the desert, near the base of the mountains, three lights flashed briefly, then extinguished.

Were they lanterns? She couldn't tell, but who would be out on a winter night in the desert? Goose bumps prickled up her arms. She remembered Trevor's warning of two-legged predators roaming in the night.

Mendez.

Her stare probed the sleeping desert but she saw no more movement. She shivered back to her bed and climbed into its warmth. Uncle Lou might want to know about this.

The next morning dawned bright and clear, all snow flurries swept away by the earlier night's winds. Gracie woke to see the sun's pastel fingers caress the jagged line of mountains outside her window. Perhaps God was not so far off after all. After her conversation with Trevor the other night, she'd finally opened her Bible since hearing of

Connie's death. Sparing the book an affectionate glance, she turned away. She dressed and headed to the kitchen, sure no one else would be awake this early.

Daddy sat in the kitchen, sipping a freshly brewed cup of coffee. "Good morning, sweetheart."

"Good morning, Daddy." She bent and kissed his cheek. She couldn't stay angry with him, not over a pair of trousers. Pouring herself a cup and then adding a liberal amount of sugar, she sat across from him. "You don't look like you slept well. Is the cold bothering your joints?"

William shrugged. "Since the polio, these old legs are always giving me fits."

"It would be nice if someone could find a cure." Bitter steam from her coffee reached her nose. She sipped the hot brew, relishing its potent burn. "It finally looks like we might be able to go out and ride around. Perhaps we could make our way into town today? Mary probably has shopping to do."

"You're fond of the servant." William looked at his daughter over the rim of his cup.

"She's a family friend, Daddy, whom they took in and helped in her time of need. Yes, I am fond of her. She's a Godly woman, a hard worker and a wise soul. She's also an excellent seamstress. Mother would enjoy her company."

He set his cup down. "Your mother tells me you have an interest in one of the hands?"

Gracie flushed. "How strange. The only hand here is James. He bandaged my knee like a professional."

"Your knee?"

"I wrenched my knee when one of the horses slipped on some ice. Don't fret, all is well now." She sipped the strong coffee, wishing she could slink back to her room and avoid this inquisition.

"It is Mr. Cruz you are interested in, correct?"

Gracie didn't know how to respond so she gulped more coffee. She could not hide her feelings from her father. Distraction might prove useful, though. "Why are you here?"

Father's blue eyes met hers. "We were concerned for you. With Connie's death we thought you might need your family near."

"I thought you came because having me here with Uncle Lou made you nervous. What's the disagreement between you two? I find him amiable. Is it his profession?"

William's forehead crinkled. "And what would you know of that?"

"I've picked up pieces here and there, but you know a good investigator never reveals her sources." She grinned at him.

"Is that so?"

"You know it is, Daddy."

"My dear, Lou's profession is his business. I'm sure you realize that for me to reveal any information to an investigator such as yourself could very well be foolhardy. It might end up in your column."

Gracie leaned forward, coffee pushed to the side. He knew something. Something big. "I stopped writing the column when you asked me to." *Compromising to her reputation* had been her father's reasoning. Disappointment still lodged in her chest, sharp and heavy. But she ignored it, knowing he cared for her despite his old-fashioned ways. Once she wrote this article, surely he would be proud of her, though.

"Gracie, honey, do you know how much I love you?" William's hand reached across the table and grasped hers firmly. "You remind me of your mother."

"I'm nothing like her."

"Oh, but you are. Strong willed, opinionated." He chuckled, then his face grew serious. "Your Uncle Lou decided a long time ago to become involved with an un-savory character who specialized in covert operations. I disapproved and tried to manipulate him by withdrawing any welcome to my home. Your uncle didn't respond well and until now we've hardly spoken."

An unsavory character? Gracie gnawed her lip. "You haven't spoken because you didn't like Uncle Lou's pro-fession?" She knew she sounded incredulous but couldn't help it. She'd never known her father to be so controlling of anyone. Except herself.

His gaze flickered down to his cup. "I am afraid your old daddy was rather prideful."

Gracie squeezed his hand. "What was the man's name?"

"Who?"

"The unsavory character."

"You've read about him in the papers. Striker."

She forced her hand to stay relaxed on his. But her mind worked furiously. It couldn't be true. Unsavory? She didn't want to believe it but Father had no reason to lie. She leaned back, hands curling tightly in her lap. "And Uncle Lou worked with him? Do you think he would give me an interview?"

William shook his head. "I don't think you should men-tion what I've told you to anyone."

"Why *did* you tell me?"

He sighed, his forefinger tracing the top of his coffee cup. "I know about your interest in Striker. It wasn't hard to spot the cut out sections of my paper."

Gracie flushed. "If you know, then why did you send me here to Striker's own territory?"

"It is?"

"Some say," she hedged. She forgot the things she knew were not common knowledge.

"You should leave the issue of Striker alone. Concentrate on pursuits that will enhance your future."

"Writing will do that."

"Not when you're chasing down a renegade lawman."

Gracie blanched. She'd tried to keep it a secret, knowing her parents would forbid her the interest. "He's not a renegade or an assassin. He enforces the Mann Act of 1910 and works with the Bureau of Investigation."

William looked like he was about to disagree, but Mary whisked into the kitchen. She nodded to them and began pulling out food for breakfast.

Gracie watched for a moment, absorbed in her thoughts. The whole reason Father disapproved of Uncle Lou was because he associated with Striker? That did not seem to be a valid reason to cut off contact with his only brother for years.

Unless Uncle Lou *was* Striker.

Chapter Nineteen

This was her chance.

Gracie slowed Velvet as they entered the stables. She shook her hair out of its tight knot. Honey hadn't been available so she'd taken Velvet and been pleasantly surprised by the mare's quick responses. She brushed Velvet, and then settled her in a stall with some fresh oats.

Trevor lingered at the other end of the stable, unsaddling Butch. It had been two days since she'd spoken with her father about Striker. Quite possibly she'd figured out Striker's true identity. Unfortunately, Mother kept up the sewing sessions and released Gracie from her sight only once a day. The schedule made her feel like a caged pet.

Hoping Mother would not come searching when today's hour respite ended, Gracie walked to Trevor. "Good morning. How are you today?"

He was kneeling down, checking Butch's hooves for who knew what, and her hand stretched toward his bent head. She snatched it back just in time.

He stood, rising above her. "Doing chores. And you?"

She forgot how tall he stood. "I am becoming desperate. I think Mother plans to keep me by her side until we leave."

"When will that be?" The question was asked in a casual voice as he moved to the other side of Butch. She could not tell if he truly cared.

"We are leaving after Christmas." She squared her shoulders. "I've missed seeing you. I hope the kittens are well."

"Well enough. Running around the barn."

"Catching mice, I suppose. Speaking of victory, I would dearly love to win another chess match." She sighed. "My parents insist ladies do not play chess."

Trevor didn't respond but she could see his hands moving quickly as he brushed long strokes down Butch's muscled flank.

"She doesn't seem to comprehend this is the twentieth century. A time of change and new ideas. Liberation, even."

Still no response. Looking around, Gracie spotted a bale of hay. She walked over and sat, inhaling its sweet freshness. The fragrance mingled with the scent of manure, mud and leather. Not altogether unpleasant. She crossed her stockinged ankles. Her gaze fastened on her skirt's hem.

"Mother recently made this skirt for me. It is abominably long, don't you think? Why, I cannot even see the tops of my calves."

"Are you always concerned with fashion?" His tone held a hint of disapproval.

"Not at all. I'm concerned with my freedom to dress as I please. I can assure you that if I marry one day, my husband will be as forward thinking as I am."

He chuckled and laid down the big brush. Butch whickered softly and Trevor gave him a gentle nudge under the jaw before coming to sit next to Gracie.

She froze. He was so near. Spicy cologne and leather

to the porch that she remembered her original reason for wanting to speak with him.

She turned to him once they neared the porch. "I have a question for you."

"Ask inside. This wind is getting real nippy."

"I cannot speak openly." Her voice lowered. "I think I've discovered the identity of Striker. What can you tell me of him?" She watched him closely and was surprised to see his face harden into something as cold and fierce as the winter ground beneath her feet.

"After months here, you think I've got something new to say?"

"I suppose it is an instinct. I feel as if you know more about this elusive man."

A palpable silence filled the air. Gracie held her breath, waiting for him to respond.

"He works for the government," Trevor said flatly. "And he's dangerous."

"Do you think you could procure an interview for me? I know of a woman's paper—"

"No." Trevor took her arm and maneuvered her up the wind-worn steps to the front door. They stepped into the house. "I have to advise you to stop pursuing this train of thought. Leave it be."

"You need not concern yourself about what goes on in my head."

"I don't. I'm worried about what's going to come out of that mouth."

"Don't be silly." She removed her coat and hung it on the rack. His expression tightened and before she could stop herself, her fingers reached to caress his face, to trace the sorrow line down his cheek.

His hand reached up and caught her wrist, but he didn't rebuff her touch.

"I hope you get over this infatuation, Gracie. And fast." He removed her hand from his face and left her standing in the darkened hall.

Gracie found Uncle Lou in his office later that afternoon. Mother had retired to her bedroom with complaints of a migraine, and the men left to look at the cattle and have, she supposed, manly talk.

But Uncle Lou had business and correspondence to attend to. By chance she heard his voice on her way to the kitchen and decided to stop and speak with him about the mysterious lights she'd seen the other night. They'd awakened her again last night and she decided he should be told immediately.

Before she could reach for the brass doorknob it swung open and Mary charged out, cheeks flushed and mouth pursed. Gracie stepped back. Mary didn't speak to her, just brushed past, head high.

Poor Mary. Gracie didn't know what it was, but she and Uncle Lou fought about something every week. And it was so unlike Mary to argue.

Gracie moved into the office, pushing a stray curl behind her ears as she entered. Uncle Lou sat at his desk fiercely marking papers with a pen. She cleared her throat.

"Uncle Lou, I have an issue to discuss with you."

"Sit down." He did not look up.

She sat warily, noting the unusual neatness of his desk. It would be nice to toss some papers on it, just to muss it a little. The Spartan quality was not typical of Uncle Lou. Neither was the unusual curtness to his tone.

It must have been a doozy of an argument.

"I'll try not to take much of your time, Uncle. I only wished to inform you that a few nights ago, as well as last night, strange lights outside awakened me. The whole experience made me quite uneasy."

His head stayed bent over the irritatingly neat pile of papers, but his fingers began to tap the pen ominously. "I fail to see your concern."

"I suppose," she said slowly, "there is no need for concern if you do not think so. I merely wanted to pass along the information, as Mendez is still on the loose."

He didn't respond but she couldn't help but notice his shoulders tense up. "You're grumpy today, aren't you?"

"No, merely busy," Lou said curtly.

"Hmm, I'd be glad to help you."

"Yes, I'm sure you would be. I've been told I have you to thank for righting my account ledgers."

"That rat." Gracie's hands clasped tightly but her words toward Trevor were without rancor. Would she be banned from Uncle Lou's house now? Had her parents been told? Another lecture on the proprieties of a lady and her upbringing would surely drive her mad. "It's true I've straightened the numbers in your ledgers. I hope that doesn't upset you."

Uncle Lou looked up, lips twitching. "Did you find anything interesting?"

To lie or not to lie?

"Numbers are always fascinating," she finally hedged. "But if I may, I would recommend noting the source of your extra income. It would better serve you to keep the books more orderly. I would be glad to check your arithmetic anytime."

"Thank you, Gracie. I'd appreciate, however, you staying away from the books here on out."

Her cheeks burned. "I'm sorry, Uncle Lou. I understand if you don't want me to straighten them, but perhaps you should hire someone." She tried to smile, but there was a sinking feeling in the pit of her stomach. He was truly angry with her. And now he knew she was aware of the unexplained income in his ledgers, as did Trevor.

She murmured her farewell and left Uncle Lou still hunched over his desk. If Uncle Lou was Striker then he could be dangerous. But surely not to family....

The swish of a broom floated through the darkened hallway. Mary must be cleaning. Gracie longed to help but Mother had been horrified by the new calluses on her palms and had forbidden her from taking part in any more cleaning activities.

Besides, Mary most likely wasn't in the mood for conversation.

She glanced up the stairs and noticed her bedroom door ajar. Leaving the steady sound of Mary's sweeping, she headed up.

She stopped in the doorway, comforted by the familiar scent of lavender perfume mixing with the airy aroma of lemon. Light streamed in from the window and the floor glowed. Mary must have polished it recently. She sauntered to the window and looked out. It was such a beautiful day, and with Mother stuck in bed, why, she could go anywhere....

A walk would be pleasant. She moved away from the window and absentmindedly shut her closet door.

On her walk she'd do a bit of reconnaissance.

Chapter Twenty

The breeze outside felt brisk but not as biting as the past few days. Gracie pulled her scarf away from her lips and reveled in the clean air before stopping to take stock of her location. The house faced north and her window sat on the east side. The lights had flickered to the left of her window, so that meant she must walk northerly.

Her cheddar and chicken sandwich swung beside her in an old lunch pail she snagged from the kitchen cupboards. It bumped against her hip as she marched toward the place at the base of the mountains where the lights had flashed again last night. Uncle Lou might put her off, but there was something strange about people wandering around in the dead of the night. There was clearly a mystery here.

Her feet made little sound as she tromped through thin layers of snow. She inhaled deeply. A sense of peace came over her. She could not remember this feeling being a part of her Boston days. The quiet she assumed would bore her to tears had instead soothed her.

Fifteen minutes later she reached the area she figured the lights had flashed from. Nothing suspicious lurked in the brown shrubs and white snow. She walked a circle around the area, scanning the ground for footprints or even horse prints.

Nothing. Absolutely nothing.

Her stomach growled and she lowered herself to a smooth stone. She'd eat, and then continue walking. If no signs of last night's meanderings turned up, at least she'd get some exercise.

Only the rustling of the wind disturbed the silence around her. She closed her eyes.

Thank You, Jesus, she found herself praying, *for this incredible land. Please bless the people who live off it. Watch over Mary and Uncle Lou. Please guide them in their feelings and give them wisdom. And I also need wisdom. I need help, Lord. I don't want to be disobedient to my parents but I need to be independent. Please teach me Your ways, patience and wisdom. Give me understanding. Forgive my rebelliousness and desires for my own ways. Help me find Striker.*

She let her words float away with the wind and sat on the rock in tranquility, content to let God speak to her heart should He so choose.

After several minutes, her stomach rumbled again so she gobbled down her sandwich. It was such a relief to be able to eat as quickly as she wanted with no thought to manners. She polished off the sandwich, brushed the crumbs from her hands and stood.

A broken shrub caught her eye. From her vantage point, the branches clearly bent. Beneath them something glinted in the sun. She picked her way over. Horse tracks indented the snow a few feet from the shrub. She knelt and traced the print. Nearby a piece of metal lay partially buried and she plucked it up. The coin glittered. Foreign, perhaps Spanish?

Snow stuck to her fingertips as she straightened and

scanned the horizon. The sun hung low in the sky. Sliding the notebook from her pocket, she recorded her position. She threw one last look at the mysterious tracks before picking up her pail and heading home.

Shivering, she let herself into the house and, with a covert glance around for Mother, headed up the stairs to her bedroom. She'd change clothes before dinner so Mother wouldn't notice the dirty wet spots on her skirt.

With the door closed to her bedroom, she went into the bathroom and washed herself, leaving her clothes in a heap by the tub. Clutching the coin, she walked into her darkening bedroom. The lengthening shadows in her room persuaded her to turn on the one dim light that hung from the ceiling.

She opened the closet door and studied the skirts. No pink tonight. Perhaps the green? She reached for it and held it up. Yes, this one fit nicely. She slipped the coin into the pocket of the skirt. Humming, she set the skirt on the bed and went back to the closet to retrieve her comfortable black shoes. As she crouched down, something glinted in the corner.

A lone ruby earring, resting near her lace-up boots, blinked at her.

Gracie knelt down and picked it up, then looked at her box. Her fingers trembled as she fiddled with the clasp and opened the lid.

An empty velvet interior greeted her.

No pearls or diamonds, even the plain gold ring she'd planned to sell was gone.

She pulled the box into the light and edged her fingers along the hidden bottom. With a quiet pull the scarlet interior gave way and revealed money. She pulled the money out and from beneath it retrieved her papers.

Safe, at least. She still had her cash and her clippings.

Her eyes burned as she replaced the items, returning the interior of the case to its original position. She dropped the earring in, set the closed box on the bed and dressed with haste.

There was a thief to catch and the sooner, the better. She rushed downstairs and could feel the hotness in her cheeks when she burst into her parents' room without knocking first.

It was a small room but the best Uncle Lou could offer the wheelchair-bound William. Her mother's things were set neatly in their places—jewels on the vanity, clothes in the closet and suitcases nowhere to be seen. A colorful afghan, similar to the one on Gracie's bed, covered their four-poster bed. All in all, despite the small size and lack of a bathroom, the room appeared cozy.

But Daddy wasn't in there.

She ran down the hall and her mind churned as fast as her legs. Who would steal her jewels?

Why would someone prowl around her room in the first place? She frowned. The only person she imagined resorting to thievery was Julia. And for Trevor's sake, she hoped desperately she was wrong.

As she burst outside she noticed a path had been cleared for her father's wheelchair. Its wheels left unmistakable indentations on the ground.

She followed the marks and reached the stables gasping for breath and sides burning. At the entrance she bent over and heaved for air a few times before she felt able to walk in and explain the situation in a coherent way.

The warm mustiness of the stable enveloped her and though she could not see her parents, she heard them. She followed the sound of their voices to the far end of the main aisle. They were in the tack room inspecting Uncle Lou's saddles. Her mother stood in a corner, features drawn.

Gracie grimaced. Mother must still have her migraine. This news would only make her head ache more.

Gracie cleared her throat. Heads snapped up.

"There is a thief in our midst." She launched into her predicament and a shocked silence filled the room.

Edith's soft white hand went to her chest and she swayed unsteadily, face pale. Gracie wanted to step forward and comfort her but knew her mother would not appreciate the outward display of sympathy.

Why had she brought the jewels anyway? It had been a silly whim, an instinct they might prove useful in her search for Striker. Boy, had she been wrong. "I'm sorry. I didn't realize…" Her voice trailed off lamely.

Trevor shook his head. "Don't be sorry. There's no reason your jewelry shouldn't be safe here." His voice held a commanding note and he seemed to rise above the others in the room. Even Uncle Lou had shrunk.

Only Trevor seemed capable at the moment of handling the situation and she wished she could go to him, rest her head on his shoulder.

"The first thing we'll do," he continued, "is find Julia."

Gracie shook her head warningly at him. Mother didn't need to know a former prostitute lived less than a mile away. Especially when that former lady of the night was the mother of the man her daughter had kissed.

"Your mother? What does she have to do with this?" Edith asked.

"I'll wager quite a bit." Trevor glanced around the little room. "Why don't you head to the house for supper and I'll get Julia."

Uncle Lou hauled a saddle off the wall as a dogged expression crossed his face. "I'm coming, too."

Gracie backed out of the tack room and into the main

aisle. Her mother followed, pushing William's chair. The men trailed after her.

Gracie was having trouble meeting her parents' eyes. Although they had not objected to her bringing her jewelry box to Oregon, she still felt horribly guilty because she'd withheld her specific motives for taking it along.

"William and I will go ahead into supper." Steel determination strengthened her mother's spine and her voice sounded stiff. "I do hope this matter is settled shortly." Nose high, she wheeled Father out. He did not speak at all.

Tension left Gracie's shoulders as they moved out of sight. She felt like a failure at the moment, as well as a debtor. The jewels were worth a great deal, enough to live on for a number of years in comfort. She let her eyes drift closed briefly, then opened them and turned to Uncle Lou. "I'm so sorry."

"Not your fault, Gracie. We'll get to the bottom of it, right, Trevor?" The grim set of Uncle Lou's mouth matched Trevor's and she could not help but feel that everything would turn out fine with these two working on it.

She looked up at Trevor and noted the new crease at the side of his mouth. It had to be troubling, thinking his mother had stolen from friends.

But they didn't know for sure, she reminded herself. She licked her lips. "Perhaps we should not immediately accuse Julia."

"And why not? She needs money and everyone here knows she can't be trusted. You better stay out of this, Gracie." Trevor stared down his nose at her and his scar seemed even whiter than usual against his dark skin.

She pursed her lips. "I'll not accept you ordering me about. These are my jewels, and I will be involved in their recovery. I'm truly unsure your mother is the culprit." She glanced at Uncle Lou. "What do you think?"

"I agree with Trevor—you need to stay with your parents. Julia will be like a cornered snake."

"No, what do you think about the thief being someone else?"

"Look," Trevor interrupted, "she's the obvious choice. I don't know why you're set on giving her the benefit of the doubt but, in any case, you need to step back and let us take care of it. Now go on to the house and get some food."

His tone set Gracie's teeth on edge. Who did he think he was? She was twenty, plenty grown to decide when she would eat.

And it didn't help that Uncle Lou lingered beside the wall, a smirk on his face.

They brushed past her and strode quickly to the entrance. She stood in the middle of the aisle, fists clenched and head feeling like it would explode. As hot as her anger was, it did not take long to simmer down and in its place came hopelessness.

How could she ever marry? Men appeared to be domineering and controlling. She hated obeying her parents. How would she listen to a husband? It was foolish to think of marriage at a time like this, anyhow.

She left the barn and picked her way through the dusky evening to the house. After finding Striker she planned to leave this place and return to Boston. Dances, dinners, theaters...

Boston was a glamorous, exciting cage.

She marched up the porch stairs. But she'd be leaving much behind. Boston couldn't offer the raw beauty or personal freedoms she found here. She sighed and pulled open the front door, the handle icy against her palm. Obedience did not come easy, and yet she felt God calling her to it.

Desires or obedience? What would she choose?

* * *

A sharp crackle woke Gracie. She rose from Uncle Lou's chair in the study and rubbed her eyes. A log lay crookedly in the fireplace. Its falling must have woken her. The fire had dwindled down to hot embers. Rubbing her arms, she went to the fireplace and tried stoking it with the poker like she'd seen Mary do. The embers only hissed and continued to fade.

She flinched as the poker was pried from her hands. Trevor stood before her, hat covered in a thick layer of snow and eyes shadowed. His silent entrance unsettled her.

"Let Trevor get the fire going," Uncle Lou said from behind her. "Can you get us something hot to drink?"

"I can try." She turned and noted the circles beneath Uncle Lou's eyes. They must not have good news, but first she would get them some food and drink even though questions ricocheted through her.

In the lighted kitchen she tried to make sense of all the knobs on the stove. Where were the matches? She groaned. It was no use. Thanks to her parents and a life of indulgence, she was almost as helpless as a baby. She opened the cupboards and found cookies and cake. Loading them onto a tray, she set it on the table. Then she found bread and, venturing onto the small porch connected to the kitchen, cheese and leftover chicken from the refrigerator. She made sandwiches, careful not to slice her finger open with the knife. Once finished, she placed the sandwiches as well as plates next to the sweets and brought it all back to the sitting room.

The men sat on the couches, warming themselves by the blazing fire. Their hats, socks and shoes lay on the hearth.

She set the tray on the table. "Here are sandwiches. I apologize, but I don't know how to get the hot water boiling on the stove. I mean, I know how to turn it on but not

where the matches are or what temperature to set it at."
She grimaced, feeling like a dunce.

Uncle Lou flashed a crooked smile. "I'll take care of
things. Why don't you sit here and talk with Trevor. He
has a few questions for you." He left as silently as he arrived and Gracie was suddenly alone with Trevor.

She sat next to her uncle's damp spot on the couch and
waited for Trevor to stop scarfing his sandwich so they
could move on to more serious matters.

She settled back into the couch. The room warmed, filling with the scent of chocolate cake. Trevor made no move
to speak but stared into the fire. His shoulders had returned
to their tense position and he bent forward with his arms
set on his knees.

His hair had grown longer since the first time she'd met
him. The strands hit his shoulders, hung over his cheekbones and she wondered if he planned to cut them soon. He
looked rugged, tough, a man not easily bested. The longer
hair did not effeminize him at all. Gracie swallowed past
the lump in her throat.

Her turned toward her, the flickering shadows from the
fire dancing over his features.

"What did you and Uncle Lou discover tonight regarding your mother?" she asked.

Chapter Twenty-One

"Julia is gone." Trevor did not look at her and his voice sounded suddenly hoarse.

"Gone?"

"Nowhere to be found. We rode for as long as we could, searching for her. Went to the stables, to the edge of the ranch. She didn't take her herbs or beans but her bags are gone."

"Beans?"

"She's always kept them for digestive matters." He rubbed at his face, brisk movements and Gracie longed to still his hands, to hold them within the safety of her own.

"How odd. Isn't it dangerous for her to walk around in this weather?"

"Yep, but she won't care. She was getting a little stir-crazy at my house anyway." He leaned back and studied her, crossed his arms against his chest and stretched out his legs.

His feet were only inches from hers, she thought numbly. "I don't understand why she would be snooping in my room."

Trevor shrugged. "As far as I can see, she had the opportunities for thievery. What I can't understand is why she didn't take anything else. This house is filled with foreign valuables. That's why I need you to tell me about those lights you saw."

"Uncle Lou didn't seem concerned."

"Tell me."

"Last night there were three again. This afternoon I walked to where I saw them and found this." She reached into the pocket of her skirt and pulled out the coin. Giving it to him, she marveled at the warmth from where their fingertips touched. He examined the coin closely and she watched his face. He was harder to read than most.

Uncle Lou reappeared with china cups and a teapot. Gracie rose and took them from him. He sat down in his former spot and she poured tea for the men, keeping a covert watch on their expressions.

Trevor handed the coin to Uncle Lou without a word, and a tense silence stretched between the two men.

"What do you think?" Uncle Lou twisted the gold in his hand, then passed it back to Trevor.

"Hard to say," Trevor answered. "Could've fallen off Julia on a ride. Could be Mendez."

"Why Mendez?" Gracie gave them their tea and sat down.

When Trevor glanced at her, she sucked in a quick breath. His expressionless look had slid away. A ferocious light gleamed in his eyes. She could see the anger, the rage, brewing within, and for the first time she felt a small slither of fear. It was as if she were seeing a different man and it scared her. She had sensed the danger in him, but she had never seen this potent power that now altered his entire countenance.

"This is a Spanish coin."

"Surely he's not the only one who carries those."

"Go to bed, Gracie."

She almost listened. Almost. His hard expression did that to her. But she recovered her resolve and said, "I'd like to, Trevor, but I really must know what you two think about the likelihood of my jewels being recovered." When both men's faces went slack, she stumbled on. "They're not only worth a small fortune, but they hold sentimental value. Some are family heirlooms."

"Unfortunately, the chances of recovering them are small." Uncle Lou's jaw twitched. "We don't know who took them or when they went missing."

"I know they were in my closet as of a few days ago. Now that I think of it, my closet door was ajar, which is what caught my attention."

Uncle Lou threw his hands up in the air and Trevor scowled.

"What? Is Julia still involved with Mendez? It is somewhat coincidental for Julia to disappear right when all this is happening." Trevor's expression darkened, and Uncle Lou looked away. Why were they angry with her? It was her jewels missing. Did they think she cared more about money than safety? That could be the case, if Mendez was involved.

And if Uncle Lou was Striker, then they couldn't speak freely in front of her.

It might be in her best interests to say good night and then listen outside the door.

She shifted on the couch. No, her jewels were still missing and she doubted Mendez would have only taken her things, which happened to be wedged in the corner of her closet in a very unassuming box. If the lights did belong to Mendez, then his presence here could only be for a reason more sinister than mere thievery.

Like taking Mary.

The thought petrified her. "You were gone for hours. You discovered nothing in all that time?"

"Like I said, you need some sleep." Trevor's voice was as frosty as his hat had been when he'd walked in over an hour ago.

"Uncle Lou, please, can't you give me any information to help me sleep better tonight?" She swallowed hard. "Surely you two did not just stumble around the ranch all night long."

"Actually, we did. Trevor's right…there's not much we can do until morning. Then one of us will drive into Burns and the other will ride the property looking for trails."

"We can also check the train station," Gracie added. "I'm certain they keep a log of passengers."

Trevor's scarred brow rose, reminding her of how he'd looked at her the first time she met him. She set her chin. They would not push her out of this adventure merely because she was of the fairer sex.

"Tomorrow I'll ride to the train station," she announced. "Uncle Lou, you should go into town and Trevor should check all the places Julia could hide on this property."

"You're not going anywhere without an escort." He spoke casually, but there was steel in his tone.

"Really, Trevor. Mendez is not after me."

"He'll snatch who he can."

Gracie faced Uncle Lou. "How big is the ranch?"

"'Bout one hundred acres," Trevor answered for him, and Gracie had to check the quick irritation that flared up. His legs sprawled in front of him in a lazy fashion, mimicking his voice.

She sighed. If only she'd locked that silly box. Too late now. The most she could do would be to hound these two men as well as follow her own leads.

"I suppose I should retire for the night." She stifled a

yawn and stood, noticing with surprise that the tray once bearing mounds of food now held only crumbs. She paused on her way out. "One hundred acres is a rather tiny ranch, is it not?"

Wariness flickered across Uncle Lou's face. "I don't plan on being here much longer, Gracie. China is calling."

"How will you make a living?" She looked from one to the other and saw immediately they were not pleased with her question.

The scowl returned to Trevor's face but Uncle Lou suddenly grinned. "Full of questions, aren't ya? You ought to go into journalism."

"It's only a matter of time and I'll be there. Perhaps we can meet after lunch tomorrow and discuss our findings?" She waited by the door for an answer.

"I don't think so, Gracelyn." Uncle Lou gave her a stern look. "Seems to me you ought to be a little more upset than excited."

"Human emotions are rarely cut and dried. I feel horrible because the jewelry means so much to Mother and Daddy. Other than that, this is quite an adventure. It's about time one came my way." She flashed them a wide smile and slipped out the door, leaving it open a crack.

She bolted up the stairs to her room, suddenly not in the least tired.

The tightness in Trevor's chest eased somewhat when Gracie left the room. He couldn't think clearly when she was near, when the scent of her perfume snaked around him. The glint of her hair, the vibrancy of her eyes. He groaned.

"You love my niece." It wasn't a question.

"Like you said, she's too young."

"I've been rethinking my stance."

His hands clenched knuckle-tight. "She's not for me." He wished she was. He wished he had the right to hold her hand, to listen to her heart. He wanted that desperately. "I can't involve myself with anyone right now, Lou. I could get her killed."

Lou snorted. "Not likely. The furor's dying down, as are your enemies. Once we take care of Mendez, you should be done. You were only a temporary agent. They don't expect more than what you signed on for."

"She's a Christian, Lou." He paused. "You ever think about religion?"

"I do my best not to think about it." Lou's boot tapped against the floor and the shadows danced across his eyes. He wasn't getting younger. Trevor had his excuses for avoiding religion, but what were Lou's? He realized with a start that in their long friendship, Lou had never said.

"I've been reading the Bible a little." Trevor felt like a fool for admitting it but confession to Lou was habit. "I've been thinking about God." He let that hang in the air. To his surprise, Lou only cocked a brow.

"A man's got to do what he thinks is best," he said carefully, then yawned. "I'm heading to bed. We've got a big day tomorrow finding that witch. James can keep an eye on the women. After you check your property, head to the train station." Lou's forehead creased. "Mary won't be happy to hear that Mendez is so close."

"Why would she?" Trevor stood and stretched his arms. "She's got reason to kill him, I'd say."

"I'll be the one to shoot...." Lou let loose a string of expletives.

Trevor winced. Lou always could curse like a sailor. So could he, but lately he'd been feeling a change inside. Maybe all the Bible reading was affecting him.

He put out the fire, then he and Lou carried the dishes

to the kitchen by moonlight. On the way there, the shadows shifted strangely. The two men exchanged a look.

Once in the kitchen, Lou dumped the tray with a quiet clatter into the sink.

Lou's voice broke the silence of the kitchen with his whisper. "Marry Gracie."

"She belongs in Boston," Trevor said quietly. He felt affection for Gracie, but that didn't mean they could marry. Her headstrong, willful ways would drive a man to insanity. But he'd heard her wisdom, seen the kindness of her heart. The glow of her eyes and the satin smoothness of her skin. He forced his thoughts away from their poetic wanderings and focused on Lou's tired eyes. "She's a risk I can't take."

Lou shook his head. "I'm getting older and there's one thing I've learned. It's not the things I've done that I regret the most, it's the things I haven't." Lou hesitated. "I was wrong about you two. She's good for you, Trevor. She wants you. Take what you can."

"She's still longing for Striker."

Lou crossed his arms. "That shouldn't be a problem."

"She thinks he's a hero, not an assassin."

"Striker finds criminals. If he took a few out, it was for the good of the country. Nothing to feel guilty about."

Trevor looked away. "Council Bluff wasn't for the good of the country."

"It was meant to be for good." A deep silence fell between them.

Was Lou remembering the screams? The child lifeless on the ground? Trevor cleared his throat.

"Those outlaws are dead now. They'll never kill innocents again," Lou said. "As for the little boy, he was an accident. You didn't see him."

"I should have." The boy had run by just as Trevor

opened fire. He'd been struck down, dead before Trevor dropped his gun. Sorrow pressed so deeply on his chest that he wanted to collapse beneath the weight of it.

Lou reached over and squeezed Trevor's shoulder. "Forgive yourself. What happened there won't be repeated." He released his grip and gave Trevor an uncharacteristic pat on the back. "Get some sleep. I'll see you in the morning."

Trevor waited in the kitchen as Lou left. He heard the creak of the stairs as Lou ascended and waited for the sound of his door. It wasn't long in coming. Trevor allowed himself a small smile. If Lou would admit to his own feelings, Mary would be married by now.

So much for advice.

His thoughts shifted to Gracie.

He couldn't possibly be right for her. She was used to servants, caviar and French silk. He could afford those things with all he'd saved, but he didn't want them. Didn't need them. From his viewpoint, she needed a rich, high-society husband.

But not Hugh.

That arrogant whelp would bore her within a week. He would stifle her sense of fun and creativity. He would slowly strangle her with propriety. She needed someone who could give her adventure, who was secure enough to allow her the freedom to explore, but strong enough to protect her.

Speaking of adventure... He started out of the kitchen.

He had an eavesdropper to catch.

Chapter Twenty-Two

The scent of Trevor's cologne showed up before he did. That spicy, slightly foreign cologne preceded the raspy creak of the floorboards only by a second, but enough to forewarn Gracie. His steps were measured and precise. He knew she was here, of course. She should've jumped up after Uncle Lou passed and escaped to her room.

The whole attempt at eavesdropping proved fruitless. She hadn't been able to hear anything they'd said over the crackle of the fire. Now she was caught. Again.

"Gracelyn, you can come out now."

She peeked around her corner at the commanding whisper. Pale blue moonlight filtering in through the front door window panes lit the tall form in the hallway. Was he angry? She slipped out of the shadows and found him at the base of the stairs, closer than she'd realized.

"Eavesdropping again?" he murmured.

"I need a bit of water." Not an outright lie, she comforted herself as her dry throat attempted to swallow. Her fingers tightened the belt on her sleeping robe.

Why did he not move? He stood in front of her, solid as the mountains outside the house.

"I will see you in the morning." She attempted to slip

past him but he caught her arm with a gentle grip of steel. She ground her teeth at the restraint. "Remove your hands at once."

"We need to talk."

"I think we've done enough talking." She yanked her arm away and put her hands on her hips.

"You might want to keep it down," Trevor cautioned.

She sighed, suddenly weary beyond measure. "What do you want?"

She could feel his eyes measuring her features, probing. An undesired thrill raced through her veins.

"I want to kiss you," he whispered gruffly.

Warmth soared through her. A hopeless warmth that couldn't stay. "Please don't." She stepped back to put space between them. "There are many things I like about you, Trevor, but we both know a relationship between us will be impossible. You have made it very clear to me."

"You'll find a nice, rich man to satisfy you with the things you're used to. Choose wisely."

"Ha," Gracie scoffed. Wariness quickly morphed into irritation. "Thanks for planning my life. For your information, I don't want a rich man. I want a good one. One I can adventure with. One who loves me for who I am and likes me in trousers. I'm twenty, the daughter of very rich, socially acceptable parents. I'll marry when God shows me I should, and no sooner."

"And your plans for Striker?"

"They are not your business."

Trevor's eyes flashed in the dimness. What was he thinking? Did he understand? "Our attraction is out of line," he said.

"Life is much different than your garden. Imperfect, uneven." Her fists left her hips and reached for his hands. She pressed his fingers against her cheek, relishing their work-roughened texture. "But one thing is similar. Our attraction will die if not watered, if not fed. That's life."

"And God?"

"What about Him?" she asked.

"His plans for you might be different than what you think, what you want."

She nodded, sadness filling her. "You're very right. I believe though there are some things He puts in our hearts that never die."

"Like what?"

"Love." She let go of his hands, missing their warmth immediately.

He reached up and rubbed the back of his neck in long, tired strokes. "I guess you best be getting to bed."

Gracie moved onto the stairs. "I guess I should," she said sadly.

Trevor didn't say any more, just raised his hand in farewell, slipped into his coat and let himself out into the bitter night.

Gracie's trip to the train station proved successful.

"Sure," the grizzled man behind the station counter said, smacking his tobacco loudly. "I seen that woman. Most perfect yellow hair I ever done seen. Boarded yesterday morning, guess 'bout before noon."

"Did you notice where she was going?" Gracie leaned across the counter.

"Now why would I know that?" He smacked again.

Gracie could tell he was lying. "If I knew where she was going I could catch up. I have a reward, of course, for whoever can point the way. I suppose I should try the porters." She turned toward the train platform but stopped at his grunt. She swung slowly back around.

"Now how much would this reward be?" He peered up at her out of crooked spectacles and his mustache twitched.

"I believe I've a dime for the person who can tell me where Miss Williams was headed. I'm certain there are porters who will remember her. Please do not consider the matter anymore." She rubbed at the goose bumps on her arms and hoped the man's greed would kick in a little faster.

His beady brown eyes held her for a moment. "I'm thinkin'," he said slowly, "that twenty-five cents might refresh my memory."

"It might, but there are plenty out there for whom a dime is more than enough for a snippet of information. Please, continue your paperwork and I'll find someone with a clearer memory."

"Los Angeles," he blurted out.

"I'll want to see proof of that." She looked down to where the little man sat and tried to ignore the distaste souring her stomach.

He pushed a record book in her face and with a grimy fingernail pointed to a signature. *Julia Williams.* As flourished and loopy as the woman herself. It was enough. Gracie plucked a dime from the pocket in her wool dress and let it clatter onto the counter.

"Thank you, sir." She marched out of the little station, down the platform, and unloosed the holding rein that held Velvet to the hitching post. She ran her hand down Velvet's smooth neck before pulling herself onto the mare's back. She adjusted her skirt. Her black silk faille hat was stuffed into her jacket pocket. Hopefully Mother wouldn't notice the crinkles in the material, but the morning was too beautiful to shield her head from the sun.

So Julia had gone to the big city. There seemed to be

little chance of retrieving the jewels. Gracie's heart was heavy as Velvet cantered the miles back to the house.

They would surely go home now and she would probably never see Trevor again. Too late she realized she loved the stubborn cowboy. Maybe falling in love with someone else was still feasible. She couldn't imagine it, though. Trevor was unique. He possessed an indefinable quality that set him apart from others. Some kind of control, an authority that other men lacked. Moreover, he did not appear to be intimidated by her dreams and goals, as Hugh was.

Yes, if circumstances were different perhaps they would've had something to build on.

Velvet released a soft whinny and Gracie looked up to see someone riding toward her. The day was clear with few clouds in the sky and the hardened snow glittered beneath the rising sun.

Trevor.

She recognized the controlled posture. He sat the horse who'd thrown him. He pulled his mount up beside her and tipped his hat. She bit back a grin. Trevor did not usually resort to such gentlemanly techniques. She nodded in return.

Together they trotted toward the ranch. "Did you discover any news?" she asked.

"Nothing. Thought we told you to stay at the house."

"You mentioned something of that nature. But it's too late to fret about it now. I have discovered your mother took the train to Los Angeles." Sliding a glance to his horse, she frowned. What if he threw Trevor again? "Have you named him?"

"Her, and no, I haven't. Los Angeles? We could intercept Julia." He said it so quietly she almost didn't hear him.

"I don't see how we could do that."

"Lou and I have friends. We'll send a post and request

them to remove her from the train and search her for the jewels."

"Are these friends reliable?" Her hair whipped into her face and she pushed it back.

Trevor looked over at her. "They're authorities. They'll handle the situation. Soon as Lou gets back I'll have to ride into town with him."

At last, a trip to Burns. "May I come with you?"

"Why?" He threw her a suspicious glance.

"I'm not going to interview the townspeople about Striker's nefarious past deeds, if that's what worries you. I simply must buy more Christmas presents. We've only a few weeks left, you know."

"I'd forgotten." He stared ahead. "Christmas is big in your family."

"Of course. It's the birth of our Savior. I suppose you don't celebrate Christmas."

"We exchange gifts," he answered lightly.

"Do you decorate?"

"Not really. Mary's usually the only female there, and sometimes Lou and I are gone on business." He held the reins loosely in his large hands, and yet she could see that the horse was under his complete control. Warmth blossomed in her chest.

"You're very special, Trevor."

"So you keep telling me." He said nothing more.

After leaving Gracie at the stables, Trevor galloped to his place. He tugged the saddle and bridle off the young mare and tied her to the post with water and oats. Like Julia had taught him. Memories of his mother washed over him. For all her faults, she'd taught him to love horses, to care for them and respect them. They'd spent hours in the desert—riding, free, laughing.

Frowning, he headed to his garden. The smell of fresh soil hadn't yet materialized and the bare, snow-dusted earth spoke of loneliness.

There were few weeds at this time of year. In fact, not much of anything was growing. He knelt down and, with reverence, touched one tiny green shoot. It was an early bloomer and probably wouldn't make it. Despite the lack of growth around the small plant, other seeds lay just beneath the hardened soil, taking in nutrients and preparing to spring up at the right time.

Gracie had been right last night. He kept his garden neat and orderly. Almost perfect. But life couldn't be that way. Why did he expect it? He glanced up at the sky as if he could find God looking down at him, but there was nothing but blue space.

What made a person able to believe? The more he thought on the things he'd been reading, the more he wanted to find the faith to trust. He sat back in the dirt and crossed his arms over his knees.

The sound of an Oregon junco floated on the winter breeze. The small sparrow perched on the roof of his house, dark head bobbing up and down as he warbled his song. Then his little body flitted away, as if he had no worries at all and knew his exact destination.

Perhaps faith was that easy, Trevor mused. The sparrow had no worries, he just lived and trusted that the One who made him would also watch over him.

But who had watched over Trevor? No one. Not one person had protected him from vicious beatings, from the taunts of hypocritical people who knew his mother, knew his father and punished Trevor for their actions.

But you're alive, a voice pressed from within. *You are alive.*

And didn't that count for something?

* * *

Mother cornered Gracie as soon as she arrived home.

"There you are. Where have you been? Never mind, go comb your hair and wash that face. Mary put out a fresh basin of water in your room. Why do you smell like manure?" Her mother's nose wiggled as she backed away from Gracie. "Honestly, Gracelyn, you would think you'd take more thought with yourself. You are a feminine, delicate lady."

Mother's hands swept through the air as she spoke and her words echoed in the empty hallway. Then her gaze traversed Gracie again and she sighed loudly, as if the burdens of the world had been placed on her shoulders. "Please clean up. We are having a tea in the study in ten minutes. And do spray yourself with perfume."

Used to Mother's melodrama, Gracie tried to hide her smile. She knelt down and unlaced her boots, then set them by the door.

"Calm yourself, Mother. There's no need for hysterics over a horse ride." She popped up and gave her mother a swift kiss on her smooth cheek and it wasn't until she flounced halfway up the stairs that she realized her mother still stood staring at her in disbelief.

Gracie chuckled. Her mother must have noticed the dirt and hay stains on the back of her skirt. She looked down at her and called out, "Don't worry, Mother. I merely fell over a pile of dirt. It will wash." She bounced the rest of the way to her room.

Once there she refused to allow circumstances to kill her positive mood. Julia's whereabouts were known, and there was a good chance Trevor's government friends would find her.

The weather was beautiful and Christmas was coming. She would ride into town, see new faces and perhaps discover exciting information. She shed her dirty clothes and washed quickly. Shrugging into a mint-green dress, she thought of the afternoon excursion. She hadn't meant to investigate when the idea of going into Burns originally popped into her head, but afterward, especially after Trevor's antagonistic look, she realized she might learn something important.

Like the true identity of Striker.

With a trip home certain, now that she'd had her jewels stolen, she needed to heighten her search for the elusive agent.

Pulling out a brush, she winced as it tugged through her hair but managed to get the chaotic mass into some kind of order. With a heavy jeweled comb she fastened the knot into the relaxed look known as the Grecian style. She glowered at the mirror.

These combs. Her unruly hair. If only she had the courage to chop it all off like Connie.

Familiar sadness tightened her chest and for a moment she let it linger. *But sorrow cannot last forever. We were made to laugh,* she thought as she inspected her face for any missed streaks of dirt. Though she didn't feel like laughing, perhaps one day she would again.

Striding out of her room she bumped into Mary "Are you coming to tea?"

"I'm serving it."

"I've had enough." Gracie fought down the anger that tightened her throat. "How can Uncle Lou let Mother treat you this way? It's shameful. I want you to sit down and join us."

Mary glanced at her, a frown crossing her perfect features. "Edith didn't ask for the tea. She won't be there."

"Then with whom am I to have tea?" Gracie followed Mary down the stairs, and then stopped midway as realization struck. "Oh, no, it's Hugh. That man! I have absolutely reached the limits of my patience, Mary."

"You'll be fine," she soothed.

Gracie edged into the sitting room while Mary continued to the kitchen. Hugh already waited for her, and when she neared the couches he rose and took her hand. A small table had been placed between the two couches for tea and pastries. She let Hugh seat her beside him, a proper distance between them, of course.

His cologne smelled on the strong side, rich and cloying. She preferred Trevor's earthiness to this odor.

"You look lovely, Gracelyn." His cheeks rounded as he took in her appearance. "I missed you while I was away. I never thought to fall in love with you, but I did. I wish you would reconsider our engagement." His hands reached for hers and she reluctantly allowed him to hold them.

"I'm flattered, Hugh. But I know in my heart that you would not be happy with me."

"How can you say such a thing?" He looked shocked. "You are the epitome of all a woman should be."

Because she wanted to snort with laughter at the intensity of his tone, she composed her features and gently removed her hands from his sweaty clasp. "I believe you're a good man. As I told you, we are simply incompatible."

"None could be more suited than we, dear Gracelyn."

The man was obtuse. She eyed him. "How do you feel about women in trousers? Or women in the workforce?"

"Why?" Caution lowered his voice. "Are you considering either?"

"I would prefer to know what you think about those issues."

"They're unimportant, Gracelyn."

Mary floated in and set a tray laden with sweets in front of them. She left without a word.

Gracie eyed the fudge. She truly wanted a piece but hated to inspire another lecture on her weight. The memory made her want to wring Hugh's neck. What kind of gentleman commented on a lady's size anyhow?

"I love you and want you to be my wife." He paused and his eyebrows dipped downward. "Were you toying with my affections only months ago?"

"We hardly know each other," Gracie sputtered.

"You led me on and now you spurn me? What game is this you're playing?" His forehead furrowed and his lips hardened into a thin line.

"I don't play games. We've barely known each other but I can assure you I am not the kind of woman you desire." She kept her tone light but inside she grew suspicious. He'd never talked this way in Boston. His sudden, persistent pursuit of her could only be due to one thing.

Money.

His family wanted her inheritance and her parents desired Hugh's lineage. She swallowed her groan as Hugh began to drone on about his blooming love for her. He must think she was completely brainless. In Boston they'd gone to a few shows, a few soirees and the only physical interest he'd ever shown had been one dutiful little peck on her cheek. His family must be desperate, indeed.

She reached for the fudge as he spoke and was shocked when his palm covered her hand and gently guided it away from the tray.

"It is my duty as the man who loves you to protect you in all ways, darling. I specifically requested no chocolate on this tray." He kept her hand in his. His light blue eyes regarded her seriously. "You must keep away from chocolate. I am sure you would not want to look the way you did before I left for military duty. You're so beautiful now." He bent and placed moist lips against her hand.

Heat rose in Gracie's face. A flash of anger sizzled across her chest. His insults deserved a slapping, most definitely. Even Mother would not fault her. She pulled her hand from him and paused. It would not be honorable or noble to hurt him as he had just hurt her. But oh, she itched to.

She rocketed to her feet instead. "I would not marry you, Hugh, were I to be condemned to spinsterhood the rest of my life. You're monstrously rude and tactless. Please excuse me, but I no longer desire your company." She made for the door but his hand on her arm stopped her.

"I've needed you for the longest time and I won't be refused. That scarred up cowboy won't be looking at you funny anymore. Not once I have you." His harsh whisper grated against her ear, and she cringed. He turned her and pressed her against him, his fingers digging into her arms, and then his wet, sloppy lips closed over hers.

Gracie's first response was outrage and she tried to step away but he was more forceful than he looked. His mouth moved over hers and to her horror she realized he was trying to pry her lips open. Fear momentarily weakened her knees but when one arm encircled her like a vise and his fingers dug into her jaw, rage kicked in.

There was no way a kiss would be forced on her. Absolutely not. And so, from the reservoirs of her memory, she employed a move Connie had taught her years ago, a tactic designed to discourage overly zealous suitors.

She kicked him in the shin.

Chapter Twenty-Three

Ignoring Hugh's groaned oaths, Gracie twisted from his grasp and raced for the door. Sunlight filtered into the hallway and cast shadows across Mother and Father's features as they met her near the kitchen.

"Are you done with tea?"

"Quite," she said, moving closer to her father.

"Are there any snacks left?" Father looked up at her.

She offered him a shaky smile. "They're on the table."

Joined by Mary, they moved into the sitting room. Everyone found a seat except Mary and Gracie. She could not make herself sit. Tremors weakened her limbs. Hugh settled next to her mother and she wanted to be sick. The energy drained from her body, making it hard to believe the respectable-looking man next to Mother could have done such a thing.

She rested against a wall, arms folded securely across her chest.

"Let me get more tea." Mary gave her a little smile as she glided out the door.

"Gracelyn, come sit by me." William patted the chair next to him. She sank down, thankful when her father's hand enfolded hers.

Perhaps her parents were somewhat old-fashioned and overly strict, but she never doubted their love for her. She clung to her father's hand and hoped the trembling in her stomach might leave soon. How silly to be nervous around Hugh. Her parents' presence assured he could do no more harm. But she refused to look at him.

She needed to wash his imprint off her face. Desperately.

Mother reached for one of the little sandwiches that still rested on the tea tray. "We have been spoiled in Boston. Did you know James uses a working outhouse?"

"Really?" Father adjusted his spectacles. "I suppose Harney County is difficult to modernize, what with all this space and the war going on. I am delighted it's over. Too many lives lost."

Discreetly, Gracie took a napkin and dabbed at her lips.

"And now well-bred girls cutting their hair and working in the factories. It's shameful," Mother added. "Did you hear of Striker turning in his resignation?"

Gracie's head popped up. "He did?"

"Oh, yes. It was in all the papers before we left. It appears that with the war over, he no longer desires to be an undercover agent for the government."

"Did they have any pictures of him?" Her fingers tightened around her napkin as she waited.

"No. Though I have heard tales of his countenance, that it strikes fear into any who look upon it."

"I don't know why everyone is in awe of this Striker," Hugh said. "The man is a killer and too scared to show his face. I can't help but wonder if he contracted the influenza, died and that's why this story is making rounds in the papers."

Gracie stared down at her hands. She hoped he hadn't

died. The man was a hero. Anyone who rescued women would be.

But the possibility posed a problem. If Striker retired, who would find Mendez hiding in the mountains? And who would keep Mary safe?

They spent the rest of the afternoon chatting and playing chess. Gracie, of course, was bid to sit near her mother and sew. No chess for her. Every once in a while she stood to stretch her legs and look out the window that faced the front yard.

Where had Trevor and Uncle Lou gone? Trevor said they might go to town.

Shoulders heavy, she stared out the window. No doubt about it. They had left her behind.

"Don't know what to make of it, Lou."

"Me, neither." The two men sat at the hotel restaurant, waiting for a return phone call. They'd polished off steak and potatoes for lunch and now had only time to pass before hearing news of Julia's capture.

Trevor had snagged Lou earlier that morning as soon as he'd seen the smoke from the car making its way to the ranch. He figured there was no need for Gracie to tag along at this time. They'd get things done faster without her constant barrage of questions.

Unfortunately no one in town seemed to know much.

Lou tapped impatient fingers against the table. "Sheriff says he hasn't seen or heard anything about new faces showing up. We know Mendez is hiding out somewhere in the mountains. Question is, who did he bring with him and will we be able to handle them when they show their faces?"

"We'll handle them," Trevor answered grimly. "Right now I want to know what Julia had to do with this. The ranch is in such a deserted area that I can't help thinking she might've struck some deal with him. Like last time."

"Mary's keeping low, eyes open. She knows he wants revenge."

"I'll feel better when George has Julia in custody. If Mendez is here Julia will know it and, for the right price, she'll spill everything." Trevor tipped his water and took a long drink, then wiped his mouth with the back of his hand. If only George would call soon. A bad feeling squatted in his gut.

"I knew she was up to no good the moment she showed up on our property. You should've made her leave, Trev."

"Wanted to, believe me. I can't figure why Mendez would bother with his revenge in the middle of this pandemic. He's a fool."

"He's a loose end." Lou eyed Trevor. "We'll tie him up, and then Striker can rest in peace."

"Excuse me, Mr. Cruz? Phone call for you."

Trevor rose and followed the waiter to one of the few telephones in Burns. He picked up the receiver. The message was quick and to the point. Trevor hung up perplexed, chest burning with foreboding. He made his way back to the table and took the hat Lou handed him.

"She claims to have no knowledge of Mendez or his whereabouts," he said.

"You offered money."

"Fifty bucks. No jewels on her, either. She showed a letter stating her new employment as a factory worker in Los Angeles." He twisted the hat in his hands. "She didn't take them, Lou."

"If she didn't, then who did?"

The thought plagued Trevor as they rode back to the ranch. He couldn't imagine anyone living there as a thief.

But the jewels were gone. Someone stole them, but who? And why?

The ranch was quiet when they returned and by silent assent they did the few chores the property required. They found James out mending a fence and gave him a hand. By the time they finished and the livestock were fed and watered, the sun rested on the mountain peaks. The men headed inside to wash up for dinner, and Trevor braced himself for Gracie's questions and her disappointment.

They weren't long in coming.

She sat through dinner silently while they explained no jewels had been found on Julia and that she carried a valid letter of employment to back up her sudden departure. After dinner everyone dispersed. Gracie's mother to her room with a headache, undoubtedly brought on by the negative news. Mary scooted to the kitchen to clean up, and Lou, William and Hugh escaped to the sitting room for cigars. As soon as Edith left the dining table, Gracie snagged Trevor's arm and practically dragged him to Lou's office.

"You went without me. That was a sneaky thing to do." Gracie paced, arms tucked against her ribs. "I specifically told you I needed to go into town."

Trevor's brow lifted.

She huffed. "I am so tired of being obedient and dutiful. These regulations are going to strangle me."

He leaned back in his chair and studied her. She crossed the room with long strides and her pretty lips twisted into a frown. He would miss her energy and erratic behavior, even if she did rattle him sometimes. "Calm down, Gracie. No one wants to strangle you. Your parents want to love and protect you, that's all."

"It's not only them." She came over and planted her

hands on the desk, leaned down until they were eye level. "It is society. Culture. You."

"Me?"

"Yes, I am perfectly capable of driving a motor vehicle but no one will let me. And do you know how much money I am set to inherit? Thousands. Do you think I'm allowed to buy my own automobile? No, because it is not seemly for a woman in my circles to drive a vehicle." She released a long, frustrated breath. "And to top things off, people keep trying to tell me what not to eat and how I look better skinnier. I have absolutely had it, Trevor. I simply wanted to go into town." She straightened from the desk, then her shoulders dropped and she sank into a chair.

"Don't you think you're overreacting a little?" Trevor asked gently.

Gracie sighed. "Perhaps, but you've never had to suffer being a female. I do apologize, however, for my emotional outburst. Between my mother and Hugh I believe my hair is turning gray."

His gaze narrowed. "What does Hugh have to do with this?"

"Nothing you need to be bothered with. We're leaving after Christmas, and then hopefully I will never see him again." She shivered. "Let us only say that Christmas cannot come soon enough."

The strangeness of her words bothered him, but he pushed the feeling aside. No need to get overly involved. "Gracelyn, I admire your intelligence. Treating you in an inferior way has never been my intention."

Her lips curved down. "I must be honest with you. I'm troubled by this situation with the jewels. If Julia did not take them, who would?"

"We're working on finding that out."

"I know...and I'm sure you have plenty of contacts. This

crime shouldn't take long to solve. Tell me, did you discover any news of Mendez?" she asked casually, probably hoping he would divulge riveting information.

He weighed his words. "No news. Looks like our worries were for nothing." He sniffed the air and gave Gracie a rueful smile. "You'll have to excuse me, but fine company is waiting for me in the sitting room." He rose from his chair and took Gracie's hand to guide her to the office door.

A strange expression crossed her face, one he couldn't interpret. Then again, he'd never been good at reading women. Just rescuing them. Not this one, though. She insisted on independence, on living her own life and taking care of herself. With the help of God, that is. Such a big part of Gracelyn. He couldn't look at her without thinking of the One she worshipped.

He hoped she stayed that way forever. His thumb lightly caressed the top of her hand as he said softly, "Don't ever let anyone tell you who or how to be, except your God."

Hours after she should've been asleep, Gracie put her book down and yawned. Starlight spilled through her window and painted the floor blue. Looking out into the night, she felt a tug within to pray.

She grabbed her wool robe and slid into slippers before hurrying downstairs. All was quiet. It must be midnight at least, she thought, as she opened the front door and stepped onto the porch. The chilly breeze threatened to whip the breath from her throat. She closed the door gently behind her.

For miles there was nothing but monochromatic landscape, broken by small shadows of scrubs glowing beneath the stars.

Thank You, Jesus, she prayed. *Thank You, thank You.* And that was all she could say for several moments.

Eventually goose bumps began prickling her skin and she knew she'd have to go back inside. Even though Trevor had said they'd been worried for nothing, that Mendez wasn't around, she shouldn't take any chances.

She'd been foolish to come out, lured by the beauty of the land.

It was as she was turning to the door that the shadow in the window caught her attention. A rabbit?

Rabbits didn't smile.

Too late. Foolish, foolish girl. She whipped around and raced for the door but the man hiding by the stairs grabbed the hem of her robe. She tried to yank away but he was faster than Trevor pulling a gun, and he grabbed her around the waist.

"Mendez is gonna be real happy tonight." Flashing her a toothless grin, he brought his hand to her face, and as much as she fought the wiry stranger, she was no match for the strong smelling cloth he pressed over her nose.

Sometime later cold nudged Gracie awake. She became aware of the thick scent of horse beneath her face. A shiver rolled through her.

"Hold still, we're almost there." A man's gravelly voice came from above, and Gracie realized she'd been slumped over the horn of the saddle. Her ribs ached where it dug into them. Dizzy and jostled by the horse's walk, she tried to straighten. Her back protested and burning around her wrists brought her to the realization she'd been tied to this horse. Kidnapped.

She forced her body to relax against the saddle, pressing her cheek against the horse's mane and allowing her body to move with the rhythm of its walk.

"Are you Mendez?" Her voice came out a croak.

"Nah. The big man ran to town but he'll be happy when he sees what I snatched." The kidnapper coughed then, and the horse stumbled. Gracie's body jerked forward and the horn bit into her stomach.

Groaning, she eased to her side. A shiver racked her. She cracked open her eyes. The moon cast an eerie glow over the land, easing shadows across the mountains and deepening crevices. She turned her head, searching for Uncle Lou's house, but she found nothing except mountains and hills around her.

The kidnapper coughed again. He tripped forward and the horse whinnied as the reins went slack. Gracie tried to breathe deeply, tried to still the violent hammering of her pulse in her ears. Carefully she turned her head to find the kidnapper.

There, to the right. He'd fallen to the ground, bent over, retching. Ever so quietly, she rocked her bound wrists back and forth, testing the strength of the rope. To her surprise, her wrists slipped easily off the saddle horn, still bound but not tied to the horse like she'd thought.

She glanced at her captor. He lay on the ground, completely still. The horse sidestepped, perhaps feeling the change in circumstance.

"Shh," Gracie soothed, using her fingers to comb through the horse's mane. She sat upright and clutched the saddle as a wave of dizziness crashed over her and faded her sight. When the dizziness passed, she pulled her leg over the saddle. Her skin stuck to the icy leather. Wincing, she pulled free but miscalculated and fell to the ground. She hit hard, the breath slamming out of her.

After a moment, she could breathe again. A rock ground into her thigh but she ignored the pain and scrambled to her feet, praying her shaky legs would uphold her.

The kidnapper moaned but didn't move.

Blinking quickly, Gracie stood still as frigid night air stung her cheeks and cut through her night robe. Snow packed against her slippers but her toes remained warm. For now.

She took in her surroundings. First things first. A weapon. She crossed to where the man lay with his head in the snow. He'd fallen into a faint of some sort. His breath sounded uneven and unnatural in the stillness of night. She looked around. He'd stopped them at the mouth of a cave.

A brisk wind blew against her again. With it came the scent of fire. The horse whinnied and spinning around, dashed away. Drat. She should've secured the horse to something.

There was nothing around them, though. Nothing but rocks and that odor of fire. It seemed to be coming from the cave. She sniffed the air. She needed a knife to cut the rope around her wrists. Maybe a sharp rock. Moving gingerly, she stepped up toward the mouth of the cave and hoped her slippers didn't rip.

The odor grew stronger, and so did the warmth. Shivers rippled through her. Was it worth the risk of exposure to get warm? She listened and heard nothing stir in the cave. Perhaps there'd only been Mendez and her kidnapper. In that case, Mendez could return at any point.

She slipped up to the cave and poked her head in.

And recoiled.

Bodies stretched across the dusty floor, unmoving and at odd angles. As she moved farther in, the bitter fumes of vomit assaulted her. Whirling, she ducked back out into the cold air.

Dead.

There could be no doubt. The stench proclaimed more than sickness. There was a stillness to that cave, a lack of snoring and rustles, that caused pinpricks to scuttle across Gracie's body.

Flipping a glance toward her kidnapper who lay unmoving in the snow, she made a quick decision. Who knew when Mendez might return? Better to be freezing and free than warm and a prisoner. Frigid air stiffened her fingers but somehow she managed to rip a swath of cloth from her nightie beneath the robe. She held it over her face and dodged into the cavern.

Warmth surrounded her immediately, mingling with the odor of death and vomit. Holding back a gag, she picked her way across the floor, using the flickering firelight to look for coats or blankets.

Death from cold was more certain than death from influenza at this point. She spotted a dark shadow against the wall and moved toward it. A body sprawled in front of her, some black, unidentifiable liquid snaking across his face. Darkness edged her vision.

She pressed the rag of cloth firmer against her mouth and took a deep breath. No fainting. She wouldn't be so weak. It took several seconds of leaning against the rock wall before strength returned in her limbs. Once she felt capable of moving, she avoided looking at the body and advanced quickly to the mound against the wall.

Coats or blankets, she couldn't tell, but she scooped up an armful and left the cavern.

Chapter Twenty-Four

A deep pounding roused Trevor from his dreams.

"Trevor, answer your door." Lou's muffled tones registered. The pounding continued as Trevor stumbled to the front door, rubbing his eyes and muttering under his breath. It better be important. He had just fallen into a troubled sleep after struggling all night with thoughts of one pesky female and what life would be like when she returned to Boston.

"What!" He swung the door open and had to squint when Lou held up a lantern.

"Gracie's gone," Lou said shortly.

Adrenaline jolted Trevor awake and he stepped back to let Lou in. Slamming the door, he stalked to the living room and sat on the very couch that only weeks ago Gracie had wept on. He'd never forget that day, nor the kiss that had preceded her tears.

"What do you mean, she's gone?" Nerves twitching, he eyed Lou.

"I'd bet Mendez has her. Mary heard a sound, looked out her window and saw a horse carrying two riders heading southwest. She said Gracie has a habit of wandering out at night. That true?"

"Yeah, told her not to. I saw her once while doing the security check." He rubbed his hands over his eyes and then took the mug of coffee Lou handed him.

"I don't know why I wasn't told about this," Lou said sternly, "but now we have a problem on our hands. We've got to find Gracie before Mendez hurts her, or worse, sells her. On top of that, I now have to deal with my brother who's never approved of my career in the first place and will never forgive me if that career gets his only daughter killed."

His jaw tightened. He wouldn't let that happen. "We need to track them before new snow falls. They won't expect us so close behind them. Did you wake James?"

"No, you'll do it while I get William and explain things to him."

"Fine, let's go." Trevor changed quickly and then, like phantoms, the two men moved into the night.

Less than an hour later, they assembled into the kitchen, everyone but Edith, who had not been woken due to her propensity for hysterics.

Lines gouged William's face and his hands trembled on the armrests of his wheelchair. Mary bustled around the kitchen with cups of coffee and leftover cake.

"I knew that girl would get into trouble sooner or later. Knew it." James frowned, his tone sad rather than proud.

Hugh sat at the table near William with a troubled expression on his face. "If you leave me a gun, I'll stay here and guard the house," he said. "I have no experience tracking and I don't know these mountains, but I can point a gun and pull the trigger if need be."

Trevor nodded his assent and felt a grudging respect for Hugh. Up till now he'd considered the man little more than a spoiled kid. He'd done nothing but complain and compare Oregon to Massachusetts the few times they'd ridden together. And there was something shifty about his blue eyes. But at least he could stay here and do his part.

"Mary, I want you to go to my room and lock the door," Lou said quietly. She nodded and left the kitchen. "Here's a rifle for you, William. One for you, Hugh. You two can take whatever positions you think best. We're ready to track."

"We'll send someone back by dawn if we haven't found her yet." Trevor pivoted and went outside. Lou and James followed, leaving the others to blow out the candles.

"Got a track here. Unfamiliar shoe," James said after several cold minutes. Lou shod all his horses with unmarked shoes, but this track held an imprint that was suspiciously unique. As if the owner wanted others to know he'd been there. They followed the track, breath blowing in front of them like clouds of smoke. Lou led James's pinto while the older man looked for tracks by foot.

Trevor tried to contain the fear that made his chest ache as they got farther from the house. What had Gracie been thinking? He told her not to venture outside at night but apparently she didn't take him seriously. If she would've listened then none of this would be happening. He wouldn't be shivering in the saddle, following a bent old man and listening to his stomach rumble. He'd be warm in bed, his biggest concern discovering who had stolen the jewels rather than hunched over a saddle, a sick worry gnawing at his innards.

They followed tracks for hours and as each minute passed Trevor could feel his jaw locking up with suppressed anger. Infernal woman. It was so cold out she could easily catch hypothermia if not sheltered soon. Thing was, they should've been close to her and her abductor by now. But the tracks showed no sign of ending.

When the sky began to lighten Lou finally broke the tense silence.

"Looks like we'll have to head back soon. These tracks are going in circles." He rubbed the back of his neck then let his hand drop to his side in a gesture of defeat.

"Someone made them on purpose," James put in. He spit a chunk of tobacco juice out of the side of his mouth before speaking again. "I'd say our best bet is to get back to the house and wait for them to contact us. Maybe I'll hide in the hills and keep watch. Could be we'll capture one of them."

Trevor scanned the horizon. "I'm not heading back. You two go without me."

"You ain't gonna find her." Lou slanted him a curious look. "It makes better sense to go back to the house, but I guess logic isn't ruling you right now."

"It doesn't make sense for all of us to return."

James pulled himself onto his horse and squinted at them. "I'm heading back now. You two work it out." He turned his mount around and galloped off, leaving Trevor and Lou to face each other in the budding light.

"I'm staying, Lou. I've got a hunch."

"Do what you have to. I need to be at the house, though."

"I know." The two friends nodded at each other and Lou left.

Trevor let his gaze drift over the rugged, deadly landscape. Fear grew in his heart again. Gracie could be already dead, but instinct told him she lived still. He wanted to let cold reason guide him but the loud thumping of his heart overruled any logical thought processes.

He grunted and pressed Butch toward the hills on the left. Where was her God now? It would be easy to blame God for another's actions, or for even creating that person. But blaming Him had been a part of Trevor's life for too long and, as far as he could tell, it had never done him much good.

As frosty air rushed past his face he found himself praying to Gracie's unseen God, begging him to spare her, pleading with him for guidance. Butch's ears turned back when Trevor started talking into thin air but then he continued on his way as if his master speaking aloud to an unseen entity was nothing new.

"Lord, I know we haven't had too much to do with each other and that's my fault, but I'm asking that if You hear me, You'd answer. I can't see You—don't feel You, either. But Gracie says You're there and that You care and right now I want her to be right. Please help her, God. I want to trust You but I need something solid to hang my faith on besides the words of another. I guess I'm asking You to keep her safe and help me find her. Thanks." The tips of his ears burned during his spoken prayer but the pressure in his chest eased and he could breathe easier. No wonder Gracie prayed so much. It really did soothe the soul.

Butch nickered and Trevor stroked his mane, then leaned down and whispered, "Okay, I asked for some divine help. Listen up and lead the way." He straightened and for the next hour they checked out every cave he knew of in the southwest section of Lou's property.

Soon the freshly wakened sun spread a glow over the land and Trevor paused in his search to take in the sight. A thin layer of snow covered the acreage and the sun's reflection made the frozen land shine as if fire burned beneath it. A few animals ventured out looking for food.

And then he saw her.

She limped in the direction of the ranch, dragging a body behind her. He dug his heels into Butch's side and tried to control the giddy relief surging through his veins. As he drew closer he could see she wore an oversize coat

over her night robe and her hair was a matted mess. A definite limp slowed her gait.

She must have heard the horse because she stopped as
he drew near and her gaze centered on him. He resisted the
urge to jump off Butch and instead dismounted slowly.

"Are you okay?" His voice was colder than he'd meant
it to be.

"Don't come near me, Trevor." She backed up a step.
"Just lead me home, please."

"Who are you pulling along?"

"My kidnapper." Her teeth chattered. "We need to get
warm soon or I don't think he'll make it."

Trevor moved forward to get a closer look at the man,
who appeared shorter than Gracie with greasy brown hair.
The man's face was turned away and he couldn't get a
glimpse of the face but he did see the empty holster at the
prone man's hip.

"They're all dead. Every single one. We need to get
home, and keep the others away when we do." Exhaustion
lined her face, sadness drew her full lips down.

Trevor pushed the anger and fear deep within and strode
forward. He pulled Gracie into his arms, letting the unconscious figure lie on the ground while he pressed her shivering body close to his warmth.

"I don't care who's dead," he mumbled into her hair.
"Only that you're alive." Her arms tightened around him.
He snapped his fingers and Butch pranced over.

In a swift move Trevor lifted Gracie's trembling form
up onto the saddle, and then he reached for the man and
hauled him over Butch. Gracie pulled the stranger closer
to her in a protective gesture.

"We're two miles from Lou's. Hold tight and we'll go as
fast as we can." The tip of Trevor's nose felt numb as they
made their way across the land. Inside, he prayed for help.

Gracie swayed unsteadily and he wondered if the man she held against her still had a pulse. They needed to get home, bad, but Butch was tired and the added weight burdened the stallion's steps.

Trevor fought the urge to interrogate Gracie. He wasn't sure who was dead or why but she looked far from able to answer his questions.

He pressed forward, snow sticking to his Levi's. A swirl of smoke in the distance caught his attention and his stride lengthened. Lou's car was heading toward them.

For the second time that day, God had answered his prayers.

Gracie could barely remember the automobile ride home, if her parents met her at the door, or when the shivers stopped. Eight hours later, according to the clock in her room, the only clear remembrance of her journey home was Trevor's strong arms and the sound of his voice, heavy with relief.

She stretched toasty warm toes against the heavy blankets on her bed and sat up. Edith dozed on the window seat, lightly resting against the curtains. Gracie whipped the blankets off, and then raised her arms above her in a full stretch. She swung her legs over the bed and, limbs shaky, dressed in a simple blue dress. She pulled on wool stockings and boots, tugged a brush through her hair until it resembled something presentable and left the room.

Legs weak, she slowly took the stairs to the first floor. She pressed a hand against her stomach. Food first? She should've stayed in bed where her mother's presence had been unexpected and strangely tender. But she wanted to relive Trevor's rescue quietly, alone.

In the icy morning, he had been out searching for her. It said more to her than a thousand kisses, and she was glad he wasn't nearby because her response to him might be uncontrollable and she couldn't allow that.

She sighed. After snagging a thick slice of cheese from the kitchen, she walked to the stables. Fresh air, familiar scents. Maybe they'd erase the horror of what she'd found in that cave. Of what she'd dragged home. Hopefully the others kept their distance. Her kidnapper must have suffered from influenza and, judging by the waste and vomit accompanying the dead bodies in the cave, so had the others.

She swallowed hard, memory spoiling her appetite. She tossed the cheese to the side and slid into the stables. Raised voices welcomed her. Hugh's swelled the loudest, soaring over the others. The noise came from the tack room at the other end of the stable.

Apparently Hugh was confronting someone about her stolen jewels. She pressed against the office door, noting the quieter tones of her father's voice and the cold rumbles of Trevor's. Her spine stiffened. Was Hugh accusing Trevor of stealing her jewels?

"Ludicrous," she muttered, and pressed her ear closer.

"It doesn't matter," William was saying. "We're leaving on a train tomorrow. Now that we have them back we'll not press any charges against you. I only ask you to refrain from ever doing business with Mr. Cruz again."

"Forget it," Uncle Lou said flatly. "Trevor didn't steal anything and if I'm reading things right, pretty boy here is the culprit. He planted them in Trevor's house for whatever reason. Nice try, Hugh, but it was an infantile move. We know this is a big setup."

"Now see here, I've known this boy for years and he would never do anything so dishonest or sneaky. He is an upstanding example of Christian virtue. Take your hands off him, Lou." William's tones rang with indignation and

Gracie grimaced. She should have told him about Hugh's previous lack of self-control, then maybe he wouldn't be espousing nonexistent virtues.

She wished Trevor would say something but imagined that he lounged against some wall, granite-faced. Perhaps she ought to march in there and set her father straight as well as defend Trevor's honor. But if Uncle Lou thought Hugh had stolen the jewels it might be more beneficial to Trevor if she found some evidence to support the charge. Besides, if she rushed to his rescue Father might not believe her, especially if he still thought she had feelings for him.

Yes, hard evidence would be better than any emotional plea, she decided as she pushed away from the door.

She turned and met the long shiny edge of a dagger. A black-haired man she'd never seen before held the blade to her stomach and grinned a yellow smile.

"Going somewhere, *princesa?*"

Chapter Twenty-Five

A scream froze in Gracie's throat, and to her horror all she managed was a mangled squeak before the man hauled her to his side. The dagger's blade pressed against her neck. Foul breath washed over her as he whispered, "Not a peep, *princesa*. One scream and I'll slice that creamy skin of yours."

He pulled her toward a stall, opened it and shoved her in. She stumbled and quickly righted herself, hating the paralysis of her vocal cords.

"You'll fetch a good price in Mexico, despite your dark hair. There's good money in women, you know." His eyes traveled down her form and a leer stretched his thin lips. He tipped the blade against her throat and with his other hand grabbed some rope hanging against the stall. The mare beside her already wore a saddle. Dread tripped a heavy foot down Gracie's spine.

Perspiration trickled down the man's forehead as he brought the rope near. "Remember, no sound or you're dead. Give me your hands."

Gracie lifted them and forced herself to watch the man carefully. Damp spots stained the fabric beneath his arms and an unnatural flush hovered on pale cheeks. He looked like he would pass out, just as her captor had.

The man removed his knife from her neck and she stood very still, resisting the urge to bolt. He pushed the knife into the waistband of his sagging trousers and advanced upon her, eyes fused to her face.

Gracie gulped as fear turned her limbs into numb extensions of her body. No doubt this man could draw his knife quickly if she tried to escape, and then she would be dead before she could scream. She swallowed tightly as his clammy fingers pulled her wrists together and wound the rope around them. His irises were very dark, almost as black as Trevor's, but the whites of his eyes were bloodshot. A tremor coursed through him as he tightened the rope. Then another.

Hope surged through her. The man looked as if he would pass out any minute. His face had gone pasty-white.

A door opened and he shoved her down onto the cold dirt floor. "Not a word."

Shivers rippled through her, and she bit her lip against the panic that threatened to overwhelm her.

"We'll be packing our bags tonight." Hugh's frosty speech floated over, followed by the telltale creak of William's wheelchair. "I have never been so insulted. Having Mr. Cruz in your employ is a huge mistake."

"Trevor's my friend and a valued business partner. Moreover, I've known him for years and trust him with my life. I'm gonna escort you to the house, just in case anything else winds up missing."

"I always knew you were stubborn, but I didn't take you for a fool," came her father's tired voice. "I wanted to work things out between us. I suppose that shall be impossible."

No one answered his last remark and Gracie listened as her hopes for rescue left the stable. Squeezing her eyes shut, she pushed the fear down. Later she could cry. Now she needed a plan of action, something to keep her sane.

She would wait on this man passing out. She shifted so she could stretch her legs.

In front of her, the stranger rose slowly and peered over the edges of the horse stall. He looked down at her with a crooked sneer. "C'mon, *princesa,* stand up."

"Who are you?" She obeyed his order to stand and boldly met his leer. He appeared not only sick of body, but sick of mind. A chill goose-bumped her arms. How would his diseased soul affect her?

"I am called Mendez," he answered as he led first Gracie and then the horse out of the stall.

Mendez? Somehow she wasn't surprised. "How did you find this place?"

A sneer twisted his lips. "Idiots. Too busy burying Smith to see me coming."

"Smith." The man who'd kidnapped her. The one she'd dragged home. Had he died? Deep breaths. Keep him talking. "Why should they care you're here?"

"They fear me."

Her mouth dried. "What do you need with me? Am I so important to you?"

His gaze flicked over her, and then he spat on the floor, close to her shoe. "You, a woman? I seek Striker and I will use you to draw him from his cowardly hole."

"Striker? I don't know who or where he is." Terror loosened her tongue and she stumbled over the words. "Have you met him? He's a hero, you know, though not many believe it. I do because I have inside sources. Do you perchance know what he looks like? I intend to find him myself, one day."

Sweat beaded Mendez's upper lip as he listened to her prattle. "What are you saying?"

She gulped, keeping her trembling voice as light as possible. "I am saying I'd be most happy to help you find Striker. He has been an object of my interest for quite some time. It is said by certain contacts of mine that he's rescued over one hundred women who were kidnapped by reprobates seeking to sell them across the border. No doubt you know all about the Mann Act." Since she could not put her hands on her hips she lifted her chin. "Horrible criminals. I would love to help you—"

"Kill Striker? For that is my intention." Mendez placed a hand on the stall behind him and she could tell he was leaning against it for support. Her wrists were not tied tightly, either.

"Get on the horse before I kill you, as well." Mendez pushed off the wall and walked around the front of the horse.

"You cannot kill Striker." Gracie licked her lips, sweat trickling down her neck.

"I can…and I will. He has humiliated me among my peers, he has ruined my business. I will have my revenge." His voice strengthened on *revenge*. He yanked the rope around her wrists up and over the horse's head, tying it so she would be forced to walk alongside the horse. "He took something from me. No one steals from Mendez. No one."

"I understand why that would upset you. I have recently had something stolen from me. It is a disturbing sensation. Perhaps I could help you get the stolen item back."

"I'll get her myself. Smith messed up with you but that can be fixed. Now I know where she is, I'll be back." He shoved her. *"Vamanos."*

They stepped out of the stall and into the stable aisle. Mendez swayed heavily and fell to the ground, jerking the rope and pulling Gracie forward. A slight groan and cloud of dirt accompanied his fall. Wrists burning, she tugged her hands free and, kneeling down, used the rope to tie his arms behind his back. He didn't move and for a moment she worried he might be dead.

She prodded him with her foot. He moaned, and she sighed with relief. The man might be wicked but she certainly did not wish death upon him now, not with the obvious state of his soul.

She stood and brushed the dirt off her hands, wincing at the stinging in her wrists.

"I guess I'm not needed here after all."

Gracie whirled around as Trevor stepped out of the stall opposite her, holstering his revolver.

"Did you know Mendez was here?" An inane question, but her relief was so acute she could hardly think.

"I should have." His eyelids flickered down to Mendez's prone form. "Stable the horse while I take care of him."

"What are you going to do?"

"Just stable the horse."

"He's sick. He needs to be taken to the house and cared for, probably by me since I have already been exposed to his influenza."

"You're not going near him. Now go to the house." Something in his tone alerted Gracie to his intentions. Her hands trembled and she pressed them against her sides, fighting the nausea trying to overtake her.

"I am not going if you plan to kill this man. His soul is in need of healing. Please, Trevor." She hated the groveling tone of her voice but could not help it. Even if Mendez was more evil than Julia and even if the insane gleam in his eyes scared the wits out of her, she still felt responsible to do what she could to help him. "If we nurse him back to health then at least he can stand and face the law."

Trevor stepped closer. "I'll take care of him, Gracie. He's not fit to live."

"Maybe he isn't," she admitted, "but he needs to live because once he dies there's no other chance for him."

"You think he deserves forgiveness?"

"No. *Forgiveness* by definition is undeserved." Her gaze slid down to the man at her feet. "Even killers can be forgiven by God. I only ask that we give him a chance."

A strange look crossed Trevor's face. A grimace of sorts. "Go to the house. I won't kill him."

"Thank you, but I still feel you should keep as far away as possible. I could not bear it if you died from this influenza."

"That won't happen," he said, eyes locked on her.

He bent and hoisted Mendez across his shoulders. "Let's go, Gracie, before your mother discovers you're missing again and her hair turns gray."

She followed Trevor to the house, carefully dodging her mother at the door.

Praying the influenza would not spread to anyone else in the house, she watched as Trevor settled Mendez on a makeshift cot in Uncle Lou's office. The man's skin was pasty and the stench of death hovered around the unmoving body. James allowed no one into the room but himself, Trevor and Gracie, much to Mother's displeasure.

Gracie washed Mendez's fevered brow with a cool cloth while James examined him. He straightened from where he'd been leaning over the prone figure. "He doesn't have influenza."

"How do you know? Looks like it to me."

"I've got my ways, Trevor. He's been poisoned and I'd say that's what killed off the rest of them outlaws." James scratched his whiskers thoughtfully. "Poison's usually a woman's method. I gotta think Julia might have something to do with this."

Gracie looked up, surprised. "Why Julia?"

"Some sort of twisted penance to make up for what she did to Mary? Maybe to stop Mendez in his tracks. Who knows?" Trevor leaned forward. "Look at the skin."

She glanced at Mendez and saw that indeed, his skin was turning a bluish color.

"What does it mean?" she asked.

"Based on the cyanosis and respiratory distress, ricin poisoning," James said.

"Is it contagious?" She scooted away from Mendez.

James took out his stethoscope and listened to Mendez's chest. "No. Lungs are full of fluid. He's not got much longer. I wouldn't be surprised if Julia poisoned their water as well as the air. You saw waste in the cave?"

"Yes, but after my abductor dropped to the ground outside in a faint, I only stayed long enough to grab some coats." Briefly she closed her eyes to block the image of her kidnapper. She'd rescued him for nothing. Throat moving, she pressed a hand to her stomach. "How could Julia poison them so easily? What's ricin?"

"Castor beans," Trevor said. "It's easy to make and there's no cure. She kept a jar in her bedroom and since she's done business with him and his men before, he probably thought she was coming for a friendly little visit." He ran his fingers through his hair. "I don't think he's going to make it."

His hands dropped to Gracie's shoulders and she resisted the urge to turn into him and hold on forever. Instead her gaze lingered on Mendez. "You said it's not contagious?"

"No, as long as you didn't inhale anything. She probably did this before hopping the train. If everyone is dead, I don't think you have anything to worry about." James tucked the stethoscope into his pocket. "I'm going to get some coffee. Best remove your hands, Trevor, before her parents come in."

The warmth on Gracie's shoulders left as Trevor stepped away from her.

"I want to stay in here, James, until he passes. Is there nothing I can do?"

"He's too close to dead." Just as James spoke, Mendez shuddered and then lay still. "Guess he's gone now. I'll be back." James let himself out as Gracie's breath sucked in.

"He's gone? Dead?" Her voice sounded shrill in the quiet room. Trevor moved behind her and touched her arm.

"C'mon, Gracie. There's nothing more we can do now."

She followed him out, a little dizzy. "I've never seen death so close before. It's unnerving."

"It can be worse. Much more ugly than that."

"Have you seen many deaths?" She reached for his arm and he stopped in the hallway. She heard murmuring in the sitting room and knew at any moment someone would come out and see them together, but she couldn't look away. She studied Trevor's face, memorizing the details so that when her parents took her from this place perhaps his image would keep her heart from breaking.

"I have seen things you can't imagine," he answered grimly. "I've done things that would shock you and yet, I'm beginning to believe those things are not enough to keep me from God." The hint of a smile crinkled the corners of his eyes. "I want you to know that sometime between yesterday and today I realized I want to believe what the Bible says about Jesus dying for my sins. About His loving me. I want to be a Christian, Gracie."

Gracie's chest tightened and she blinked tears from her eyes. "I am so glad for you. Have you told Mary?"

"I will."

Their gazes locked and she could hardly breathe. How would she ever leave him?

His eyes glinted, knowing. "Your parents want to head out tomorrow. I guess you heard Hugh accusing me of taking your jewels."

Indignation shot through her. "A preposterous accusation. I am quite positive he took them. He is out for my money, that's the only reason he wants to marry me. Don't worry, Trevor." She inclined her head and whispered, "I'll find evidence he took those jewels and planted them at your house." She straightened. "Why was he there in the first place?"

"Claims he was looking for me."

"An unlikely explanation." She swallowed hard, knowing they had only seconds of privacy. "Tell me honestly, is Uncle Lou Striker? I simply must know because, if he is not, I intend to go at once into Burns. Mendez was looking for him, you know." She scrunched her nose. "He wanted to kill him. I only wish to interview Striker."

"Aren't you afraid?"

"Should I be? Striker is a hero, there is no doubt of it." She quirked a brow at Trevor and couldn't resist adding, "Sometimes I think I'd like to marry the man, as long as he's not Uncle Lou."

"You shouldn't make rash judgments on hearsay."

"I believe I've heard this lecture already." She smiled at Trevor, who looked stiffer than the corsets Mother used to wear. "You must admit that not only is the man an exciting adventurer, but a person of honor and integrity, as well."

"More information from your sources?" Trevor leaned against the wall and regarded Gracie quizzically.

"Of course," she answered.

"And those relationships tell you Striker is a good man?"

"Absolutely."

"Better than Hugh?"

Heat suffused her face. "Striker would never attack a woman."

"Hugh attacked you?" Trevor stiffened and his eyes glittered fiercely.

She backed up a step. "Perhaps *attack* is too strong a word. Not really attack—more of a forceful kiss—but never fear, I took care of the matter. He will not try anything like that again."

Trevor reached out and pulled her to him, his fingers a vise on her arms. "Did you tell your parents?"

"Really, Trevor, it is none of their business."

"Are you insane? You need to tell them."

She shoved away from him. "I will not. It is quite embarrassing."

"What's embarrassing?" Her father wheeled out from the study, followed closely by Edith and Hugh.

"This," Trevor said, and with long strides he reached Hugh, drew back his right arm and punched the golden boy squarely in the jaw.

Hugh crumpled without a sound.

Chapter Twenty-Six

"You've made a huge mistake."

"Think so?" Trevor rubbed sore knuckles along his jaw, watching as James drove his Ford away.

Lou rolled a toothpick between his teeth. "Yep. You'll regret it."

"Being a Christian isn't the worst thing in the world, Lou."

"Maybe not." A grudging response. "Now we have to hope Gracie doesn't share her thoughts on Striker's whereabouts with all her friends at the paper. This place has been a sanctuary."

"She doesn't know who he is."

"She knows you're close. Thinks you're me. If trouble comes, we'll face it. But becoming a Christian?" Lou spit the toothpick over the edge of the porch. "That's a whole 'nother can of worms. I figured you might do it to get the girl. But you're letting her ride off into the sunset with her parents and that fancy-pants thief. I can't figure it, Trevor. What's in religion anyway?"

"Not much," Trevor answered ruefully. "You gotta read the Bible. This isn't about religion." He paused. "And much as it irks me, we've got no proof Hugh took those jewels so you might want to curb your accusations."

"I found this when I was sweeping his room a few minutes ago." Mary held up a small pearl earring. "He looked so squeaky-clean. I'm glad he's gone, as well as Mendez. It's a relief to be out from beneath that cloud. And now you're free, Trevor."

"I guess so. Lou can keep up with the government, and I'll watch the ranch."

"I don't understand why you punched him," said Lou. "It didn't set well with William and Edith. They bustled out real quick. At least I don't smear people's characters without reason." He smirked.

"Gracie didn't mind the punch."

"Her parents did."

Trevor scowled. "They're gone now and we can go back to our lives. After Christmas we'll go to the bank and I'll buy half the ranch." He looked across the acres stretching in front of the house, at the rapidly disappearing smoke from the truck.

James had offered to take the family to the train station, and they'd left immediately after breakfast.

Trevor shoved his hands into his pockets and leaned back against the house. Everything would be strangely silent without Gracie around. Empty, even.

"This means we won't be having a Christmas tree, doesn't it?" Mary glanced over at Lou. "I'll miss her."

"You can have a tree if you want." Lou stood next to Trevor, arms crossed. "Trevor and I need to see about finding a place to stick Mendez. Then we'll find that cave and clear it out. Hopefully, there's no poison floating around. I suppose we're going to have to find Julia and get things straightened out. You ready, Trev?"

"Yeah." He ignored the strange tightness in his chest and hoped he wasn't coming down with anything.

It wasn't until nightfall that Trevor returned home. His house sat dark and silent, as somber and quiet as dinner at the house had been. He couldn't believe Gracie made that much difference in the atmosphere, but apparently she had.

In his bedroom a package lay in the middle of his bed and he approached it cautiously. No telling who Julia was going to poison next and he wouldn't put it past her to kill her own son. Thank goodness they'd gotten a telegram out to George, telling him to pick her up as a possible murder suspect. Mendez might've been a criminal but taking the law into her own hands was plain wrong, even if she was somehow trying to atone for past sins.

The handwriting on the package was not Julia's, however, but Gracie's. He recognized the small, precise writing from letters he had brought to town for her. Picking up the package, he hesitated, then ripped it open. A paper floated down to the floor and he ignored it as his eyes lingered on the gardening tools and heavy book. The tools lay partially encased in a leather pouch that filled the room with the scent of wood smoke and lavender. He pulled out a small hoe and saw his name engraved at the base of the handle. His throat constricted and he set the gift on his bed before reaching down for the letter.

Dearest Trevor,
I'm leaving today. I plan to visit in the summer but in the meantime I am on a quest to find the elusive Striker. You do know he has retired? I have decided that if Uncle Lou is not the man, then he knows who is. If you have any information, please write to me,

as I will be resuming my search for Striker in order
to land a job with the *Woman's Liberator*.

Perhaps the next time we meet I will be wearing
trousers and will no longer bore you with my obsession for finding Striker. I do hope I was not too much
of a bother to you.

Thank you for those amazing kisses. It will be difficult, no doubt, to find another who kisses as well
as you.

May God bless you in all your endeavors.

Forever in my heart,

Gracie

Trevor carefully folded the paper and placed it in his
top drawer. His gaze fell on his Bible, opened to Jeremiah,
chapter twenty-nine. His finger found verse eleven.

*Lord, I still don't know You too well, but I gotta believe
You've got something good planned for my life.*

He closed the Bible and readied for bed.

Boston moved more busily than Gracie remembered.
The crowd bustled around her, pushing and jostling, and
she held more tightly to her Dotty bag. As she and her
family waited for a taxi, she spotted a woman huddled in
the corner of a shop. Her face, dirt-grimed, seemed frozen
with misery. She was shivering.

Gracie looked away and swallowed. Her own hands
were loaded with clothes, jewels and money. That woman,
from all appearances, had nothing but thin rags on her
back.

She glanced down at the leather jacket Mary had
so kindly given to her and made a quick decision. She
stripped it off and, pushing through the small crowd waiting for taxis, went to the woman.

Rounded eyes the color of her mother's sapphires gazed up at her.

Gracie knelt down and draped her own coat across the woman's bony shoulders.

"Why?"

The whispered question brought a lump to her throat.

"Gracelyn!" her mother's voice called her.

She patted the woman's shoulder. "Because you're deeply loved. May God bless you."

She sprang up and headed back to the taxi waiting for her. She squished into the backseat, Mother in the middle and Hugh behind the driver. A last look, and then the automobile pulled away from the curb.

"Really, Gracelyn." Mother sniffed and handed her a white-linen handkerchief. "Wipe your hands."

"You could catch something from that riffraff," Hugh added.

She ignored him, as she had the entire train ride, despite the nudges, pinches and scowls from her parents.

Snobs, all of them.

Not like Uncle Lou, Mary and Trevor.

She had not known her heart would feel this heavy, that at any moment tears might spring from her eyes. Somehow Trevor had captured her heart and she remained chained by her feelings.

The only enjoyment she'd experienced on the way home had been seeing the purple mark on Hugh's jaw. She wished she had put it there instead of Trevor.

No doubt Hugh had stolen her jewels in order to discredit Trevor, as well. The man was completely ruthless. A coward.

"We're almost home, dear. It will be good to have our electrical amenities again. And we'll have plenty of time to decorate the tree." Mother slanted her a sidelong glance from her position between Gracie and Hugh.

"I really don't feel like celebrating."

"Nonsense. You are the most ardent of us all. We will celebrate the birth of our Savior as we always do."

"While others mourn the deaths of their friends? Didn't you see the papers? The death toll is astronomical." Gracie returned her face to the window.

It was bad enough she'd face this Christmas without her dearest friend, but now she would also be forced to celebrate while dealing with the loss of her love.

"Come now, Gracelyn," her mother admonished. "You did not know Mr. Cruz long enough to pout about his absence. He is a scoundrel and best left in that desert where he belongs. Hugh here is a shining example of all that a hero should be."

"Hugh wouldn't know heroism if he tripped over it." Gracie faced the shock etched across her mother's face and ignored Hugh's sputtering. "Striker is the real hero and as soon as Christmas ends, I'm getting an interview with him."

William turned from the front seat to face his daughter. "I thought I forbid you to write for that scandalous, liberal poppycock."

"I have not written for them, Father. But I'm twenty, unlikely to marry and unwilling to live beneath your social restrictions any longer." A deep fire spread through her bones. "You're smothering me. The paper will pay me for my work as well as offer me a staff position should I succeed."

"But, Gracelyn," gasped Edith, fingers reaching for her embroidered handkerchief. "What will people say? We cannot have it. We forbid it."

"This is a topic better discussed at home," William said

with a meaningful jerk of his head. The driver flushed and stared straight ahead.

"Very well," Edith muttered.

Gracie shifted closer to the door and away from her mother. They could not keep her in this gilded cage forever. Surely God had nothing against her procuring a job and standing on her own two feet. There must be some sort of balance between obedience and following one's calling.

Two months. Not quite as long as Gracie thought it would take to find Striker.

After a morning of helping out at a small church in the poorer section of the city, Gracie went home, changed and headed to her appointment with Striker.

Now she paused outside the ramshackle house, double-checking the address on the note clutched in her gloved hand. This must be it. She darted a look to each side before going up the steps and knocking briskly.

Who would have guessed that searching for Striker would have yielded results so quickly? This could be the beginning of a real, paying job. Thanks to the minister of her parents' church, William and Edith had come to the conclusion that a job would be the very thing to lift Gracie's spirits and take her mind off the many changes in her life. Astonishingly enough, they had put aside their social niceties and gave their blessing to her pursuit of the elusive agent.

After much research and many interviews, she'd received a tip from a trusted source that should she appear at this address at this time, she might very well meet Striker himself. Of course, she'd informed a few fellow writers of her plans on the chance the meeting somehow went awry.

She pushed her scarf higher over her nose. Boston during February did not inspire any feelings of loyalty, but she also kept her face covered for protection. Although cases of influenza had slowed considerably, it would be wise to be cautious.

Whatever was Striker doing in Massachusetts? Uneasy, she determined to be on her guard until his identity was established. Should this be a trick of some ruffian…she fingered the small blade hidden in the folded pocket of her skirt. She'd not be without means to protect herself.

She knocked on the door again and shuffled her numbing feet. The door opened as her hand poised for a third hit and a square-shouldered butler appeared.

"This way, ma'am." He led her to a surprisingly chic sitting room and closed the door. She stood uncertainly for a moment, then went forward and sat on one of the expensive couches facing the fireplace.

She wished, after all this time, that she felt more excitement. The sad fact was she longed for Trevor…and Striker could hardly hold her interest. She seemed to see Trevor everywhere. Even here the patterned rug covering the hardwood floor and the fireplace made of rocks reminded her of Trevor's home.

She hadn't heard from him at all. The first few nights she had not been able to stop her tears, both for Connie and for Trevor.

Christmas had been hardest. She visited Connie's parents and that had been depressing. Then she'd come home and been forced to endure her mother's cheerful clucking and rock-hard fruitcake.

At least it was all over. Even Hugh had found another heiress and gone on with his life.

She took out her papers and writing utensils and set them beside her on the couch. She pulled off her coat, scarf and gloves. If this was Striker's house he sure knew how to hide. The outside looked ramshackle and disreputable but inside everything shouted money.

Her knees bounced and she glanced at the clock on the wall. Why didn't Trevor want her? After all this time, after those kisses and insightful conversations, he still did not want her. Mother insisted that looking at Trevor was like staring at a blank wall. Utterly useless. But Gracie had thought she could see past the wall. Had thought she'd seen love.

She grimaced. Boy, had she been wrong.

This very afternoon Mother informed her that Uncle Lou had left for another jaunt to the Orient and had probably taken Trevor with him. Gracie did not believe it.

Trevor wanted to sit at his ranch and take care of the horses, the property and Mary. He didn't want China and he didn't want her.

The funny thing was, Gracie longed for Oregon. She missed the quiet sunsets and the crunch of Velvet's hoof in the snow. She even missed listening to Mary hum while mopping the floor. Perhaps she'd grown too old to enjoy the city now. Whatever the reasons, the desert called to her as surely as God called Abraham and when her quest to find Striker ended, she would go back as an independent, employed woman.

The door opened and Gracie rose immediately. This was it. She smoothed her hair and frowned when a stray strand fell into her eyes. She blew it away and watched as a tall, dark man let himself in. He shut the door with a thud and stepped toward her. The scent of exotic spices filled the room.

"*You!* What are you doing here?" Pulse pounding through her body, she looked around his broad shoulders at the closed door. "Where is Striker? I have this note delivered to my house expressly granting me an interview at this address." She glanced down. "Perhaps I got it wrong," she muttered.

"No, Gracie. I left that note."

"What prank are you pulling, Mr. Cruz?" She backed away but was all too aware of her heart thumping loudly against her chest, of the dampness in her hands. Her legs trembled.

She thought when she saw him again she would be composed, but her body betrayed her. She swallowed past riotous emotions and set her shoulders. "I am waiting for Striker. Do you know him or did you lie?"

"I know him." Trevor advanced closer and grasped her shoulders, pulling her tightly against him. "But right now, I only want to know you, Gracelyn Riley."

"What game is this? I demand an answer." She pushed against his chest halfheartedly. His cologne floated around her and she was afraid to look into those heavy-lidded eyes. The knowledge shook her.

Since when did she back down when frightened? She forced herself to meet his gaze boldly and trembled at his look. His eyes glinted savagely with uncontained emotion.

"You love me," she breathed.

"I will love you forever." He lowered his head to kiss her.

This time she did shove him forcefully, though she doubted it did much good. He loosened his hold, however, and she stepped back.

"We have been here and done this before, Mr. Cruz." Her hand waved wildly as she paced back and forth. "I must know your intentions."

"I intend to marry you."

"Do you plan to ask first?"

He slanted her a mischievous grin. "Will you say yes if I do?"

She wet her lips, loving him, wanting to pinch herself to see if she truly lived this or if it was but a dream. "My parents will never accept this."

"You once told me you'd defy them for love."

Her heart fluttered. "I still would," she said quietly.

"Good. By the way, I paid a visit to Hugh. He'll be straightening things out soon enough with your parents. If I were you, I wouldn't worry about them."

"I hope you did not hurt Hugh too badly."

"He'll live." He smiled and before she could react, dropped to a knee. "Will you marry me?"

Marry? Pulse roaring through her, Gracie pivoted and paced the room. This was a shock, a dream come true, a nightmare. She couldn't sort her feelings. Marriage to him would be wonderful. She was in love with him, but what if he restricted her the way her parents did? Love could quickly turn to bitterness.

She stopped in front of him. "Perhaps we ought to try a courtship first."

"You're afraid."

"What nonsense," she sputtered, then caught herself. It would not do to sound exactly like mother. "This is simply so—oh, who am I trying to fool?" Dropping down to her knees, she wrapped her arms around him and buried her face into his shoulder. "I've missed you so much and of course I'll marry you. We'll be wonderful together," she babbled. "I don't want to be a spoiled socialite. Please don't back out now. I don't think I'll ever feel about anyone the way I do you."

Her tears wet his shirt and she felt his hands stroking her hair, her back.

"I won't ever back out." His voice was gruff.

She nodded against his shirt.

"Come, sit with me." He led her to the couch.

Wearing trousers, writing scandalous articles, they would never take the place of love. If Trevor didn't like those things, then she would deal with that but she would not stop loving him.

At least playing chess was acceptable to him, she told herself.

He handed her a handkerchief and she finished drying her eyes.

"I've been learning a lot lately. I couldn't get you out of my mind. Mary finally suggested maybe God wanted me with you, that He sent you to us for a reason. I prayed and I felt peace inside." His teeth flashed, even and white, maybe the first real smile she'd ever seen him wear. "You introduced me to a God that makes you laugh, that gives wisdom and strength. Thank you, Gracie."

"I love you, Trevor." She sniffed. "I'm sorry I was such a snob when we first met. God has changed me, as well. He has shown me love in my darkest times. I do hope you realize I will never be like that Eunice."

"That's history." He chuckled. "I loved her briefly. Her and the dream of a wife and a family. I never cared about her the way I do you. I've changed."

It was true his face looked different now. Smoother, more malleable, as if spring had finally arrived and softened the winter deadness of his soul. Something like hope blossomed inside her. A lovely silence ensued until the clock struck the five o'clock hour. Startled, Gracie realized she hadn't seen a trace of Striker.

She smoothed her hair and patted her cheeks with a lacy hankie. "When will Striker be here?"

"Do you want background on him first?"

She arched a brow. "How would you know those details?"

"We're close, very close."

Ha. He must be Uncle Lou. "But I asked you about him."

"I was not at liberty then to speak."

"But you are now, because he's retired?"

"Something like that. You know he received government contracts that sometimes led to assassinations?" Trevor leaned against the back of the couch and stretched his legs out beside her.

Disappointment spiraled through her. "I had hoped not."

The look on his face confirmed her fears. "Council Bluff?" she asked.

He nodded. "The government sent him after persons of interest, mostly for capture but sometimes to take out. Council Bluff changed things. The women and the children weren't expected. An unforeseen calamity." A raw edge caught his voice.

Suddenly, the truth hit her. Of course. The rug and fireplace so similar to Trevor's. The heaviness in his tone when he spoke of Council Bluff.

Uncle Lou wasn't Striker at all, though he'd protected him all these years.

She leaned forward, longing to hold Trevor's hand. "What he did for our country has not changed, Trevor. Perhaps Striker killed criminals, but he also rescued innocent women countless times. He cannot be held responsible for what evil men did at Council Bluff. This is what I know of him, this American hero." She angled her body to face him. "The government made him a part of an elite group of agents designed to enforce the White Slave Traffic Act of 1910. Later he was based near the Mexican border to collect intelligence and reduce smuggling. He did so well, however, and rescued so many women being transported for immoral purposes, that the government asked him to help with espionage."

Trevor's eyes remained fixed on her. "You have quite a bit of information there. But nothing personal."

"I know." She gave him a gentle smile. "Tell me his story."

"He followed Mendez when he kidnapped a close friend. He rescued her and that was how he met an older agent who recruited him to begin work with the government. He enjoyed his job. The justice of it. The thrill of hunting out the perfect stock. The honor of rescuing others, however anonymous it was. But he didn't like death. He retired, tied up all his loose ends and now lives how he wants."

"Hmm." Gracie looked down at her notes. "All interesting information but I think I should wait for the interview." She stood and let the papers float to the floor. "At the moment, I really don't care about interviewing Striker. I shall marry you, Trevor. How soon can we get it done?"

Trevor rose and chuckled. "Soon as possible, but I imagine your parents will want a fancy wedding."

"Two weeks. We can accomplish it, assuming they'll agree."

"They will."

"You seem overly confident, Trevor." She glanced around the spacious room. "I suppose the fact that you have money and a decent living bodes well."

Trevor handed her a piece of paper. "Let's discuss this."

"What is it?" She took it. "I don't understand."

"I love you, Gracelyn Riley. I love your spirit and ideals, the way your hair curls around your face when it escapes from your hat, the way your cheeks pink when you're caught eavesdropping. I never want to smother you with propriety. I want us to grow old together and discover all the wonderful joys God has in store for us."

His words warmed her. Caught her on fire actually. Squealing, she leaped into his arms, squeezing and kissing his shadow-rough neck. The paper he'd given her crinkled. Whatever it was, it couldn't be better than what he'd just said. She dropped back and scanned the contents of his note.

She couldn't stop her grin. It was probably the most foolish smile she'd ever worn, but she didn't care. There was no doubt now. God had placed them together.

"This is quite romantic, Trevor." She studied the paper in her hand. "Let's see, I must wear trousers whenever the mood is upon me, must always write forward-thinking articles, must never lose at chess. Now, Trevor, that last one is hardly fair." Her smile widened until her cheeks hurt. She flung the list to the floor. "I would have married you anyway, Mr. Cruz."

"I know."

"There is one thing." She pulled back from his embrace. Would he say it? Would he tell her the truth? She'd love him no matter what, but did he know that?

"Name it."

She tilted her head up. His face sharpened as he leaned toward her. When his mouth hovered inches above hers and her legs felt like molten mush, she pulled back and whispered, "Who is Striker?"

Trevor's hands tightened on her back. "They call me Striker."

Relief weakened her knees. Or perhaps the love shining in his eyes did that. She smoothed a dark lock of hair from his brow. "I know. And I love you, Striker."

* * * * *

Dear Reader,

Thank you for reading *Love on the Range*. I loved writing this book. It's actually the first manuscript I ever finished and I'm so excited that Love Inspired Books offered to publish it.

The origin of the FBI is fascinating and I enjoyed exploring the historical agents who served our country. Giving my hero the occupation of a secret agent for the FBI was fun. The story of Gracelyn going west formed when I first read about the Spanish influenza pandemic. After World War I the flu began taking thousands of lives. By the end of this pandemic, millions around the world had died.

Nineteen eighteen was a scary time, and yet it was also a period of great inventions and changes in American culture. Trevor and Gracelyn, two characters from completely different backgrounds, captured my imagination and kept me hostage for many years. I hope you enjoyed their story. I've done my best to reflect historical details accurately and hope you'll forgive any mistakes I have made.

I adore connecting with readers! I can be found at my website, www.jessicanelson.net, or you can send me an email at jessicaenelson@bellsouth.net.

Hope to hear from you!
Jessica Nelson

Questions for Discussion

1. Gracie and Trevor come from different backgrounds. Do you think a romantic relationship like theirs can last? What common values do you think create a satisfying, lasting relationship?

2. Mary and Gracie are both Christians and yet share their faith in different ways. Do you think one way is more effective than another? Why?

3. Although Gracie does not come from a troubled home, what conflicts does she face in her life? How can she resolve them?

4. At the beginning of *Love on the Range* Trevor has trouble with forgiveness. How does he view forgiveness and how does his perspective change by the end of the story?

5. Everyone has felt shame. How does Trevor deal with his shame?

6. Gracie tends to be an optimist, which can cause her to appear shallow and unrealistic at times. Could you relate to her? Why or why not?

7. Uncle Lou doesn't talk about God or seem interested in Him. Do you know people like that? What makes someone uninterested in God? Is there a sensitive way to share faith with a person like Lou?

8. Because of Mary's Paiute heritage, she was treated badly. Have you ever come across prejudice? How did you deal with it?

9. Gracie was raised in a wealthy household. Although she is an avid supporter of women's rights, until the end of the book she hadn't given much thought to helping the poor. How does she come to realize this lack in her life? Who influences her change in perspective?

10. Trevor's mom, Julia, has hurt others for her own benefit. How does she try to rectify her mistakes? Do you think she's changed by the end of the book? Is it possible to make up for bad things you've done to others?

11. What do you think about the characters' attitudes toward Julia? How would you treat someone like her?

12. Each character in the story has personal values. Who did you relate to the most? Why?

13. Some people appear more admirable than others. Who did you admire in this story? What qualities did they display that you admired?

14. Some people are difficult to like, or even to relate to. Was there a character in *Love on the Range* whom you disliked? What traits made that character unlikable?

15. Forgiveness is important. Have you ever had to forgive someone for something they did to you? Have you ever had to forgive yourself? Explain.

INSPIRATIONAL

Love Inspired

celebrating 15 YEARS

HISTORICAL

COMING NEXT MONTH
AVAILABLE MAY 8, 2012

MISTAKEN BRIDE
Irish Brides
Renee Ryan

HOMEFRONT HERO
Allie Pleiter

THE HOMESTEADER'S SWEETHEART
Lacy Williams

THE MARSHAL'S PROMISE
Rhonda Gibson

REQUEST YOUR FREE BOOKS!

2 FREE INSPIRATIONAL NOVELS
PLUS 2
FREE
MYSTERY GIFTS

Love Inspired
HISTORICAL
INSPIRATIONAL HISTORICAL ROMANCE

LIH11B

PRESENTING...

More Than Words

STORIES OF THE HEART

Three bestselling authors
Three real-life heroines

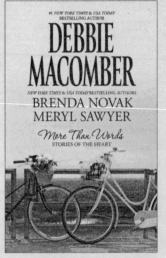

Even as you read these words, there are women just like you stepping up and making a difference in their communities, making our world a better place to live. Three such exceptional women have been selected as recipients of Harlequin's More Than Words award. To celebrate their accomplishments, three bestselling authors have written short stories inspired by these real-life heroines.

Proceeds from the sale of this book will be reinvested into the Harlequin More Than Words program to support causes that are of concern to women.

Visit

www.HarlequinMoreThanWords.com

to nominate a real-life heroine from your community.

www.Harlequin.com